The Wild Ones

The Wild Ones

M. LEIGHTON

BERKLEY BOOKS, NEW YORK

A BERKLEY BOOK
Published by the Penguin Group
Penguin Group (USA) Inc.
375 Hudson Street, New York, New York 10014, USA

Penguin Group (Canada), 90 Eglinton Avenue East, Suite 700, Toronto, Ontario M4P 2Y3, Canada
(a division of Pearson Penguin Canada Inc.) • Penguin Books Ltd., 80 Strand, London WC2R 0RL,
England • Penguin Ireland, 25 St. Stephen's Green, Dublin 2, Ireland (a division of Penguin
Books Ltd.) • Penguin Group (Australia), 707 Collins Street, Melbourne, Victoria 3008, Australia
(a division of Pearson Australia Group Pty Ltd.) • Penguin Books India Pvt. Ltd., 11 Community
Centre, Panchsheel Park, New Delhi—110 017, India • Penguin Group (NZ), 67 Apollo Drive,
Rosedale, Auckland 0632, New Zealand (a division of Pearson New Zealand Ltd.) • Penguin Books
(South Africa), Rosebank Office Park, 181 Jan Smuts Avenue, Parktown North 2193, South Africa •
Penguin China, B7 Jiaming Center, 27 East Third Ring Road North,
Chaoyang District, Beijing 100020, China

Penguin Books Ltd., Registered Offices: 80 Strand, London WC2R 0RL, England

This is a work of fiction. Names, characters, places, and incidents either are the product of the author's
imagination or are used fictitiously, and any resemblance to actual persons, living or dead, businesses,
companies, events, or locales is entirely coincidental. The publisher does not have any control over
and does not assume any responsibility for author or third-party websites or their content.

THE WILD ONES

PUBLISHING HISTORY
Kindle edition / July 2012
Berkley trade paperback edition / March 2013

ISBN: 978-0-425-26780-6

An application to register this book for cataloging has been submitted to the Library of Congress.

PRINTED IN THE UNITED STATES OF AMERICA

10   9   8   7   6   5   4   3   2   1

ONE: *Cami*

Sipping my beer, I look around at the familiar scene. If the honky-tonk music blaring from the speakers in the ceiling hadn't been enough to scream *COUNTRY BAR*, the sea of cowboy hats would have been. I smile as I adjust the black one that sits atop my own head. I love being incognito. Even if, by chance, someone I know stumbles into the smoke-filled dive, they'd never believe it was me looking out from beneath the brim.

Something hits the back of my bar stool—hard—just as I put the glass to my lips. Ice-cold beer pours down my chin and straight into my cleavage. I suck in a breath.

"'Scuse me," a deep voice rumbles in my ear. Two hands grip my upper arms and pull me back, keeping me from tipping right out of my seat. I'm looking down at my soggy jeans and T-shirt when I feel the hands disappear. Half a second later, a face appears in my line of sight. "I'm so sorry. Are you okay?"

My fingers stop plucking wet cotton away from my chest and

I stare. Quite rudely, I might add. I'm speechless. Literally. And that, like, *never* happens to me.

The most amazing eyes I've ever seen are staring back at me. They are pale greenish-gray, rimmed in sooty lashes and filled with concern.

A sharp jab to my shin makes me let out the breath I hadn't been aware of holding. I see my best friend Jenna's head poke out from behind the mystery face. I know she kicked me and I know she's trying to get my attention, but I can't look away from these eyes long enough to glare at her.

God, his eyes! I've never seen eyes that make me want to gasp and giggle and do a striptease all at once. But these do.

They flicker down, letting me go just long enough to collect my wits. I find very few of them. They are well and truly scattered. When he looks back up at me, his eyes are wrinkled at the corners. He's smiling. And holy hell, what a smile it is!

"Does it make me a bad person for liking your shirt better this way?"

I glance down at myself. My dark pink bra is plainly visible through the now-wet paper-thin material of my pale pink shirt. So are my very erect nipples. I blush, mortified.

Why, oh why did I wear a light pink T-shirt with a dark pink bra?

Because you can't see your bra through it when it's dry, dumbass.

A thumb brushes my right cheek. "God, that's sexy," he whispers. Against my will, my eyes fly to his face. His smile has died to a lopsided grin that is devastation in its purest form. "I've never made a girl blush before."

I laugh nervously, struggling to find my voice, to find my dignity. "Somehow I doubt that," I say softly.

"Wow! The hair of a devil, the face of an angel, and the voice of a phone sex operator. You really are the perfect woman."

To my utter humiliation, my cheeks burn even hotter. Curse my fair skin!

Reaching into his pocket, Hot Stranger pulls out a couple of bills and slides them across the bar. "Another of whatever . . ." He trails off, looking at me in question, waiting for me to fill in the blank.

"Cami," I say, trying to hold back my grin.

Smooth way of getting my name. Chalk one up for Hot Stranger.

"Another of whatever *Cami* is having." He turns back to me, a wicked gleam in his smoky eyes. "Sorry about your drink. Not so much about your shirt, though," he admits candidly.

Willing myself not to blush again, I tilt my head. "So, do clumsy strangers have names in this place? Or are you just called Bull in China Shop?"

The lopsided grin comes back. "Patrick, but my friends call me Trick."

"Trick? As in trick or treat? That kind of trick?"

He laughs and my stomach flutters. It actually flutters. "Yep. That kind of trick." He sobers and leans in close to me. "Cami, can I ask a favor?"

I'm breathless again. He's so close I can count every hair in the stubble that dusts his tanned cheeks. For just a second, his clean manly scent overrides the cigarette smoke and stale beer smell of the bar.

I lose my voice—again—so I nod.

"Pick 'treat.' Please, for the love of God, pick 'treat.'"

Like an idiot, I say nothing. I do nothing. I simply stare. Like a . . . a . . . well, like an idiot.

He makes a disappointed noise with his lips, then starts shaking his head. "Too bad. Woulda made my night."

He straightens, takes a step back, and smiles at me again. "Nice to meet you, Cami," he says, and then he turns and melts into the crowd.

"Earth to Cami!"

Tearing my gaze away from the broad-shouldered, slim-hipped view of Trick walking away, I turn to Jenna. "What?"

"Is that all you have to say? 'What?'" She's grinning.

"What would you like me to say?" I'm still a little addled. Or is it bedazzled?

"Um, I'd like to hear your plan for getting your lame ass off that stool and going over there to collect on that treat!"

"Eavesdrop much?"

"He was practically sitting in my lap while he hit on you. What was I supposed to do?"

"Uh, *move!*"

Jenna snorts. Not a great sound, but somehow she makes it seem cute and girly. "And miss that view? I was all but catatonic just look-ing at him. He is seven kinds of hot, Cam!"

I giggle. "Listen to you. You've got a boyfriend. Or have you con-veniently forgotten that we are meeting people here?"

"I haven't forgotten. Have you?"

I nod at her. "Touché, pussycat."

In truth, I had. From the time I'd looked up into Trick's eyes, I hadn't thought of Brent one time. And that can't be a good sign. Brent has *never* made me feel what this guy has in three minutes.

"Meh," she says, waving her hand dismissively as she sips her own beer. "Don't give it a second thought. Looking at him is kinda like staring at the sun. You see spots and you're dizzy for a while, but then it goes away."

I wonder to myself if I really *want* it to go away. I can't ever remember a guy making me feel this way.

I can't stop myself from looking into the crowd again. I scan the endless ocean of hats until my gaze stops on one dark head. The hair is longish and has a slight wave to it. I know without having to see his face that it's Trick. It just seems right that he'd be the only guy in the place not wearing a cowboy hat.

Almost like he can feel my eyes or my thoughts on him, Trick turns around. His gaze locks with mine like there isn't a room full of people between us. We stare at each other for a few seconds, and then, real slow, he grins.

Good God, he has dimples! I might die!

Right on cue, my cheeks get hot. Here we go again.

His grin widens into a smile, and he winks at me. I'm pretty sure my toes are numb. I watch him turn away. Before his head completely disappears, I consider what Jenna said. Maybe I should go and ask for the treat . . .

I jump when I feel fingers at my neck, brushing my hair back. "You looking for me?"

I recognize the voice. It's Brent. I sigh. It's not right that I should feel a little disappointed. But I do. The time for me to be reckless has passed. The door of opportunity has officially been closed. By Brent.

I turn on my stool. I smile up into the face of Brent Thomason, my boyfriend. He's everything a girl should want in a guy and certainly everything my father wants in one for me. But he's never really set my world on fire. And I've never really noticed. Until now.

Brent is no slob in the looks department. His sandy hair has that purposefully messy look and his dark brown eyes have an exotic tilt I've always found very appealing. But even as I stare into them, I'm picturing smoky greenish-gray ones.

"Were you looking for me?" he asks again.

I dodge the question, playfully poking him in the chest. "You're late!"

"I can't be *too* perfect. Gotta keep a girl like you on her toes." He kisses the tip of my nose and then brushes my lips with his.

"Did you get the 'Vette running?" I ask, leaning back.

"No. That's why I'm late. I just talked to the guy who was supposed to take a look at it for me. Since I couldn't even get it here, he agreed to look at it tomorrow night instead. I'll get it out there even if I have to have it towed," he growls in determination.

As usual, I find Brent's passion about his car a little bit of a turn-on. One of my father's obsessions is vintage cars. We have a garage full of them, and I know enough about them to talk like I've got some sense.

"Out where?"

He shrugs. "Eh, some sort of field thing. You know how country people are."

I feel my frown but can't stop it. I know Brent doesn't really mean anything by the comment, but it still bothers me. Unlike most of my friends, I know what life without money looks like, feels like. Granted, it was a long time ago, but some things a girl never forgets.

Sexy eyes drift through my mind . . .

"I want to get that thing running so I can drive you around and show you off. I mean, drive *it* around and show *it* off." He grins at me. I grin back. The sad thing is, I think he had it right the first time.

TWO: *Trick*

Tiny hands tap on the bare skin of my back. I feel the thump of them echo through my throbbing head.

"Uuuuuuuugh," I groan into the pillow.

I hear a giggle. "You sound like a monster when you do that."

I groan again, louder this time. Another giggle. Grace loves it when I sleep in. She gets a kick out of waking me up.

"I neeeeed foooood," I growl in my best monster voice. Then, as fast as I can manage to move first thing in the morning with a hangover, I turn over and loop my arm around her tiny waist and throw her onto the bed.

I grab her foot and start tickling it relentlessly. She jerks and wiggles, rolling around on the bed, giggling the whole time.

"Stop it! Stop it! Stop it! That tickles," she cries breathlessly.

"You know this is what happens when you wake the sleeping giant."

"I'm sorry! I'm sorry! I didn't mean to!"

I let her foot go and throw my legs over the side of the bed. "I'm letting you off easy this time, but only because you remembered the magic word."

"I'm sorry?" she asks as she sits up and pushes her dark brown bangs out of her eyes.

"No, that's two words. The magic word is *hippopotamus*."

She grins. "I didn't say *hippopotamus*, silly."

"You didn't? Well then . . ." I lunge at her and she scoots off the bed, squealing all the way out the door.

I sit back down on the bed, my head pounding painfully. *Not having* a ten-year-old sister in the house and *having* a bedroom door that locked were two of the major benefits of college life.

Don't go there. Too little, too late.

Pushing myself off the bed, I head for the bathroom.

At least it has a functioning lock. Thank God!

After a couple splashes of cold water to my face, the night before comes back in a rush. Amazing near-violet eyes come to mind and, right after that, a blush that makes me hard just thinking about it.

Cami. She was gorgeous!

Damn!

Not that it matters. Girls like that *always* have boyfriends. Possessive ones who know what they've got and are willing to throw down for it. I certainly would. She's the kind of girl you fight to the death for.

Damn.

"Hurry up, slowpoke. Breakfast is almost ready."

I hear Grace's little feet scampering away from the door, no doubt thinking I might come charging out after her. I smile into the mirror above the sink. Even though she can annoy the daylights out of me, I still love her. Hell, I practically raised her. I'm the only man in her life, the only father figure she's ever really had. Or at least the only one she can remember.

My thoughts turn bitter and angry, so I splash a little more cold water on my face before I head for the kitchen. Big, homemade breakfasts are one of the benefits of *not* being at college.

"Mornin', hon," Mom says with a bright smile.

"Mornin'," I return, sitting in front of the place she has set for me, the place that used to be my father's. "I told you, you don't have to do this, Mom. I can make myself breakfast."

"Not like this, you can't."

I grin. "Good point."

Her smile fades as she sits down with her own plate. She looks at me from the corner of her eye. "You out drinking again last night?"

I sigh. "Yeah. Why?"

"I'm not fussin'. It just seems like you've been doing an awful lot of that since you had to come home."

"Mom, I didn't have to come home. I *chose* to come home."

We both glance at Grace, who is pretending not to pay us any attention.

"I know it's not what you wanted and I feel—"

"Well, don't. Don't feel that way. I *wanted* to do it, Mom. You and Grace are all I've got. It just makes sense."

Her smile returns. "I knew all along you'd grow up to be this kind of man. I'm so proud of you, Patrick. I just wish . . ."

"Mom, college isn't going anywhere. I can finish up later. Right now, this is more important."

Her smile turns sad, and she nods. I know she feels guilty, like she ruined my life by telling me the insurance money had run out. For the first part of the last year, I felt that way, too. But I meant what I said; she and Grace are the only family I've got. If I don't take care of them, who will?

"Just promise me if it all gets to be too much, you'll say something. I don't want to see you drink yourself—"

"Mom!" I interrupt sternly. I soften it with a grin. "I'm fine. Really. It's just some fun with the boys. No big deal. There's nothing else to do around here, remember?"

She shrugs one shoulder and shoots my line back to me. "Good point."

THREE: *Cami*

The smell of bacon pulls me out of my dream with both hands. My first thought? *Where am I?* Once I realize the canopy above me was mine from childhood, my second thought comes in. *Drogheda's making me breakfast.*

I smile. One of the best things about spending the summer at home is Drogheda, the housekeeper and my oldest confidante, and her wonderful cooking.

As I lie in bed, enjoying the familiar smells, my third thought rushes in, disturbing the peace of the morning. It comes in a vision— two twinkling greenish-gray eyes and a sexy grin.

Trick.

I should *not* be thinking about him. Still. But somehow that boy got under my skin. Big-time.

Pick "treat." Please, for the love of God, pick "treat."

Just remembering those words makes my stomach do a flip. What is it about him?

I hear a loud clank come from the kitchen. I smile. Whenever I sleep longer than I should, Drogheda "accidentally" drops things in the kitchen. A lot. And very loudly. Eventually it wakes me up and I go down for breakfast. She's devious like that.

Throwing back the covers, I stretch before tiptoeing across the room to quietly open the door. Ever since I was twelve years old, Drogheda and I have played a game of cat and mouse the first day I'm back from school, before she gets used to me being home for the summer. I make a point to pop up unexpectedly and scare her at some point during that first day.

We did it all the way through prep school, and we've done it since I've been in college. It's one of those traditions that, no matter how childish it is, I'll always continue. And I'll always treasure.

This morning, I'm getting started early. I creep in through the back entrance of the kitchen, making my way silently through the butler's pantry. I peek around the corner and see Drogheda standing at the stove, her back to me. She's humming softly as she so often does when she cooks. She has a spatula in one hand, flipping pancakes.

I wait until she flips the last of the four and moves to set her spatula aside before I pounce. In three long strides, I wrap my arms around her.

"Drogheda!" I cry, squeezing her tightly and kissing her rounded caramel cheek.

Drogheda screeches and reaches around to smack my butt with her palm. She lets out a string of words in her native language before she says something in her thick accent that I can understand. "*Chica*, you scare an old woman half to death!"

"Oh, you love it and you know it." I reach around her and take a piece of bacon that's draining on a paper towel. "Aren't you happy to see me?"

Drogheda turns to me, one hand holding the spatula and the other on her hip. "Of course I'm happy to see you. The house is so empty without my *picaro*, my *poco diabla*."

I stop chewing, pointing my half-eaten strip of bacon at Drogheda. "My Spanish is a little rusty, but didn't you just call me a little devil?"

"Me?" Drogheda asks, feigning innocence. "No, *chica*. You must've misunderstood. Why, I would never call such a sweet, innocent child a name like that."

I snort. She snatches the bacon from my fingers and pops it in her mouth, then points her spatula at me.

"Ladies don't snort."

I grin. "Yes, ma'am."

"Now, you go sit down. Breakfast is almost ready."

As Drogheda fixes herself a cup of coffee and carries it to the table to sit with me while I eat, I think back to the days when Mom used to do all these things for me—cook for me, talk to me, listen to me, participate in my life. Since Daddy became *the* Jack Hines, Mom had to become Cherlynn Hines, the wife of *the* Jack Hines. And that entails much more time spent at the country club than it does sharing breakfast with me. I would be bitter if I didn't feel sorry for her most of the time. It's not always easy being a part of my father's immediate family.

"So, tell me about your plans for the summer," Drogheda urges.

"You mean besides attending every party within a hundred-mile radius and working on my tan?"

She swats at me. "Oh no! *Mi Camille* isn't going to grow up to be one of those useless rich women. Tell me what you're *really* going to do."

I smile. Drogheda knows me well.

"Actually, I'd like to learn a little more about the business. I mean, I've always loved horses, and somebody's gonna have to take over once Daddy gets too old to oversee it all."

"Ha," Drogheda laughs. "Your *papi* will never be too old. You will have to prove to him that you can be his *partner* first. And then, maybe one day . . ."

"That's some awfully sage advice from a pretty young thing like you, Drogheda. When did you get so smart?" At fifty-two, while she certainly isn't young, Drogheda definitely doesn't look her age. Her rich golden skin is still smooth and soft.

"What about that boy? Do you still see him?"

I smile. "Drogheda, his name is Brent, which you know. You are so ornery!"

She curls up her lip. "I don't care. I don't trust that boy. He is after something."

I grin devilishly. "I can tell you exactly what he's after."

Drogheda's face gets all stern, and she points a finger at me. "Don't you dare let him spoil you, *chica*! He's not worth it. Save that for someone who loves you."

It's my turn to roll my eyes. "I know, I know. I've had the lecture a thousand times, Drogheda. You *do* realize that I can't stay a virgin forever, right?"

She'd kill me if she knew it was a moot point.

"I'm not saying stay a virgin forever. I'm saying wait. Just wait."

"For what?"

"Not for what, for *who*."

"But I told you. Brent loves me."

"No, he doesn't. Not like he should. He loves your beautiful face and your young body and your father's company."

"What else is there?"

"One day, someone will love you with or without all those things. You just have to find him. You'll know when the time is right, *mi Camille*, when *the boy* is right. And trust an old woman, *that* boy is not the right one."

FOUR: *Trick*

I move out from underneath the hood of the Hemi 'Cuda and reach for a bottle of water.

"Damn, it's hot under there!"

"Six months at the new job and already you're a pansy," Jeff ribs good-naturedly.

"Pansy, my ass! Stables are just a lot bigger and cooler than this rinky-dink garage."

"I guess the next time you need to work on your Mustang, you'll just have to find a fancy garage to work in, then, won't you?"

"Who are you kidding? That car is cherry, man! She doesn't need any more work."

"It *looks* cherry, but I happen to know the guy that restored it. Freakin' pansy. Hell, that thing could fall apart on the road somewhere in BFE."

"Not gonna happen. I hear he's brilliant."

"A brilliant pansy?"

"Yep."

"And humble, too. Or so I hear."

"Seriously, Rusty," I begin. I've called my best friend, Jeff Catron, "Rusty" ever since his freckles started coming in around the third grade. Even though he'd long since outgrown them, the nickname stuck. "I just don't know if a fuel injection system is gonna work with this model. I don't think it's gonna fit, bro."

Rusty growls and runs a hand through his dark red hair. "Seriously?"

"You're the expert. You should know. I mean, I could be wrong, but I just don't see it happening."

He sighs. "I thought it was worth a shot. But I think you're right. I knew if there was anybody that could make it work, though, it'd be you."

"The brilliant pansy?"

Rusty grins. "The humble brilliant pansy." He wipes his hands on a towel and comes around to lean up against the grill of the 'Cuda. "I gotta check out a car for a guy tonight. Out in the field. You coming?"

I shake my head. "You're not talking me into this again."

"I'm just asking in case I run into trouble with it. It'd be nice if you could at least be there. I wouldn't ask if I didn't need you, man. This could be a big deal for future restorations, though. This kid comes from money. I helped out a friend of his, and now he's willing to give me a shot. Who knows where it could lead?"

Rusty's dream since we were kids has been to be a world-class muscle car restoration expert. I know his garage makes good money, more than enough to pay the bills, but he has dreams.

Just like I had dreams.

"If I let you sucker me into this, you owe me, Rus. Big-time."

Rusty nods. "Done. Anything."

I sigh. "All right. What time?"

"Nine thirty."

"I'll meet you there."

His face breaks into a huge smile.

How do I let him talk me into this shit?

FIVE: *Cami*

"Jenna, you should totally get that, especially if you want to make a little extra money," I say as she twirls in front of me.

She stops spinning and stares at me, confused. "Make a little extra money? Huh?"

"Sure. If I had some singles, I'd be trying to stuff a couple in your G-string right this minute."

"Oh. Ha. Ha," she says caustically, turning toward the bank of mirrors behind her. "Is it that bad?"

"Good Lord, Jenna! That skirt is so short I can see London, Paris, and France from right here."

Her lip pooches out in a pout. "Well, what about the shirt?"

"Shirt? Is that what you're calling it?" Although I do like the soft pink color and the lettuce edge, the top needs at least two more inches of material to *not* be considered one half of a bikini.

"God, when did you become my mother?"

"When you started dressing like a stripper," I tease with a wink.

Jenna's shoulders slump. "Is it really that bad?"

She isn't finding my teasing funny, which isn't like her at all. She usually gives as good as she gets. "You know I'm just picking on you. It's just . . . different. That's all. I love the color and the trim. And the skirt is really cute, it's just a little shorter than stuff you usually wear. That's all. Who are you trying to impress, anyway?"

She comes over and sits in the chair beside me. "Trevor and I have dated since our freshman year in high school. I know he loves me, but lately, I can't help but feel like I'm losing him a little."

"And this is how you plan to win him back?"

"Of course! What hot-blooded American guy doesn't love a stripper?"

"For the night, maybe. But for longer?" I look at her skeptically.

"So you're saying I shouldn't try to spice things up?"

"Spice things up?"

"Yeah. You know, spread my sexual wings a little."

"Exactly where are your wings located?" I kid as I look down at her short skirt.

She flips me the bird.

"Jenna, I'm not saying that at all. You know I, of all people, have zero advice to give. I'm just saying if it's a temporary thing, fine. But if you feel like you're losing him, like if it's an emotional thing, I don't think this is gonna help. At least not long term."

She screws up her face and sticks her tongue out at me. That's the Jenna equivalent of *Cami, you're right*.

"You're so smart it makes me sick." She shoves her shoulder against mine in that gentle way that friends do.

"Have you talked to Trevor about any of this?"

Jenna wrinkles her nose and shakes her head.

"You should, you know."

"I know, but it's not that easy."

"Well, find a way. He's a nice guy. Maybe it's fixable."

"I hope you're right," she says, sighing. Jenna stays slumped in her chair like Eeyore for a few more seconds before she perks up. She looks at me. "You totally get me, you know?"

"I know. And it scares me."

She grins, which is always a good sign. "So, stripper or no?"

I laugh. "Maybe one night as a stripper wouldn't hurt anything."

"And it might be fun." She waggles her eyebrows comically.

"All right, all right. Settle down. I think we're about to go into territory that makes my brain bleed." I have a strict policy about Jenna grossing me out with her TMI tendencies.

"You shouldn't think of it that way, Cam. You should look at my life as your own personal 'What Not to Do' manual." She turns to me with a wicked smile in place. "Of course, it more often serves as the 'What *to Do*' manual."

I roll my eyes as she struts back to the dressing room.

"It looks gorgeous," Jenna says from the edge of my bed as she watches me curl my hair. "If you keep messing with it, you'll ruin it."

I push the handle to release the last curl. It falls into a gentle spiral. My hair has a natural wave. It's not curly in that enviable loose-curl way and it's not straight in that enviable poker-straight way. It's just wavy, wavy in that has-a-mind-of-its-own way. Basically, I have two options in life: a curling iron or a flat iron.

"Why are you so worried about it, anyway? You never go to this much trouble for Brent."

"What? I can't spice things up, too?"

"Since when does your relationship with Brent need spicing up?"

"It's not that it *needs* spicing up. I just thought it could use a little . . ." Greenish-gray eyes flash at me from my memory. It could use some of *that*, some of what Trick made me feel in less than five minutes.

"Since when?" Jenna's perceptive stare pins me from across the room. "Unless this isn't about Brent at all."

I look away from her eyes. "I don't even know what that's supposed to mean." But I do. I know exactly what she means. And she's right.

"Camille Elizabeth Hines, are you still thinking about that guy from last night?"

"No! What guy?"

Jenna's mouth drops open and her eyes get wide. "You are!" She slides off the bed and walks toward me, her hands on her hips. "You're still thinking about that hot guy from the bar."

"You're crazy. I have—"

"You are such a liar! I know you too well, Cami. Tell the truth."

I turn toward her and lean against my vanity. "Okay, so what if I am? It's not like I'm ever gonna see him again. What's the big deal?"

"The big deal is that you finally found a guy who really does it for you. Good God, I've been waiting for years for this to happen." Jenna steeples her fingers in front of her mouth, her forehead wrinkled dramatically. "My baby's growing up."

I throw my brush at her. "Oh, stop!"

Her expression turns serious. "Listen to me. You're my best friend and I love you. I'm not saying that you need to chase after some guy you met once in a bar. But you should give this some thought, Cami. If Brent doesn't make you feel all that and more, something's wrong. I'm just sayin'."

Deep down, I know she's right. I love Brent, but he doesn't turn my insides to mush or fill my thoughts day and night. But he's a great guy who treats me well and has my father's approval. And he's hot. Who doesn't like to have a hot date to kiss?

"Well," I begin, straightening. "None of this affects our plans for the night. How do I look?"

Jenna scans me from the top of my dark red curls to my black shorts and cowboy boots.

"Hot enough to go trick-or-treating," she responds with a wink.

SIX: *Trick*

Even in the dark, with only the glow from the lights around the makeshift stage that used to be the floor of a barn, I see her. The instant she walks through the gate, she draws my eye like honey draws a bee.

Her hair is all wild around her face, making me want to run my fingers through it. She's wearing a skintight shirt and a pair of shorts that show off the longest legs I've ever seen. I can't help but get lost in the thought of what those legs would feel like wrapped around me. And the best part is, she's with another girl. The same girl she was with at the bar. Not a guy.

"Hey, Leo," I call to the guy setting up the keyboard. He plays for the cover band that's entertaining in the field tonight. "If Rusty comes looking for me, tell him I'll be right back."

I make my way around the edge of the crowd, back to where Cami and her friend have stopped to watch the band set up. As I come up to her left side, she turns to look at me.

Now, I've got an ego just like any other guy, but I also know when a girl is attracted to me. And this girl is attracted to me.

Her eyes light up and her lips spread into the most beautiful smile this side of heaven.

"You really should stop following me," I say with a grin.

"Apparently I can't seem to help myself," she replies, her eyes twinkling.

"I'm unfortunate in that way. So much animal magnetism, the ladies just lose all control."

She laughs, a deep, husky sound that makes me want to groan. "And so humble, too."

"That's the second time I've heard that today. I'm not sure what it means."

"That you know two delusional people?"

"Most likely."

She smiles. I smile. I could just look at her all night long.

"So, what brings you to a field party? I'm pretty sure I'd remember if I'd seen you here before."

"Oh, really? Come to a lot of field parties, do you?"

I shrug. "Not anymore, but if I'd ever seen you at one, I would remember. Trust me."

The glow of the stage lights is enough for me to see her blush.

"You're really gonna have to quit doing that."

"Doing what?" she asks coyly.

"Blushing like that."

"I assure you, if I could avoid it, I would."

"But then I'd just have to make it my mission in life to make you blush. By whatever means necessary."

Her smile falters a little and her eyes dart to my mouth.

God help me!

* * *

"So, what did you say you were doing here?"

"I didn't."

"But you were going to."

"Was I?"

"Well, it's either that or you were going to take me up on my offer."

I hear her soft gasp, even above the noise of the crowd around us. It squirms in my stomach and makes my palms itch to touch her.

She clears her throat. "Actually, I'm here with my boyfriend."

"Damn. I knew you were too beautiful to be unattached. It's just a shame you're dating an idiot."

"An idiot? Why is that?"

"Any guy would have to be out of his mind to leave you alone at a party for one second."

"I'm not alone."

She turns around to her friend, but she's gone. "Well, I *wasn't* alone."

"But now you are."

She nods but doesn't try to make any excuses to leave. She just watches me. And I watch her.

This might be the only chance you get, Trick.

I take a step closer. She doesn't move away. "There is one thing I should've told you last night," I say, taking one more step toward her. I reach out and loop one long fiery curl around my finger and bring it to my mouth. It feels like silk and smells like strawberries.

"What's that?" she asks, her voice a little breathless.

"I don't mind a little competition."

"You don't?"

"No, but I hate to lose."

"Do you lose often?"

I lean down, my face only inches away from hers. I watch those incredible eyes as they flit between my mouth and my eyes over and over again.

"Never," I whisper.

And then I press my lips to hers. They're soft and warm and just as lush as they look. I keep expecting her to pull away, but she doesn't.

Deciding to make the most of my one shot, I slide my fingers into her heavy hair and tilt her head to the side. Her lips part and I slip my tongue right between them.

The inside of her mouth tastes like sugar and mint. I tease the tip of her tongue and it flirts back a little with mine. What really surprises me is when I feel her hand at my waist. Her fingers fist in my shirt. She's holding on for dear life.

I wind my arm around her tiny waist and pull her body in close to mine. I feel her melt against me. It's all I can do not to throw her over my shoulder and carry her off into the dark. But a throat being cleared behind me ruins my fantasy.

She tenses in my arms and I know without opening my eyes that it's her boyfriend. I ease my head back, breaking the contact with her lips, missing it immediately, and I smile down into her eyes.

"That was worth what's about to happen next."

I turn slowly around to face my aggressor. His face is red with fury.

I preempt him. "All right, you get one freebie. Make it count."

I tuck my hands behind my back and I stand there and wait. The guy looks like he has no idea what to do.

Hell, if that was my girl, I'd be on you like stink on shit.

Finally, after looking behind me at Cami, he balls up his fist and makes a passable attempt at a punch. It's so slow, I turn my head and his knuckles glance off the side of my face. Probably won't even leave a mark.

"Fair enough. Now, you go your way and I'll go mine."

I pull my hands out from behind my back and start to walk off. From the corner of my eye, I see him lunge at me. I sidestep him and he nearly loses his balance and falls on his face. When he turns around, I know it's more about pride now, which means he's getting ready to get stupid.

"Look, man, I gave you a free shot for kissing your girlfriend. Don't push it."

The guy comes at me swinging this time. I block his first punch, duck his second, and then put my fist in the center of his gut. He doubles over and I lean down to speak quietly to him. "Stay down. If you don't, this won't end well for you."

With that, I nod to the guy's slack-jawed friend, wink at Cami, and walk casually away.

Smart guy. He stayed down.

SEVEN: *Cami*

It takes me a second to recover after Trick winked at me. It doesn't help when I hear Jenna mumble behind me, "Mother of hell! That was effin' hot." Finally, I snap back to my senses and go to Brent.

"Are you all right?"

I put my hand on his arm, but he jerks it back. "What do you think you were doing?"

In the face of the emotional hurricane that's blowing around inside me—guilt over thinking about Trick, guilt over wanting him to kiss me, pleasure over being in his arms, disappointment that Brent doesn't make me feel that way, shame for cheating on my boyfriend—I latch on to the one defensive thing I can find—indignation. I would call it righteous indignation, but the way I'm still trembling after Trick's kiss, I think *righteous* might be a stretch. *Indignation* will just have to do.

"You're mad *at me* because someone else kissed me? I had

absolutely nothing to do with it! It's not like I sought him out. I suppose it'd be my fault if I got hit by lightning, right?"

And that's kind of what it felt like, like I'd been struck by lightning. Delicious, toe-curling, hair-raising, belly-stirring lightning.

"Well, it didn't look like you were fighting very hard."

"Did you ever consider that it might've taken me by surprise? I mean, it's not like I came expecting some random guy to come up and kiss me."

But if I'd known Trick would be here, I would've wished for it.

"I'm sorry," Brent said, hanging his head a little. "You're right. I don't know what I was thinking."

Guilt stabs at my conscience again. "Can we just forget about all this and enjoy the band?"

Brent sighs. "Yeah. I don't want this to ruin your whole night."

"Good," I say with a smile, winding my arm through his. "Let's get a drink and go watch the band."

"Where's Trevor?" Jenna asks, as we turn to make our way to the keg.

"He's still talking cars with that guy out front. He'll be here shortly."

A few minutes later, each of us armed with a red Solo cup full of beer, we make our way toward the stage. The band is getting ready to go on.

They're a local group called Saltwater Creek. I happen to know of them because they played a couple of college gigs that I attended. They're a really good cover band with a few original songs that aren't half bad.

The lead singer and guitar player, Collin, walks to the microphone. "All right, all right, all right," he says in his best Matthew McConaughey drawl. "We're one man short, but I think we could go ahead and get started if y'all can help me talk our friend, Trick, into coming up and filling in for a song or two. Come on up, Trick."

Every eye in the crowd turns toward the foot of the stage. Trick is there. He starts shaking his head and backing away from the stage, his hands held up in a *stop* gesture.

"Aw, come on, man. Do it for the people. They're here to rock and roll. Let's give 'em what they want."

He's still shaking his head, even though several guys around him are pushing him toward the stage.

"Let's hear it for Trick, everybody!" Collin shouts. "Trick! Trick! Trick!"

The crowd joins the chant and Trick looks around, a slow smile curving his lips. For just a moment, his eyes meet mine. I look away before Brent notices.

"Yeah!" Collin yells as the crowd starts clapping.

I look back toward the front. Trick is walking onto the stage. Someone hands him a bass guitar and he puts the strap around his neck. He takes the pick and starts testing the tune of the instrument. The crowd quiets until they hear the familiar chords of "Cat Scratch Fever" begin to emerge. Then they go wild.

Walking to the front of the stage, Trick picks the notes effortlessly. When his solo riff is over, the rest of the band chimes in, beginning with the heavy beat of the drum. Girls start screaming, guys start hollering, and I can't help but smile.

I'm really beginning to enjoy myself when, all the way across the throng of partiers, Trick looks up and his eyes meet mine. I am a deer caught in the headlights. I am a girl charmed by the cobra. I am breathless and mesmerized.

And then he grins.

Just like that, I'm his. Whether he knows it or not.

EIGHT: *Trick*

"I want Titan looking his best. A trainer with a syndicate out of Alabama is coming at the end of the month to look at him. I happen to know they pay top dollar for a bloodhorse and Titan is our best two-year-old."

I look at my boss, Jack Hines. His dark brown hair is styled like a man who uses hair spray, his fingernails are clean like a man who gets a manicure, and his eyes are hard like a man who gets what he wants however he can.

Jack Hines. Self-made man. Millionaire. Champion breeder. Dumbass.

"Yes, sir," I say as I continue to rub down Revere.

"They're willing to look at Knight-Time. I think if they give him a shot, they'll want him. Maybe even over Titan."

I nod. I totally disagree, but I nod, anyway. "What about Highland Runner? Have you given any more thought to—"

He shakes his head once. I've worked here only six months, but I know what that means. I grit my teeth.

"That horse is still too wild. If I make the decision to race, it will be one from my own stock. A horse born on this farm, like Knight-Time. If he's not sold before then, that is. If anything, I foresee Highland Runner ending up staying here to stud. His bloodlines are good, but . . . These are the kinds of things you need to learn, Patrick, the subtle nuances of this business that will serve you well if you continue on in it."

The jab hits its mark. He's putting me in my place. He's the expert; I'm not. I get it. He knows how much faith I have in Runner. And he thinks I'm crazy.

But *I* think *he's* blinded by money. Because Runner didn't cost him much, Jack thinks he's worthless. He couldn't be more wrong.

"Just have them ready," he commanded, turning and stalking away in that arrogant way he has. Before he gets out of the stable, he stops and hollers down to me. "My daughter is home from school now. She likes to ride most every day. See that you help her if she needs it. But nothing else."

What the hell?

"Yes, sir."

I'm a hired hand, which means I'm also a rapist? His daughter is probably all of, what, sixteen and goes to, like, a prep school or something? No doubt she's as arrogant and detestable as he is. Like I'd touch that with a ten-foot pole!

I finish rubbing down Revere and take him back to his stall. As I pass Runner's stall, I feel even more frustrated.

Dammit!

"Sooty!" I yell for the breeder-slash-trainer. I hear his faint voice from somewhere at the other end of the stable. "I'm taking Runner out." He mumbles something else. It doesn't sound like a no, so I grab Runner's tack.

I took up with Highland Runner the first time I met him. He's an amazing horse. Yeah, he's a little wild and unruly, but he's come a long way since I've been here. All he needs is a firm hand and someone who's not afraid to ride him. And I'm just that person.

After I get him saddled, I lead him out to the round pen to put him through his paces. I shorten his normal routine so I can ride him out in the fields. The Hines ranch has acres and acres of smooth grassy fields perfect for riding the two year-olds and breeding horses, and for letting them out to run alone.

I let us through the gate and get back onto Runner. His muscles twitch. He knows what's coming. And he's ready for it.

Runner responds to me perfectly, just like he always does. Jack Hines just never takes the time to watch him. Not really, anyway. His mind is set and that's that.

But I know. I know Runner. I know his potential. It's a gut feeling I have. And my gut is rarely wrong.

Just like my gut wasn't wrong about Cami.

Cami.

Like she has a dozen times over the last day and a half, she pops into my head. It happens at the strangest times.

I smile. That girl . . .

Her boyfriend better keep an eye on her. If I get hold of her again, I'm liable to steal her away.

I smile. The thing is, I think I probably could. That's just not really my way. Now if she leaves him *for me* . . . that's a whole other story.

Just the thought of those lush lips and that tight little body makes the crotch of my jeans shrink about two sizes. And that's not a good thing when I'm on a horse's back.

I guide Runner back to the stable. From the corner of my eye, I see a flash of dark copper catch the sun. I feel the grin tugging at my lips when I see none other than the object of my daydream walking toward the stable with her friend.

How did she find me?

Doesn't matter. She found me. Now she's as good as mine.

When Runner reaches the stable doors, I hop off his back and walk him the rest of the way in. I stop him in front of his stall so I can bathe him and groom him after his run.

I peel my sticky shirt off and run my fingers through my damp hair.

"This is gonna feel good for both of us, huh, Runner?" I say to the horse. He puffs once. I always get a little wet when I bathe the horses. Guess I'm just a messy guy.

I get everything ready and I'm just starting to hose him off when she comes into the stable. I look up and she's watching me. She looks fresh-faced and sexy as hell in her worn-out blue jeans, boots, and little red shirt. Her hair is wound up in some sort of loose bun-type thing on top of her head. I can imagine her taking it down and shaking that red mess free, real slow. Makes me want to pound something just thinking about it.

The strange thing is, she looks confused. Like she's surprised to see me.

But why would she be surprised when she *came here looking for* me?

NINE: *Cami*

Jenna mumbles exactly what I'm thinking.

"Holy shit! Will you look at that!"

I know I'm staring. Rudely. Again. But I can't help it. At the other end of the stable stands Trick. He's shirtless, hatless, and wet. And I'm pretty sure I've never seen anything hotter.

His arms are long and muscular and his shoulders are wide. When I look at them, one word comes to mind—*powerful*. He's a lot like the horses in the way his muscles move and bunch under his smooth skin. And his chest! Dear God, those pecs are just begging for my fingers to dig right in.

His stomach completes the perfect package of his upper body. It's rippled like the surface of the lake when I drop a rock into it, every abdominal well-defined.

His skin is tan, like he spends a lot of time outdoors without his shirt on. And, considering the weapons this boy is packing, I think he's doing the world a favor by going shirtless.

My eyes travel to his big hands as he rubs them over Runner's side.

"What the hell is he doing here?" Jenna whispers, again voicing what is going through my mind.

He's bathing a horse. One of my father's *horses. What the . . . ?*

I had been heading for Firewalker's stall, but now I veer toward Trick and Runner. As I approach, he looks up, his gray eyes raking me appreciatively from head to toe. He grins up at me. It's lopsided and just about the sexiest thing ever.

"What are you grinnin' at?" I ask.

"You are a walking, talking wet dream in those jeans." I blush. Of course. His grin turns into a smile. "You sure that's how you want to start this conversation? Remember how it ended up last time?" My cheeks burn and I know they're fiery red. He chuckles. "Maybe I just should've said hi instead."

I ignore him and come back with my own question. "What are you doing here?"

His smile falters a bit, and he frowns. "Isn't this where you expected me to be?"

"Um, no. Why would I?"

"That's a good question. You came looking for me. I figured you'd have a reason."

"No, Jenna and I came out to go for a ride. Why would I look for you here?"

I'm fascinated by the string of emotions that flit across his face. At first he looks confused, but then he looks like he wants to laugh, like it's a joke. Then he looks more confused and that turns into disbelief, like in his mind he's saying, *No way!* But then, much to my surprise, he looks aggravated. No, scratch that. He looks downright mad.

"You're Jack's daughter."

It's a statement, not a question. And he is *not* happy about it.

"Yes, I am."

"Damn!" I hear him mutter under his breath.

"But that still doesn't explain what you're doing here."

He pauses, running his fingers through his damp hair.

"I work here."

"Oh," I say, deadpan.

A long, uncomfortable silence stretches between us. His reaction tells me all I need to know about his position on flirting with the boss's daughter. I wonder if he's as disappointed as I am. I don't even know why I feel that way, but I do.

You have a boyfriend, dummy! Why does it even matter?

"Well, if you need any help getting your horse ready, just let me know," he says dismissively. He gets right back to spraying down Runner as if Jenna and I aren't standing two feet away.

I do my best not to stomp off, but it's hard. I feel like throwing a fit that only a two-year-old could be proud of.

Jenna's scrambling beside me. She looks back and then grins over at me. "He's totally watching you leave."

For some reason, that makes me feel a little bit better.

TEN: *Trick*

"**M**an, I haven't seen a girl get under your skin like this since high school."

I look at Rusty over the top of my mug. "Who're you kidding? She's not under my skin."

"Riiiiiight," he says with a grin.

Ignoring him, I glance around the bar for any familiar faces. Lucky's is the only bar in the area, and me and my friends have been coming here since we got our first fake IDs. Since the fairly small town of Greenfield started growing a few years back, I'd begun seeing more and more strangers in the smoke-filled room. But tonight, I'm not looking for a stranger.

My eyes stop on the back of a blond head. I recognize the girl standing at the bar, her curvy figure barely concealed in a pair of tiny shorts and a tank top. It's ReeAnn Taylor. She's always been into me. She's good-looking and, more important, she doesn't have a boyfriend *or* a father who could fire me.

"Don't even think about it, Trick."

"Think about what?"

"ReeAnn. Tappin' that won't get the rich girl out of your head. Only one thing will."

Cami.

I growl into my beer.

Why does she have to be his daughter?

"Look at it this way, you can always find a job someplace else."

"Like where? The Hines ranch is the only Thoroughbred farm for a hundred miles or more."

"Well, do something different."

"Like what? Without my degree, I can't get a job doing anything else that pays as well as Jack does. And we need the money. I didn't leave college to come home and get a job because I had nothing better to do. You know I had no choice."

"Well, maybe you could—"

"Just forget it, Rus," I interrupt. "It is what it is. I'll just stay away from her and everything will be fine. It's not a big deal. She's just a girl."

In an effort to prove my point (as much to myself as to Rusty), I get up and walk over to ReeAnn. When I stop beside her, she turns around, almost right into my arms.

She looks up at me with her pretty brown eyes and smiles. "Did you come to ask me to dance?" she asks.

"Would you have said yes?"

She nods and slips her hand into mine. I lead her out onto the dance floor just in time for a slow song. She plasters her body against mine and winds her arms around my neck. I can feel her breasts rubbing my chest and her hips swaying suggestively against mine.

It would be too, too easy, wouldn't it?

*   *   *

I ignore the fact that I don't want easy and I tighten my arms around ReeAnn's waist. She tucks her face against my throat and snuggles in, purring like a contented cat. Her perfume smells nice, but it's a little strong. I try not to notice how it smells nothing like fresh strawberries.

I push that thought right out of my head as soon as it arrives, and I let my hands trail down ReeAnn's back to her hips. I feel her fingers dive into my hair and she leans into me, rubbing her lower body against mine. I think to myself that I could probably get into this if she keeps doing what she's doing.

That thought stops in its tracks when I look up and my eyes crash into the violet ones I've been seeing far too often. Cami and her friend Jenna are standing not ten feet away, underneath the Lucky's sign. They must've just arrived. Cami's staring at me like I have two heads.

Right on cue, ReeAnn wiggles in my arms like she's trying to remind me I should be thinking about her, not someone else. I look away from Cami and try to focus on the girl trying to crawl inside my shirt. But it's no use. Suddenly, ReeAnn's perfume is suffocating me, her skinny arms are choking me, and her sexy-little-kitty noises are just plain annoying me.

With a sigh, I loosen my hold. I finish the dance with ReeAnn, but only just. All I can think of is getting away from her, getting out of this bar and getting into a nice, warm bottle of tequila. I know from experience there's a special kind of oblivion at the bottom of the bottle, and that's just what I need on a night like tonight.

ELEVEN: *Cami*

The sun is streaming through the window right into my eyes. Normally, I wouldn't mind waking up to that, but today . . . not so much. Like unwanted flashbacks from war, the scene I stumbled upon last night won't let me be. Even when I squeeze my eyes shut, I can't seem to stop seeing Trick and that girl all wrapped around each other.

Makes me sick!

I refuse to consider why it bothers me *at all* or how pathetic it must've seemed when I left Lucky's less than thirty minutes after arriving. I should've known the night was gonna blow. Jenna didn't even want to go to begin with. Me and my bright ideas.

That's what you get for going to a place like that when you've got a boyfriend, anyway. You wanted to run into him, and you got what you asked for.

I roll over and pull my pillow over my head. I'm not ready to face the day yet.

"Cami! Cami!" It's Drogheda and she's shaking my shoulder. Something must be wrong for her to be in my room waking me up.

"What?" I ask, sitting straight up in the bed, startled.

"You sleep like the dead this morning, *chica*. I've been banging around in the kitchen for over an hour and still, you sleep."

"Sorry. I didn't get much rest last night and I'm still tired." I must've dozed off after I woke up the first time, because I didn't hear all of Drogheda's finely honed skills of annoyance.

"What's the matter, *mi Camille*?"

That actually makes me smile. Drogheda is the only person in the world who can get away with calling me Camille, and only because she makes it sound like an endearment rather than the name I hate so much.

"Nothing," I reply, with a shake of my head. I don't look her in the eye. Drogheda's got some kind of crazy sixth sense, and she can tell when I'm lying to her. I've learned it's best to avoid eye contact.

She stares at me, moving her head when I move mine until I'm forced to look at her.

"You tell me now, missy!" Drogheda can be very no-nonsense when the occasion calls for it.

I sigh. "It's nothing really. Just this guy." I sit up and tuck my hair behind my ears. "And I mean, I've got a boyfriend, which makes the whole thing just really stupid."

"What whole thing? Tell me from the beginning."

So I do. I tell Drogheda all the not-so-sordid details. It surprises me when she grins. And, for Drogheda, it's a pretty devilish grin, too.

"What did I tell you? *That boy* is not the right one for you. Didn't I tell you you'd find the *right boy*?"

"Drogheda, Brent is a great guy. Didn't *I* tell *you* that?"

"Ay-yi-yi! That's all I hear for years now, but *this* is what I want to hear. I want to hear you tell of a boy who gets in your head," she says, tapping my temple with her finger, "and in your heart, too." She taps my chest over my heart.

"But Brent—"

"Pssssh," she says, waving her hands at me. "I don't want to hear any more excuses, *mi Camille*. Keep that boy around if you must, but don't turn your back on this new one. You have to give love a chance. When it's real, it will find a way."

My laugh is short and bitter. "Can it find a way around Jack Hines?"

"Have faith, *chica*. Love can even find a way around your father."

Drogheda's smile is sweet and encouraging, just what I needed this morning whether I knew it or not. Impulsively, I lean over and wrap my arms around her neck.

"What would I do without you, Drogheda?"

"You'd be lazy all day, that's what." She slides off the bed and swats at me with the dish towel she's still carrying. "Now, come eat your breakfast so I can clean up the kitchen."

"I'm coming, I'm coming! Give me a minute," I complain good-naturedly.

Drogheda rolls her eyes in exasperation and walks away, muttering something in Spanish that I can't understand but sounds awfully cute.

Somewhere between my bedroom and the kitchen, I decide to go see my father, the only person I can think of who might know more about Trick than I do, which isn't much. Much to my surprise, I pass my mother coming out of his office. She nearly runs me over.

"There you are, baby girl! I was afraid I'd miss you again this morning," she says, leaning in to kiss my cheek. She smells like fresh linen, just like she always has. Now the linen is just more expensive.

"What are you still doing here?" I ask, looking into eyes so much like my own as she leans back.

"Is it so terrible to want to see my daughter for five minutes when she's home for the summer?"

I smile. "Of course not. You're just usually on your way to the club or at some kind of meeting by now. I'm just surprised. That's all." She looks a little wounded, so I hurry to continue. "I'm glad you stayed. Wanna go out for lunch later? Maybe after, get a mani-pedi and do some shopping?"

"I wish I could, but I've got a day full of meetings and appointments today. Can I take a rain check?"

Some things never change. "Sure, Mom. Later."

She smiles and glances down at her fingernails. "I might regret putting this off. What will the ladies think if I'm all chipped?" We look at each other and then both burst into laughter. Mom rolls her eyes. She plays her role well, but my mom is still in there. Somewhere.

As she leaves, I make my way into the office. My father is sitting behind his desk. This is the first time I've seen him since I got home. I notice a little gray at his temples that wasn't there at Christmas. Otherwise, he looks the same—short dark hair, tan skin, and sharp blue eyes that see right through me when he looks up.

I smile brightly. "Morning, Daddy." I lean against the doorjamb and yawn.

"I was beginning to wonder if I was going to get to see you at all," he says with a smile, laying his pen to the side. He leans back in his chair and steeples his fingers as he watches me.

"Sorry. I've been with Jenna the last few days and I guess you've been . . . what? Checking out new horses?"

He shrugs. "Nothing you need to be concerned about."

"What if I want to be?"

He frowns. "What's the supposed to mean?"

I walk on into his office and sit down in one of the big leather armchairs that face his desk. "Daddy, I'm thinking of spending the summer learning more about the business."

"Why?"

I shrug. "Because I want to. You know how much I love horses. But I've always just loved riding them. I've never really seen the business side of things, and it's something I'm interested in."

His smile isn't very big, but it is full of pride and pleasure, which makes me feel good. Maybe he's been waiting for this day all along. Who knows?

"I think we can arrange some kind of internship, then."

Internship. Inwardly, I roll my eyes. I should've known Jack Hines wouldn't throw the least bit of nepotism my way. "Sounds good. I thought maybe I could make a couple of trips with you this summer. You know, check out new horseflesh and meet some of your contacts."

He nods. "I've got one coming up next month that would be a good place to start."

"Just let me know when and I'm on it."

He continues to nod. I can practically see the wheels turning. And the expectations rising. "You should make some time to start looking into the genetics of Thoroughbreds, then. Financial investment, too. You need to have a good understanding of both those aspects before you start meeting other breeders."

"I can do that." There's a long pause, during which I know I'm being appraised. That always makes me uncomfortable. "So, I met the new guy yesterday. What's up with him? What happened to Ronnie?"

"Found out he was mixed up in some . . . undesirable affairs. I let him go."

"So where'd you find his replacement?"

"Some locals knew of him. He grew up around horses. Supposed to be real good with them. Has some veterinarian training. Thought I'd give him a try. He's young. Twenty-three, I think. If he works out, he could have a long career with us."

"How long has he been here?"

"About six months, I guess."

"How's he working out?"

Daddy nods in that way he has that says he might be a little impressed. Might be. "He's doing pretty good so far. I think he has a lot to learn, but I don't see any problems with him being able to do that. Eventually." Sharp blue eyes narrow on me. They make me want to squirm. That look always precedes something I don't like. "Why the twenty questions?"

I shrug and try to be as casual as I can, even though nothing about Trick makes me feel casual. "Just normal curiosity about the new guy. Nothing special."

"I'm sure Brent wouldn't want you hanging around with the young male help."

I feel my hackles rise. What a snob! It amazes me that Daddy, having come from a meager background, can act like he's had money all his life. Drawing lines between us and "the help," like some of us were born with silver spoons in our mouths.

I hold my tongue for a minute so as not to say something defensive that might give away my interest in all things Trick. "I don't plan to hang around with the help, Daddy. Any more than I ever have. But you know I love to ride."

"Well, you can do that in the evenings, then. Between enjoying your summer and learning some of the business, your days will be pretty full. Speaking of which, I think Brent is coming over with his father later today. Perfect day for a swim."

Thwarted! Damn!

I smile. I hope it's not as tight as it feels.

TWELVE: *Trick*

Why did I drink so much last night?

Four Tylenol and nearly a gallon of water into the day and my head *still* hurts. I've already taken Titan through his paces and groomed him, exercised Knight-Time and groomed him, and rotated Revere to a different pasture for a few hours. Surely that's a whole day's worth of work in about four short hours.

I'm walking Lonesome, the broodmare, out to the north pasture when I hear a splash. I look toward the house and I see a dark head break the water in the pool. As I walk, I watch its owner swim across the length and then stand up in the shallow end.

It's Cami.

Wet, her hair is much darker. Like a rich coppery brown color. As she walks through the water and more of her body emerges, Lonesome and I both stop in our tracks.

She slicks the water out of her hair and mounts the couple of steps that bring her all the way out of the water. And then, God help me, she turns in my direction to walk toward a lounge chair where her towel is lying.

My stomach aches a little at the sight of her. She's wearing a shiny bronze bikini that looks like it was made for her. The bottoms are high-cut to show off her long legs and flat stomach. The top is nothing more than two tiny triangles that hang on to each perfect breast.

Oh hell! She looks even better than I thought she would in my head.

I'm standing here, kind of spellbound, watching her rub the water from her arms and legs when she looks up. Her head snaps up fast, almost like she can feel my eyes on her. I wish she could. I'd *really* give her something to smile about.

She stops drying off and just stands there with her towel in her hands and looks at me. I feel like there's a piece of yarn tied between us and the longer she stands there, the tighter it gets. Like it's drawing me toward her. I can't go to her, of course. But God, I want to!

She jumps, like something startled her, and she turns back toward the house. I see her boyfriend walking around the pool toward her. I don't really want to see them together, but for some reason, I'm still not moving.

He stops in front of Cami and throws his towel on the chair where hers was. Slowly, he reaches up and takes her towel from her hands. He's going to kiss her. I just know it. And my teeth are gritted. I don't know why I should even care, but I do.

He lays her towel aside, too, but rather than kissing her, he bends down and throws her over his shoulder and jumps in the pool. I hear her squeal just before a big splash that's followed by their laughter.

I move around to the other side of Lonesome and tug on her reins. Their playful voices follow me all the way to the second gate. I imagine what Cami looks like when she laughs, when she's as happy as she sounds.

I almost wish he'd kissed her instead.

I'm walking back to the stable after dropping off Lonesome, doing my dead-level best not to look in the direction of the pool. The fact that it's awfully quiet makes me wonder what's going on in the water. It also makes me want to punch that rich prick right in the face.

I grin at the prospect.

"What're you up to?" Sooty asks me from the doorway of the stable when I get within sight.

"Nothing. Why?"

"You're smiling like the cat that ate the canary. Why would that be?"

I shrug. "Just thinking."

Sooty eyes me with his shrewd faded blue gaze. I'd be willing to bet they don't miss a thing. That perceptiveness, that attention to the smallest detail is part of what makes him a great trainer. He doesn't miss anything with the horses, just like he doesn't miss anything with people.

Finally, he smiles. His yellowed teeth are a dead giveaway of his lifetime love of tobacco.

"Wouldn't have anything to do with a girl, would it?" He spits into the dirt floor and scuffs at it with his boot. He's one of the few people I've ever met who chews tobacco between cigarettes. I can't help but wonder if he ever sleeps.

"Yeah, it does. A mare. By the name of Lonesome. I just put her out in the north field."

He inclines his head, his way of saying he's respecting my privacy. "Fair enough. Females are females, don't matter the species. You'll learn that soon enough when you see us breed Lonesome in a few weeks. Doesn't matter how much she likes that stud, she'll kick at him at first. It's nature's way."

"That's all fine and good for horses, but females don't kick at me, Sooty."

"Don't be surprised if you find one along the way that does, though. Just means she's worth a little extra effort."

Playfully, I punch the old guy in the arm. "Sooty, you dog! I never figured you for one that likes it rough. You don't take any of these riding crops home, do you?"

Sooty snickers a little and shakes his head. "Boy, you're not right in the head."

"Isn't that a job requirement for working here?"

He gives me one short bark of laughter, which is like striking humor gold with Sooty. "So it is, Patrick. So it is."

As he's walking off, he spits again and then turns back to me. "Mint Julep ought to be ready to foal in the next week or two. You're welcome to hang around here during the night until she gives birth if you want to. There's another room up in the loft. Up to you. You can tell Jack I said it's okay."

I nod to Sooty. This is a big deal. It's his way of saying he's taking me in, that he thinks I'm worth his time to teach a thing or two, even though I've seen just about everything there is to see. Sooty likes things a certain way, though. The fact that he's willing to show me *his way* means he trusts me. "Thanks, Sooty."

He nods once and walks off. I'm thinking *that* plus seeing Cami in a bathing suit makes this not such a bad day after all.

THIRTEEN: *Cami*

Ohmigod, would you leave already?

First of all, I know this is not how I should feel about having my boyfriend around. But today, I totally do. He was far too attentive in the pool; he was all hands. That was fine while Trick was watching, but after that . . . not so much. I know it sounds crazy and ridiculously childish, but it's true. In a perverse way, I wanted Trick to be stuck with the image of me wrapped around someone else, kind of like I was stuck with the image of him and that blond girl.

I hope he doesn't sleep a wink!

Now Brent is determined to stay and kiss my father's butt. What's worse is Daddy *wants* him around. The son he never had, the ideal mate for his daughter—whatever the real reason, if we lived in medieval times, I'd be betrothed to Brent. You know, beneficial alliances and all. Blech!

Not that Brent's a bad guy. He's really not. He's actually a great guy. Smart, handsome, well educated, comes from a good family, treats me well. And I love him. But there's just something missing, something I never knew was missing until I met Trick.

Brent is sort of like dark chocolate. If you try it first, you're going to love chocolate. And that's fine. You could go your whole life loving it. But if you ever taste milk chocolate . . . oh boy! From that point on, dark chocolate will never be quite as good. You'll always crave milk chocolate.

All in all, Brent was just much more appealing *before* I met Trick. I realize now I just didn't know what I was missing.

But Brent doesn't deserve that. He deserves someone who thinks he's milk chocolate.

I watch him laugh with my father and I feel terrible for sitting beside him, thinking about another guy.

Maybe I just haven't given him a chance to curl my toes. Maybe Trick just caught me off guard. Maybe I just need to try harder to make it work with Brent.

I slip my fingers into Brent's where they rest on the couch between us. He looks over at me and smiles, and my conscience immediately feels a little better.

He turns his attention back to Daddy, commenting on something he said, and I realize he looked surprised by me holding his hand.

What's wrong with me? Why don't I do this more often? Why don't I feel like I can't keep my hands off him?

Greenish-gray eyes laugh at me from the back of my mind. If it were Trick sitting beside me, my heart would be pounding and I wouldn't be able to stop looking at him. I would be thinking about him without his shirt on and remembering what his lips felt like on mine.

"Wouldn't it, Cami?"

Daddy's voice brings me back from my fantasy. He and Brent are both staring at me, waiting.

"I'm sorry, wouldn't it what?"

Daddy shakes his head and smiles at Brent. "Is this how she always acts when you hold hands?"

Brent laughs and looks over at me. He winks and squeezes my hand. I smile. I *want* to feel something, but the only thing that stands out is the guilt I feel over thinking about Trick again.

Dammit!

"I was saying wouldn't it be nice if Brent stayed for supper."

"Oh, of course. I'd love it if you'd stay." I put on my brightest smile and push Trick right out of my mind. Now if I could just get him to stay out . . .

"Why don't you take him out for a ride? You've got time beforehand."

I feel my smile waver. "Yeah, yeah. That sounds good."

"You'd better get going then," Daddy prompts, leaning back in his chair. His smile looks awfully smug, which makes me immediately suspicious. But then I realize why it's smug. First he tells me to ride in the evenings, his subtle way of saying *Stay away from Trick*, yet now he's practically pushing me out the door. The difference? Now I've got Brent with me.

You sly devil! You want *Trick to see me with Brent, for him to see I'm taken.*

If it meant Brent making me his, Daddy would probably be okay with him peeing on my leg to mark his territory.

Men!

I excuse myself to go put on some jeans. A few minutes later, Brent and I are making our way to the stable. I'm really nervous for some reason. Excited, too.

I swallow a growl of frustration. It irks me that Trick gets under my skin like this. I'm supposed to be focusing on Brent.

Brent, Brent, Brent!

It's my mantra all the way to the big stable doors. I know I should be holding his hand, but for some reason, I just can't make myself do it. That irks me, too.

Sooty is in the office area that sits just inside the entrance.

"Well, look who it is," he says when he sees us. Sooty walks over to us and holds his hand out for Brent. "Haven't seen you around in a while, son."

Brent smiles. "Just been busy with work, Sooty. How you been?"

"I'm still kickin'."

A throaty motor starts up at the back of the stable. We all turn in that direction just in time to see Trick pulling away in a badass classic Mustang. Probably something like a Boss or a Cobra. I can't get a good enough look at it, but it's definitely something my dad would like.

As he passes the open side door of the stable, I see him look in. His eyes meet mine. Even across the distance, I feel the . . . turbulence. That's the best way I can describe it. It takes my breath for a second.

When he drives on, I turn back to Sooty, hoping Brent didn't recognize Trick. Sooty is watching me closely. Very closely. The edges of his thin lips turn up the tiniest bit.

"Well, well, well," he says.

I look away from him, too, back at Brent. His eyes are darting between me and Sooty.

"Well, what?"

Sooty clears his throat. "Well, I guess we'd better get you two saddled up and out the door before dinnertime. You came to ride, right?"

Sooty winks at me.

What's that old man up to?

Sooty acts perfectly normal after that, leaving me to wonder if I had just imagined his strange behavior.

FOURTEEN: *Trick*

If a car could be a soul mate, my Mustang would be mine. She's a Boss 429, and nothing in the world can soothe me like doing fifty-five on a curvy road with the wind pouring in and the music pouring out. She responds quickly to my slightest touch—I've tweaked the steering to near-perfection—and she hugs the turns as we snake our way through the country.

I don't really have a destination in mind. I just want to drive for a while and clear my head. It's not a matter of not being able to have Cami. Not really. I'm pretty sure if I pursued her, I could have her. At least I think so.

No girl is worth losing this job, though. No girl! You're the only thing standing between Mom and Grace and destitution. And they've lost enough already. We all have.

After almost two hours of reiterating my priorities, which keep getting hijacked when Cami enters my thoughts, I find myself at Rusty's garage. The lights are on and his car's out front. Rusty's always working. Well, to Rusty, it's more like playing. Kind of like me working with horses. When you're doing something you love, you can't really call it work.

"What up, man?" He rolls out from under the front of a T-Bird and greets me with a cockeyed grin.

"Just . . . out." I sit in a chair that he'd obviously been resting in at some point, drinking a beer.

"Uh-oh. Don't want to go home. Can't stay at work. You're homeless for the moment. That it?"

I shrug even though Rusty's already wheeled back under the car. He rolls back out and frowns up at me.

"What are you doing here so late?" I ask.

"Got a guy coming in with his 'Vette in about a half hour or so."

"The guy from the field party?"

"Yep."

I nod.

Rusty narrows his eyes on me. "All right. What is it?"

I lean back and exhale. Rusty knows me too well.

"I'm just still getting adjusted to the way things are now. That's all."

"Is it about the money?"

I close my eyes. It seems that everything boils down to the money. My entire life has been reduced to the singular pursuit of money above all else.

"That must be a yes. And she still won't let you sell the car?"

"Nope. You know how she's been about some of Dad's stuff. I think she wants to hang on to him as long as she can, even though selling it would solve everything."

"Well, you can't really blame her in a way, though."

Actually, I don't blame her at all. Not really. The car holds dozens of hours of memories and hundreds of physical reminders that my father and I pieced it together for more than two years. Yes, it was his pet project, but it was also something he wanted to give me when I turned sixteen. Something I could treasure. Something we'd built together.

And I do treasure it.

But still . . .

"Yeah, but there's a time when sentimentality has to take a backseat to practicality."

"Nice! Spoken like a true college kid."

I can't help but wonder if I'll ever get to finish vet school.

So close . . .

"Well, it is what it is. I just need to see us through the next year or so until I can get some things worked out. Maybe then . . ."

"I hope so, bro," Rusty says. We sit in silence for a minute, something Rus is rarely comfortable with, before he casually slides back under the car without another word. He's already overextended himself.

As usual, he has music on while he works. I close my eyes and listen for a few minutes before my thoughts start crowding in on me again. I'm just not the type to be idle with my musings unless they're about some sort of trouble I can fix. Right now, there is no fix. This *is* the fix.

I get up and pull my shirt over my head. No sense risking getting grease stains all over yet another shirt.

"What can I help with, man? I'm tired of thinking."

"Why don't you get under the hood and loosen the bolts from those brackets."

Grabbing a socket set from the workbench, I pop the hood and get to work.

After about five minutes, Rus and I start talking shop and my mind is adequately occupied. The garage bay doors are open and the slightly cooler night air is coming in, the music is still playing, and my troubles are, for the time being, somewhere else.

Until the breeze carries in the faint scent of strawberry. I rise from under the hood and there, standing in the garage entrance, is Cami.

FIFTEEN: *Cami*

I can't decide whether I'm thrilled or frustrated when I walk into the garage with Brent and I see Trick come out from underneath the hood of the car he's working on. I *am* a little frustrated; constantly running into him is making it harder to concentrate on Brent. And it's certainly not helping me to *not* think about Trick, which is what I really need to do. But mostly, I'm thrilled. Excited. I hate to admit it, but I am.

He's shirtless. Again. He's not sweaty or dirty or anything. He's just all bare skin and well-defined muscles. And there's something so sexy about the way his jeans hang on his hips. I can even see those little dents at the bottom of his stomach. If I'm being honest, I really just want to walk right over to him and touch them. With my tongue.

Cue the blush.

I feel the heat working its way up my neck and into my face.

You idiot! What did you think would happen if you thought about things like that?

But it's not like I intentionally thought about doing that. It was almost involuntary. Most of my reactions to Trick have been. It's like something else takes over and I'm sort of helpless to stop it.

I see his eyes flash and a grin pulls at one side of his mouth. That's how I know he noticed my blush.

I turn and look at Jenna. She's always a lifesaver in situations like these. Only Jenna isn't paying any attention to me. She looks kind of stunned herself.

I look back toward Trick and I see that another guy has emerged from beneath the car. *That's* what caught Jenna's eye. Or, rather, that's *who* caught her eye. And boy, did he ever!

"What's he doing here?" Brent asks of Trick's friend.

"He's a friend of mine. And he's great with cars. Is that a problem?"

I think I see Trick cringe a little. Obviously his friend doesn't know about his run-in with Brent.

Brent doesn't answer at first. I can almost see him weighing his options, weighing his pride. "I guess not, if he keeps his hands and his comments to himself."

"He won't be a problem."

Brent nods. "Trevor wanted to bring his car out to let you look at it. He'll be driving us back."

Brent had talked to Trick's friend (was his name Rusty?) about doing some work on the Corvette. He'd heard Rusty does some of the best work around when it comes to the classics. Trevor had then talked to him about doing some work on *his* car. When Jenna had called and asked me to ride out with Brent and then us ride back with her and Trevor, I'd agreed. I didn't want too much time to think. Besides, I have to spend more time with Brent if I'm ever to be crazy about him. So I agreed.

Well, that plan's shot to hell!

I make a point not to glance at Trick, standing a few feet away.

I try to pretend I don't know him, that he doesn't work for my father, and that I haven't given him a second thought since that night.

But I have! Ohmigod, he's practically all I can think about! It's ridiculous.

I search immediately for something else to concentrate on. Thoughts like that will only make me blush. And he'll notice. And he'll smile that sexy smile. And Brent might notice. And that won't turn out well for anyone.

I turn again to Jenna. She's standing at Trevor's side, trying her best not to stare at the garage owner. I look at him again.

He's tallish and lean with dark reddish-brown hair. His eyes are bright, bright blue and they continually flicker to Jenna. Looks like she's not the only one with an interest.

Who wouldn't be interested in Jenna, though? With her Greek heritage, she's very striking with her shiny black hair and bronzy skin. Very exotic. And her personality? Psssh, forget about it!

Ohmigod! You know you're off your rocker when your thoughts sound like a sixties mobster's.

Trevor, Brent, and Trick's friend head out of the garage to go look at Trevor's car. As they pass, the owner stops and sticks out his hand, which is surprisingly clean considering what he was doing when we arrived.

"Jeff Catron," he says, nodding at me. His voice is nice. Deep and gruff. I shake his hand. I notice his eyes have already moved on to Jenna, long before his hand does. And they stay there. "My friends call me Rusty." He shakes her hand, too, holding on to it a little longer than he should, but not long enough to alert Trevor. I don't think it matters. In my opinion, *anyone* would have to be an idiot not to see the sparks flying!

"I'm Jenna. And this is Cami." He casts a quick smile in my direction and then turns all that heat back on Jenna.

Might have to take a step back from that! Wow!

I look up, between them, and Trick is watching me. That heat, I know I need to stay away from.

Rusty moves on and the three men exit the garage, leaving me and Jenna alone with Trick. He walks to the door, no doubt to make Brent feel better about being out there when he's in here with me.

Trick is watching the guys out in the lot. I can tell Jenna is itching to go over there and watch them, too. Well, watch Rusty, I should say. That's the only one she's interested in at this point.

And then there's me. I'm left . . . floundering in the silence.

I walk to the car Trick was working on when we came in. Although my father collects the very high-dollar classic cars now, it hasn't always been that way. I can remember when things started to change, when money became more plentiful and Daddy started buying mostly restored vintage cars to work on. He graduated from partially restored Mach I Mustangs, Camaros, and GTOs to fully restored Shelbys, Jaguars, and Ferraris. And, being the daddy's girl that I was back then, I learned some of the ins and outs with him. That's why I can walk up to a car like this and be somewhat familiar with it.

I'm looking under the hood at the engine they're rebuilding when a shadow falls across the car.

"That's the part that makes the car run," Trick says dryly. I start to take offense until I look up and see his pale, twinkling eyes. I smile.

"Is that what it is? Because it looks to me like a V-8 Thunderbird Special for this . . ." I walk around to the side of the car and take a step back, appraising it from front to back. "What? Fifty-seven T-Bird?"

I look back at him. His expression shows disbelief. I arch one brow. A slow smile curves his chiseled lips.

My heart picks up when he walks over to me and grabs my hands. He curls my fingers over the backs of his and examines them, rubbing his thumbs over the nails.

"I wouldn't have taken you for a grease monkey. What gives?"

I'm having trouble breathing with him standing so close. I glance nervously at the garage doors behind him, knowing Brent is out there and I shouldn't even be talking to Trick, much less . . . this.

He gently lowers my hands and lets them go. I wiggle my fingers. I can still feel him touching them, even though he's not.

"My father. He's a collector. Has been for a long time. I used to like hanging out in the garage with him back when he liked to work on them."

Trick smiles at me. "All girl with a little bit of tomboy. Just when I thought you couldn't get any sexier." He says it quietly, almost like he's thinking to himself. I see his eyes flicker to my lips.

I want him to kiss me. So badly. Brent is the furthest thing from my mind.

But obviously not the furthest thing from Trick's. His smile fades and his face sinks into a frown. He backs away from me just before we hear Rusty's voice getting closer.

Trick walks back to the door and I rejoin Jenna. When I stop by her side, she turns to look at me. I know we're both thinking the same thing.

SIXTEEN: *Trick*

"I don't even need to ask who that was," Rusty declares as we watch Cami and her friends drive away. "She's pretty hot."

I throw him an incredulous look. "'Pretty hot'?"

Rusty shrugs. "Yeah. She's pretty hot. But her friend . . . damn!"

"Yeah, what's up with that? Could you be a little more obvious?"

"What? I barely looked at her!"

"Dude, you needed a freakin' bib! You all but drooled all over yourself. I'm surprised her boyfriend didn't kick your ass."

Rus snickers. "Like that could've happened."

Rusty has always been scrappy. He's a big guy now, but that hasn't always been the case. Even when he wasn't, he was not the kind of guy you wanted to mess with. You just didn't. Still don't. Unless you're me, of course. We've been in our share of drunken brawls with each other. I think we've both won a few and lost a few.

"Missing the point, man."

"I got this, Trick. Calm down. Holy balls! You're worse than my mom."

I drag my fingers through my hair. "Sorry, Rus. I don't know what's wrong with me lately."

"You put too much pressure on yourself, bro. You've got some kind of hero complex, thinking you gotta save everybody."

"Feeling responsible for my family does not mean I have a hero complex."

"But it's more than just that. It's like you think if you can save enough people, it'll change things. Or change you somehow. Make you feel less guilty."

"Nothing can make me feel less guilty. If I hadn't bitched about watching Grace, Mom could've gone to the store and Dad wouldn't have been rushing to get Grace's medicine home. I was such a little asshole."

"Trick, it wasn't your fault! Accidents on slick roads happen all the time. How many times do you have to hear that before it sinks in?"

I laugh bitterly. "Apparently a few more, because this is only making me mad."

"You and that temper. Why is it that you've learned to hide it from everyone but me?"

"No one else makes quite as good a punching bag as you."

"Oh, so that's how it's gonna be. You wanna go a round, ace?"

Rusty starts dancing around, shadowboxing like some sort of prizefighter who's just entered the ring. It gets even better when he starts humming the *Rocky* tune.

I can't help but laugh at him. More often than not, he's just what I need.

"Bring it, firecracker." I stand up and hold out my hands. Rusty taps each palm with quick jabs and then smacks me upside the head.

"Oh-ho-ho!" I say. "Enjoy that one, 'cause it's the only time those hands are gonna touch me."

Despite my six-foot, two-inch frame, I'm agile. Always have been. Quick and light on my feet. I bounce around him a little and then, *bam!* I land a solid slap to his right cheek.

Rusty's eyes flash. His temper is much more easily stirred than mine, but it burns out quickly. Unlike mine. I've learned to control my temper, but once it's fired up . . . well, let's just say the blast radius is usually pretty wide and devastating.

Rusty reaches out with his left hand. I dodge it and tap his ribs with my fingertips. He comes in next with two lightning-fast right jabs. I dip to the side and avoid both, then pop up and brush his chin.

"Looks like *rusty* is more than just a name for you," I tease, knowing I'm pushing my luck.

Much to my surprise, Rusty stops, drops his hands to his sides, and smiles at me. "You're not gonna get to me, Trick. Not this time. I'd rather break open that bottle of Patrón over there and think about the hot chick I just met."

I relax as well. "That *does* sound like a lot more fun, doesn't it?"

I move over to Rusty and, just as I'm getting close, he sucker-punches me in the stomach. It's not hard enough to really hurt, but it's hard enough to knock the wind out of me for just a second.

"You're such a dick," I sputter.

With a laugh, Rus slaps me on the back and leads the way to his stash of my favorite tequila.

The door creaks as it opens. I crack an eyelid to look around. My brain hurts. I think it's actually dizzy. And trying to differentiate drunken dream from sobering sunshine is not helping.

My head clears a little and I open my eyes all the way to glance at my bedside clock.

It's already seven o'clock? Damn!

I hear soft footsteps as Grace sneaks up to the bed. I guess waking up before me twice in one week is like pure heaven for her.

Even though I'd rather go back to sleep, I should technically already be gone, heading to work. Regardless of either, I wait patiently for her to get closer.

When I see her feet come into view, I reach out and tickle her stomach. My scaring her makes her happy, so yeah, I make a big roar for added effect.

She squeals in delight and takes off.

Mission accomplished.

"Mom says your phone's been ringing," she says from the doorway, a nice safe distance from my reach. She's still smiling.

I look on the bedside table and, sure enough, my phone's not there.

Must've dropped it on my way in last night.

I sit up and realize that my headache has a headache. I groan, genuinely this time, and Grace runs off screaming. Painfully, it echoes around in my skull.

Note to self: Don't make her scream after half a bottle of Patrón.

Before I even make it to the bathroom, I see pink-slippered feet appear. I squint up at Mom. She doesn't look happy. I can almost see the lecture hanging around her tight lips.

Thank God, she saves it for later.

"Your boss called. Four times. Something has come up. He wants you to plan on being around the stable tonight and maybe for the rest of the week."

Great! Not just any day with a hangover, but a *long* day. Working with horses. Riding them. I'm an idiot.

"I hear ya. I'm getting up."

She shakes her head at me.

"Son, I just . . ."

"I know, Mom. I'm fine. Just a bad day yesterday."

"And drinking didn't change that, now did it?"

Good point.

Without another word, she turns and walks away, leaving me to get ready for the longest, most uncomfortable day of my life. I head straight for the Tylenol.

SEVENTEEN: *Cami*

Even though it's what I said I wanted, I'm bored looking at the books for the business and the bloodlines of our horses. I really do want to learn it, but today my focus is elsewhere.

I've been at it all afternoon, trying my best to stay away from the stables. It hasn't been easy. Yes, partly because I've always loved my early-morning rides, but mostly . . . well . . .

Not again! Dammit, Trick! Why are you so . . . ugh!

I can't even finish that thought. I don't know how to describe him, really. He's charming for sure. He's funny and witty. He's obviously intelligent. He must be good with horses. He's apparently dedicated to his job. He seems like a good friend. Evidently he can box. Or maybe he's just been in a lot of fights. And he's definitely hot. Whew! Like hotter-than-the-ninth-ring-of-hell hot.

I think of those smoky eyes and that sexy smile. I feel steamy and realize I actually get all flushed just *thinking* about him.

Ridiculous!

None of those words adequately describe Trick, though. I've met guys before who are all those things, and none of them have had such an effect on me. Not one.

I lean back in Daddy's chair and prop my feet on the desk. I give in to the urge to think about Trick. Fully. Intently. Just for a minute.

Trick is different. He's hard to pigeonhole. And what makes him so unique is not so much a blatant, identifiable characteristic, like *hot* or *funny*. It's more like a *way* about him. He's magnetic. Dazzling. Mesmerizing.

And then it hits me.

Addictive. Trick is addictive.

Yes! That's totally it! The more I see of him, the more I want to see. The more I think of him, the more I can't stop thinking of him.

Yes, that's exactly the word I would best use to describe him— addictive.

I'm lost in a daydream about him when a knock at the door startles me. I look up to see the very object of my ruminations standing in the hall just outside the study.

I stare at him. It takes me a minute to adjust to seeing him when I'd been thinking about him in such depth. Then he smiles at me and all I *can* do is stare. I'm sure I look just like a deer caught in an oncoming car's headlights.

"So this is what you do all day," he says, leaning one shoulder casually against the doorjamb. He's wearing old jeans with a hole in the knee, boots, and a white T-shirt with the sleeves cut off. A red baseball hat is dangling from his fingers and his hair is messed up, like he just ran his fingers through it.

I'm sure I've never seen anything more mouthwatering.

"What?" Ohmigod, I'm actually dazed.

He chuckles. "I said, 'So this is what you do all day.'"

"Oh, uh, no. I was just, um, going over the books."

"Yeah, that's exactly what it looks like."

I slide my feet off the desk, smiling as I rack my brain for something clever to say. "I work better off my feet."

One dark eyebrow snaps up.

"Um, I mean, I think better with my feet up."

The other brow shoots up to join the first.

"What I mean is that I . . . I'm . . ."

I feel the blush rising into my cheeks as I stammer. It doesn't help that Trick is smiling in such a playful way.

Hot damn, he's sexy!

"I know what you meant," he says quietly.

My face gets even hotter.

"Please don't do that."

"Do what?" I ask.

"Blush. You have no idea how hard it makes it."

"How hard it makes what?"

He doesn't answer immediately. He cocks his head to the side and studies me before he answers. "Staying away from you."

I look down at the ledger I'm holding and bite my lip to keep the smile of pure pleasure from emerging.

You shouldn't be happy about that comment, you idiot!

But I am.

"Good God, that's not helping, either."

My eyes flicker up. He has straightened and is running his fingers through his hair, his head bowed.

"What did I do now?"

"You're biting your lip and . . . God! It just makes me think of what you taste like." He sounds almost pained. And I get the feeling if he could get his hands on me, he'd kiss me.

Something hot and exciting builds in my stomach.

I know I shouldn't ask. He works for my father. And I have a boyfriend. But none of that seems to matter. I can't help myself.

"Why are you so determined to stay away from me?"

"I'm the help. Your father wouldn't like it. And I need this job."

I'm not sure how I feel about that reasoning. It's sound, yes. Sound, responsible, respectful, all those things. But . . .

"And I have a boyfriend."

It's perverse that I would remind him of that.

He laughs.

"I'm not worried about him."

"Why not?"

"Because if he was all that stood in my way, I'd make it my mission to take your mind off him. For good."

"Just like that?"

"Just like that," Trick repeats. He takes a step into the room. Then another. I see his expression change and my pulse picks up. "I'd be all you could think about. You'd think about my smile all day and my lips all night." He takes another two steps into the room. Two steps closer to me.

I'm actually breathless with anticipation. The air between us is thick with . . . something.

And then I see a shape move in the doorway. I look past Trick, and there stands my father. He clears his throat.

I've got to hand it to Trick. He doesn't really get flustered. His expression falls a little bit, and maybe cools down from the heat he was wearing a second ago, but he doesn't jerk like he's guilty of anything. He just watches me for another second and then turns around to face Daddy.

"Sir, I was just looking for you. A family emergency has come up and Sooty will be out the rest of the day. He thinks he might be able to get back by tomorrow night, but he isn't sure."

I watch my father's face cloud over. Not thundercloud cloud, but close. He hates surprises.

"So what does he plan to do for coverage in the meantime?"

"He's asked me to stay and keep an eye on things, which I'm happy to do."

"And what if Mint Julep goes into labor?"

"Sir, I've seen dozens of births, even had to assist with a couple during practicums in school. I *was* going into my final year. There won't be any problems."

"Did Sooty leave a number where he can be reached?"

I see Trick stiffen the slightest bit. He doesn't like being undermined, but he doesn't say anything.

"Yes, sir. And I have the on-call number of Dr. Flannery as well."

"That's as it should be, but I'd like to talk to Sooty. The number?" he says as he strides across the office to the desk.

Trick rattles off a string of numbers and Daddy writes them down, then tears the paper off. "Can you two please excuse me?"

I come out from behind the desk. Trick is already at the door. He is waiting for me, but not looking at me. He's looking straight ahead, at the wall. When I pass him, he shuts the door behind us.

I turn to say something to him, although I have no idea what, but he's already walking away.

Crap balls!

EIGHTEEN: *Trick*

*J*ust *get the hell out of there! Just get the hell out of there! Eyes forward, eyes forward!*

I fuss at myself as I walk away. Anything to keep from looking back at Cami and doing what I want so badly to do.

How can a female be that frickin' distracting? She's like Kryptonite! I can't think straight when I'm around her and I lose sight of everything important. And that shit ain't gonna fly!

I give myself a good talking to all the way to the stable. I need to focus on getting the rest of the horses exercised and then check on Mint Julep. This job is important. It has to be *the most important* thing. *Has to be!*

In my head, I plan out the evening, an evening that does *not* include Cami Hines. After I check on Mint Julep, I'll spend the rest of the night going through her record and getting to know everything there is to know about her and her condition. If that jackass boss of mine asks me anything, I want to be able to answer him immediately and without hesitation.

I'm still thinking of anything and everything except Cami as I saddle Highland Runner. I can tell by the way he twitches when I buckle it on that he's as unsettled as I am. That's one problem with spending so much time with a wild horse. He responds to me and my moods. And right now, he's every bit as restless as I am.

"Calm down, boy. It's all right. I'm gonna take you out and run some of that off." I stroke the side of his muscular neck as I prepare to lead him out of the stable.

I turn toward the door and there, with the sunshine streaming in behind her, stands Cami. I can't see her face at all. She's a black silhouette backlit by blinding brightness. It's a halo around her.

Like the angel she is.

I stop. Neither of us says anything until she starts walking toward me. I can feel my body reacting to her the closer she gets. My pulse picks up. My breathing gets a little shallow. I feel the need to fidget as I think about pushing her up against the wall and making both of us forget all the reasons I shouldn't look at her the way I do.

I rationalize to myself that it actually makes perfect sense. I want her so much because I can't have her. It's human nature.

I console myself with that knowledge as I watch the sway of her hips as she walks.

Damn, but she's hot!

She stops in front of me, her hands stuffed into the back pockets of her jeans, making those delicious breasts of hers strain against the material of her shirt.

"What are you doing down here?" I ask.

I hear her take a deep breath before she answers. "Look, I know you need this job. And you know I have a boyfriend. But we can't avoid each other completely all summer long. I love to ride and I'm trying to learn more about the business and the horses. And now Sooty's gone, leaving you with extra work. Seems to me like we ought to be able to at least be friends so we can be around each other, right?"

I don't want to tear the clothes off any of my friends!

I think that, but I don't say it. Instead, I quietly consider what she said, what she's proposing. It's a logical thought. I'll give her that. And if she thinks it's going to be so easy to be around me without sparks flying, then far be it for me to act otherwise. If she wants to pretend we're just friends, then I'll give her what she asks for.

Until she's begging for something else, my mind finishes perversely. I mentally chastise myself before answering her.

"Just friends?" I shrug. "Sure. I just hope your father's okay with it."

"Don't worry about him. He's fine."

I doubt that, but then again, she might be his Kryptonite, too. I can't imagine that she's heard the word *no* an awful lot in her lifetime.

"If you say so," I say casually. "Did you come down here just to tell me that?"

"No, I came to help. I can kill two birds with one stone. I can help you and I get to ride. Win-win."

"And why is it so important that you help me?"

I know I shouldn't goad her, but I can't seem to help it. And I have to pay dearly for it when I see her cheeks turn pink before she turns away from me to stroke Highland Runner's nose.

Her and that blushing!

She must know she's blushing and I'm reacting, because I can see her pearly white teeth biting into her bottom lip. I clamp my mouth shut against the urge to pull her against me and suck on it for her.

"Well, it helps me, too. I get to learn the horses a little better. You know, the newer ones. Recently I've mostly been riding Firewalker, so . . ."

"Ahh," I say noncommittally. "So you're using me, is that what you're saying?"

Her head whips toward me and her expression shows regret, as if she really thinks she might've hurt my feelings. It just makes her all the more appealing.

"No! That's not it at all!"

I laugh. She's adorably gullible, too. It occurs to me that if Cami has any flaws, I can't seem to find them.

"Ohmigod, you're the devil," she says, trying to conceal the curve of her lips.

"So I've been told," I say, winking playfully at her. When blood rushes to her cheeks again, I bite back a groan. I'm really going to have to quit teasing her or we'll both end up regretting it.

She clears her throat, obviously searching for a change of subject. "Which other horses need exercising? I can take one, too."

I'd been planning to ride Titan in the round pen, but hitting the trails with Cami is just too appealing.

"Titan. I was going to take him and Runner both out on the trails today."

"Okay, then I'll take Titan."

"Are you sure you can handle him?"

Her eyes sparkle and she sticks her chin out proudly. "I can handle any horse in this stable."

"Any horse except Runner, you mean."

"Any horse *including* Runner."

"No offense, but you're not getting on Runner. He's still too wild."

"Daddy says he'll never be ready."

"Then why would you think you can ride him?"

"I saw you riding him the other day. He looked fine."

"He's used to me, but it'll probably be another couple months before anyone else can ride him."

"You think?"

"I know," I say, trying not to let her get my hackles up. "I can feel it in him. He's coming around."

"I guess time will tell who's right about Runner."

"I guess so."

There's a short and slightly uncomfortable pause before she speaks again.

"I'll take Titan today, then."

"Fine," I say, as if she had any other choice. There's no way in hell I would have let her anywhere near Runner's stirrups. "I'll get him ready for you."

"I can do it."

"I'm sure you can, but I'll do it while you talk to him."

I don't want to add that my presence will help soothe Titan before she mounts him. Only a person with an affinity for horses like mine would understand. My father used to talk about my "connection" to them all the time. He'd say I was born to work with horses.

Apparently he was right.

Taking Runner by the reins, I motion for Cami to follow me. "Come on."

We walk the length of the stable to the other end, where Titan's stall is. His big, black head is sticking out over the open top half of his stall door. I stop to rub his nose and blow softly into his face before I hand Cami Runner's reins and go to grab Titan's tack. By the time I come back, Cami is feeding Titan a sugar cube out of her other hand and whispering to him. I can barely make out the words, but the tone says all I need to hear. Her love of horses is clear in every syllable she utters.

I watch Titan's ears. Although he's no danger to Cami, he's not quite at ease with her, either. I stroke his neck and chest as I prepare to bridle him, hoping he'll settle.

"Good boy, Titan. Let's get you ready for Cami. We're going out for a ride. You'll like that, won't you, big guy?"

All the while I'm stroking him, my voice is calm and soothing. He nickers quietly at me, and I slide the bit into his mouth. His muscles shiver beneath his shiny coat and I can almost feel him relax afterward.

I lead him out of his stall to where I can put his saddle on. I don't stop talking to him. Titan is highly trained and accustomed to the presence of people, even people unfamiliar to him. But when it comes to Cami, I'm not willing to take a chance. I want him calm before we leave the stable.

When he's saddled and ready to go, we lead the horses outside, where I reach for Runner's reins and hand Titan's over to Cami. She's watching me with an odd expression on her face. I'm not sure what to make of it.

"What?"

She narrows her eyes on me. "You really are good with horses, aren't you?"

I shrug. "Who told you I was good with horses?"

"My father."

I can't keep the shock from my face. The only thing Jack Hines has ever shown me is a mild disdain.

"That surprises you?" she asks.

"Uh, very much."

"Why?"

I shrug again. "You'd just never know that by talking to him. Or at least I wouldn't."

"Maybe not, but that's what he told me."

"And why were you talking about me?"

My jeans feel a little tighter when she blushes and licks her lips nervously. "He was just telling me about the new staff, that's all."

Why don't I believe her?

"Is that right?"

She nods.

"Maybe neither of you will be shocked, then, when Runner turns out to be one of the best horses this stable has ever turned out."

"You're that sure of him?"

"I'm that sure of him."

I don't know her well enough to say for sure, but it looks like she might be a little impressed. And, even though it shouldn't, that makes me want to smile.

NINETEEN: *Cami*

*M*aybe this was a mistake.

I can't help but doubt myself as Trick and I lead the horses out of the stable. I thought I could handle just being his friend, especially when he is so determined to keep me at arm's length to preserve his job. I mean, his interest in me is obviously not *that* strong or he wouldn't be thinking about his job first, would he?

For some reason, that makes him all the more appealing. And then seeing him with the horses . . .

Ohmigod! Think about something else!

I can feel my face get hot. Again. I don't think I've blushed as much in my entire life as I have since meeting Trick. And it makes it even worse that I know he likes it. For some reason, that excites me. I *want* him to like it. I *want* him to like me, *want* him to want me. I shouldn't. But I do.

Without another word, we stop just outside the huge stable doors and mount our horses. Trick looks at me and smiles. He pauses and

I see his eyes dart to Titan's head. I'm not sure if he's worried that I'm upsetting the horse or that I might be *riding* an upset horse. Either way, he looks satisfied to see that Titan's expression and body language are completely devoid of any signs of temper.

"So, where are we going?"

"I thought we'd take them up to the lookout."

I'm impressed that he knows the land so well. He must've explored the trails quite a bit to know where the lookout is. I'm also a little thrilled by the idea.

Even though you shouldn't be. You know this is a bad idea.

"Sounds good," I say, ignoring the voice of reason.

Trick urges Runner into a slow trot around the yard to warm him up. Titan and I follow suit. Trick tries to pretend he's not watching me, but I can feel his eyes on me. I can always feel his eyes when they're on me.

After a few minutes, he stops and I pull alongside him. I wonder what he's up to when I see his cockeyed grin and twinkling eyes. "So, you think you can keep up across the open field?"

I feel Titan shift beneath me, his muscles bunching like he's telling me he's up to the challenge. Runner is prancing anxiously under Trick, too. "You're on."

Without giving him a chance to respond, I tap Titan's side with my heels and he takes off. I urge him into a gallop. Fast as lightning, we blaze a trail across the grass. The brisk wind is whipping my hair, the setting sun is warming my face, and carefree happiness is bursting from my heart. I don't question it; I just go with it.

Titan's rippling body is nothing but power beneath me. He's carrying me away from the world, with only Trick at my side. I glance to my left and see that he's watching me. He smiles, a smile that could nearly unseat me, and then, much to my surprise, he moves easily ahead of me.

I urge Titan faster and he responds. But not enough. With every second that passes, Runner moves farther and farther away.

When he reaches the tree line at the trailhead, Trick pulls Runner to a halt and turns to wait for me. I'm only a few seconds behind, but still . . .

"Wow!" I say when I bring Titan to a halt. "He can run!"

Trick leans down and pats Runner's neck lovingly. "He's got what it takes. He's just a little rough around the edges, is all."

Trick's expression makes me wonder if that's how he sees himself—like he's got what it takes, but he's a little rough around the edges. Obviously, people see something in him or he wouldn't be here. My father is picky about who he lets work with his horses. But he's also one of those people you can rarely satisfy. It makes it hard, especially for those who don't know him like I do.

"Still up for a trip to the lookout?"

"I'm game if you are," I reply.

Trick grins, that grin that makes me want to eat him up even though I barely know him. "Oh, I'm game, all right."

With that, he nudges Runner onto the trail, and I follow. When the path widens, Trick moves to the left so I can ride alongside him.

The horses are enjoying the leisurely walk. The woods are quiet around us, but I feel like every living creature in a ten-mile radius ought to be able to feel the tension between Trick and me. It's practically tangible and completely irresistible.

"So how long have you lived around here?" I figure the question is innocuous enough, hopefully enough to camouflage my intense interest in him.

"All my life. Well, except for the past few years."

"Where were you then?"

"Vet school."

"Seriously? Where?"

"Clemson."

"What's your area of concentration?"

"I *was* planning to be a large-animal vet."

"Was? Aren't you going to finish?"

Trick shrugs. The gesture is nonchalant, but his face tells the real story. This is a sore subject, something he's not very happy about.

"Maybe someday."

"How much longer do you have?"

"Less than a year. Just a few classes, actually."

"What? Why would you not finish, then?"

"Things happen. I'll finish one day."

"What could be so important that it can't wait a few months until you finish school?"

He glances over at me, his expression unreadable. "Family," he says, deadpan.

"Surely they understand. I mean—"

"It's not a matter of them understanding. It's a matter of a dispute against my father's insurance money after all these years. The company that services the policy was taken over by a larger group, and they're reviewing old case files that are still active. They're questioning the circumstances of his death and, until they get it resolved, they've stopped payment. Unfortunately, my mother is unable to make it on her own."

I flinch a little at the bitterness in his voice. Of course, I'd probably be bitter, too.

Pieces of Trick start clicking together. The sad thing is, the more I'm around him, the more I get to know him, the more fascinating and perfect the picture becomes.

"So you put your life, your future on hold to come back and work to help your mother until . . ."

"Exactly."

We both get quiet after that. I'm lost in thought, as I'm sure Trick is. Even though I feel bad for him—having to give up his dream when he was so close—I respect him for putting his family first. I don't know many people who would do that, especially not people his age.

I think of Brent. He's a good guy, but can I see him doing something so selfless? Sadly, I can't say for sure that he would.

As I'm thinking back over the conversation so far, something occurs to me.

"Your dad's insurance money? What happened?"

Trick says nothing, just looks over at me. His face is pretty much blank. He doesn't look mad. Or sad. Or irritated. He just looks . . . like he's thinking. I wonder if he's considering how much to tell me.

"I'm sorry. That was a really nosy question, wasn't it?"

His lips twist into a wry grin. "It's all right. I, uh, I just . . ." He trails off, and his discomfort with the subject starts making me uncomfortable, too. He continues before I can change the subject, though. "I don't know if you would remember the name, but my father was Brad Henley. He died in a car accident almost ten years ago. The insurance company is claiming he killed himself."

And he drops the bomb. Just like that.

TWENTY: *Trick*

I watch Cami's mouth open and close a half dozen times. It was mean to do that to her. I know how hard a time people have trying to find something to say after that. But she asked.

I'm not sure if I wanted her to know so it would scare her off or because I don't want her thinking I'm a complete loser. The problem with the second is that I shouldn't care.

But I do. Too much.

"Trick, I . . . I'm . . . I really . . ."

"Look," I say, stepping in to let her off the hook. "It was a long time ago. Don't worry about it. It is what it is. Doesn't change what's happening now."

"Your poor mother . . ."

"Yeah, she's had it kinda rough. Grace, too. Luckily, she was pretty young, so she's doing all right now."

"Grace?"

"My younger sister."

"How old is she?"

"Ten."

"Does she . . . I mean . . ."

"Nah, she's doing great. She's a freakin' mess, but in a good way, I guess." I laugh, thinking of how excited she gets just waking me up. That's proof that she missed me, that she needs me at home. At least for a little while longer.

I can tell Cami's still uncomfortable. She's frowning like she's trying really hard to think of something to say.

"So what about you? Where are you going to school?"

"University of Georgia. I'll be a senior next year."

"What's your major?"

"It was pre-law, but I changed it to business."

"Ahhh, planning a hostile takeover of the family business?"

Cami laughs. I love the sound. It's throaty and sultry. Makes me want to do more things to make her laugh just so I can hear it.

"Knowing my father . . ."

"So *that's* what you were doing earlier, going over the books."

She squints over at me, a little smile playing along the edges of her lips.

"How do you know? Maybe I was lying in wait."

"Waiting to charm the first person through the door. Is that it?"

Her grin develops, showing off her pretty teeth. "Did it work?"

"Yes, but it was a wasted effort."

"And why is that?"

"You already had me with that wet T-shirt of yours."

She giggles and looks away, but not before I can see her cheeks turn pink. Oh God, how I'd love to drag her off that horse and onto mine, have her wrap those long legs around me and . . .

I adjust in my saddle. Thoughts like that aren't going to do me a bit of good.

She clears her throat. "So, how is it that you came to know so much about horses?"

"My father used to be in the business."

Her head jerks toward me. "Really?"

I nod. "He had a financial partner, but he did all the work with the horses on a rented farm. I went with him a lot at night and on the weekends. He used to tell me I was meant to work with horses. Seems like he was right. Here I am."

"Do you like it? I mean, working with the horses here?"

"I love working with horses. It's what I was going to specialize in after school. I always wanted to work with them. Maybe even own a few to race and breed one day. As for working here . . ." I pause, just to see what she does. After a few seconds, she glances at me from beneath her lashes.

She just can't help but be sexy.

"I'm discovering it has its definite . . . benefits."

She grins. "Is that right?"

"Yes, ma'am," I say in my best Southern drawl.

"And what would those be?"

Good God, she's teasing me!

"The view around here is very nice for one thing. Rounded hills; lush valleys; gently curving roads; tight, firm . . . turns." I look over at her from the corner of my eye and grin. "And sometimes there's a hint of strawberry in the air. Makes my mouth water."

"Wow, it, uh, it sounds pretty spectacular when you put it like that. But I'm sure it's just a plain ole place, much like any other."

"See now that's where you're wrong. This place is special. I knew it from the start. This is the kind of . . . place that gets under your skin and won't let you have a moment's peace until you give in to it."

"But you don't want to give in to it."

"I didn't say that. I said I *couldn't* give in to it. There's a big difference."

She looks away. I see her chest rise and fall like she sighed. "I guess it's for the best, then."

"We'll see."

If I had been watching the trail and not looking at Cami, I'd have seen the snake in enough time to warn her. But I didn't.

Cami and I are both relaxed on our horses, neither prepared for Titan to freak out. But he does. It happens so fast, I can't stop it.

I hear Titan snort just before Runner feints to the left. Titan screams and rears up on his hind legs, tossing an unsuspecting Cami onto the ground before he starts backing up.

My heart leaps up into my throat. It's like I see him backing up in slow motion, making his way toward Cami, who is lying in the dirt, stunned.

Reaching over, I slap Titan's hindquarter as hard as I can, sending the horse barreling forward. One big foot mashes a hoofprint into the snake's body. I doubt he'll be doing much striking in the future.

I hop off Runner.

Cami is sitting up, trying to catch her breath. I'm sure landing the way she did knocked the wind out of her.

She's gasping when I reach her. I squat down and pull her gently into my arms.

"Are you okay?" I rub soothing circles on her back. Her breathing grows deeper and more even as she calms down.

"I-I've n-never been thrown off b-before. I don't know wh-what happened," she stutters, still a little breathless.

"You were overcome by my wit and charisma. It's my fault. I should've warned you."

She smiles up at me, and I know she's fine. She scared the shit out of me, but *she's* fine and that's all that matters.

"Those were some pretty stunning acrobatics you did there. I'm impressed."

"Yeah. The product of a lifetime of working at Cirque du So-Lame."

Her comment catches me so off guard, I throw back my head and laugh. Hard.

"Smart, beautiful, and witty—the feminine trifecta!"

"And apparently outrageously good on a horse," she quips as she tries to stand.

I grab her under her arm to help stabilize her. She loses her balance a little and leans into me for support. Being the guy that I am, I can't help but use the opportunity to put my arm around her waist and draw her in closer.

"Let me help you."

"Thank you," she says, putting her hand over mine where it rests on her side and grabbing my free hand with her other one.

"It wasn't your fault, you know."

"Of course it was. I've had horses buck on me before and I've never been unseated. I should've listened to you."

"You weren't paying attention. I shouldn't have been distracting you so much on a horse like Titan."

Cami looks up at me, her violet eyes sparkling in the evening sun. "You *are* pretty distracting."

"You ought to see me juggle."

"Juggle? So you *are* familiar with the Cirque du So-Lame."

"Baby, there's nothing lame about me."

When we stop in front of Runner, who didn't follow Titan very far, thank God, Cami looks up at me, her face as serious as a heart attack.

"You know, that's one of the things I admire most about you."

"What's that?"

"Your humility," she replies, deadpan. And then she starts laughing. Hard.

"Do you *really* want me to throw you over the saddle and make you ride all the way back with your ass in the air? Because that sorta sounds like what you're getting at."

"Would you really do that?" she asks, doing her best to look wide-eyed and innocent.

"Damn straight. And I'd love every minute of it"

She laughs, but I can tell it's got a nervous edge to it. I don't think she really knows what to say. For some reason, I like the thought that I unsettle her.

"Don't be shy! Tell me how you really feel," she teases.

I come around behind her and put my hands low on her waist. I know I shouldn't be flirting with her, but God help me, I can't seem to stop myself.

I bend down and whisper in her ear. "Trust me. You're not ready to hear that."

I'm thrilled when I see goose bumps break out on her neck and arms. It still has to be every bit of eighty or eighty-five degrees, so I know it can't be the weather. It's me. She reacts to me like I react to her.

But I'm not sure that's a good thing *at all*.

Before she can speak, I continue. "Let me help you up on Runner."

I hold on to Cami as she stretches to put her foot into my higher stirrup and then swings onto Runner's back. I'm proud of myself that I resist the temptation to palm her ass under the guise of "helping." I might be able to keep my job after all.

I climb up behind her and tap my heels against Runner's side to urge him forward. As we walk by the snake, Cami shivers.

"Not a fan of snakes?"

"Not particularly," she admits.

"Well, that one's not going to be doing much harm now."

As if it's trying to argue my point, the snake rattles its tail and its broken body writhes.

"You're not going to leave it like that, are you?"

Actually, I was. After that snake had gotten Cami tossed on her back and nearly trampled, I would gladly have left it to suffer. But I can't now. Not only because it would make me *look* callous, but it would really *be* callous. And callous I'm not.

Pulling Runner to a halt, I hop off his back and look for something I can use to put the snake out of its misery.

"Don't look," I call to Cami over my shoulder. Even after I'm done and am once more sitting behind her on Runner's back, she keeps her head averted. "Let's get you home."

Cami scoots forward in the saddle to give me room, but when she relaxes, her butt is rubbing me in all the right places. I bite my lip to keep from thinking things that will give . . . ahem, "rise" to certain body parts. I'm torn between wishing the ride could last a lot longer and wishing we were already back at the stable.

TWENTY-ONE: *Cami*

*O*f all the times for Trick to get quiet, why does it have to be now?

It seems like, without my mind concentrating on his flirting, all I can think about is his body behind me. How it feels to have his strong arms wrapped around me, how his chest moves against my shoulders, how his thighs and his crotch feel rubbing against my backside. His clean soapy scent surrounds me and, with his face so near mine, I can't help but think of turning my head just enough to kiss that strong jaw.

Ohmigod! This is the longest ride ever!

After we've gone a ways, I have to say something.

"Thank you for doing that," I say quietly.

That was the wrong thing to do because he has to practically press his cheek to mine to hear me.

"Pardon?"

Even though I know I shouldn't, I let my head fall back farther and turn it slightly to the side to speak closer to his ear.

"I just said, 'Thank you.'"

He leans in farther and looks down into my face, his lips literally a couple of inches from mine. I see his grayish eyes flicker to my mouth and his tongue sneaks out to wet his lips. I think I might die.

"Any time," he says softly.

Although I don't want to, I turn my head away. But I don't lean forward again. Instead, we ride the rest of the way back with me reclining against him, my head sort of tucked in the crook of his neck.

Once we leave the trail, Trick doesn't pick up speed as we cross the field. I wonder if it's because he likes me nestled against him as much as I like being there. I sigh a little in disappointment when the stable comes into view.

I wish I could stay like this forever.

My eyes are closed and that's what I'm thinking when Trick stiffens behind me. I sit up and look around. My eyes immediately go to the thing that has him suddenly uptight. There's no question why.

My father is standing at the entrance to the stable, holding Titan's reins. And wearing a thundercloud on his face.

Other than stiffening when he saw him, there is no other evidence that Trick is the least bit affected by Daddy. He guides Runner right up to him, brings him to a stop, and dismounts. He even ignores him while he helps me down off Runner. Then, very calmly, he turns to take the reins from my father.

"I'll take those, sir."

"What the hell is going on here?"

I'm surprised my dad waited that long to lay into him. I think he's a little thrown by Trick's demeanor, too. Most people tremble in their boots and kiss his ass. Trick does neither.

I can't help but think that's hot!

"Cami was nice enough to come and help me exercise the horses.

Unfortunately, a rattlesnake startled Titan and he threw her. I was just bringing her back."

He turns his murderous expression on me. I see it soften, but only minimally. "Are you all right? Did you get hurt?"

"No. Just took my breath for a minute, but I'm fine."

That's all he needs to hear. He's furious again, and it's directed toward Trick.

"Is this how you show you are responsible enough to take care of things in Sooty's absence?"

"I wanted to make sure Cami got back safely. If you don't mind, I'll check Titan now," Trick says, holding Titan's reins while he runs his hands down each knobby leg to assess him. Daddy and I watch Trick as he walks Titan in a loose circle, closely observing the way he moves, looking for signs of injury. When he turns to my father, I can see the relief on his face. He was worried about Titan, too.

"Sir, the horses are fine."

"What was my daughter doing on Titan, anyway? Both of them could've been seriously injured!"

My father loves me. I know this. But I'm not fool enough to think that he puts me *that* far above his horses, his business. It's times like this I'd like to strangle him.

Angrily, I step between Trick and him. "It was my idea. I insisted that I could ride Titan. I told you I want to learn more about the business and the horses. You said it was fine."

"I told him to stay away from you," he fires back at me.

I see red.

"You *what*?"

I can see him retreating the instant I call him on it.

"I mean, I told him just to—"

"Let's get something straight here, Daddy. I'm an adult. I can do what I want, when I want, with whomever I want. Unless you want me spending my summer elsewhere, you'd better just back off Trick. He didn't do anything wrong. I told him I could ride any horse in this stable."

"And what's worse is you bring her back on Runner, when I've told you a dozen times he's too wild," he says, turning his anger on Trick again.

"Why did you even hire Trick if you don't trust him? Trust his opinion? I've spent all of a couple hours with him, Daddy, and I can tell you he's good. Very, very good. And that horse minds him perfectly. Now stop treating me like a baby and stop harassing Trick." With that, I turn to Trick. "Thank you for letting me help and for bringing me back. I'm sorry to have caused you so much trouble." I loop my arm through my father's. "Daddy will walk me to the house, but I promise you I'm fine."

Trick, still seemingly unaffected, nods to me, then nods to my father. I might be crazy, but I think I see a little admiration sparkling in his eyes.

And even though it shouldn't, that makes my stomach all warm.

As I walk away, I want to look back to see if he's watching me. I feel like he is, but I can't be sure. I make myself face forward, though. Daddy doesn't need anything else to bitch about.

"Promise me you're not going to fire Trick because of this."

He says nothing. And, truthfully, I'm a little alarmed. I will never forgive myself if Trick loses his job because I couldn't stay away from him.

"Daddy, he really needs his job. And I really want to learn more about this place. Just give us both a chance."

He stops and looks down at me. His expression is still dark and I must admit he can be pretty intimidating. He's six foot three and has dark hair, dark skin, and light blue eyes. He's handsome for sure, but his ice-cold eyes can be bone-chilling. Especially when he feels something important to him is being threatened. Fortunately, I grew up with it and I've learned to deal with it.

Somewhat, anyway.

"Please, Daddy," I add for good measure.

Finally I see that I'm making a dent.

"No more screwups, young lady. And I mean it."

"Yes, sir."

Hours later, I'm standing at my window looking down at the light shining from the windows in the stable. I really want to go down there and see what Trick's doing. And just talk to him some more. But there are a thousand reasons that's not a good idea. One of which is that I have a boyfriend, a boyfriend whom I've thought of very little all day.

I'm going to have to keep an eye on that.

I sigh, mainly because I just can't help it. Lately, I feel like I'm chained to Brent. Or maybe it's that Brent represents chains to me. There are tons of great things about him—he's from a good family, he's smart, well educated, successful, handsome, doting. He's also my father's choice, which makes things much more difficult in some respects. Easier in others.

But lately, since meeting Trick, my relationship with him just seems . . . constricting. And my feelings for him seem . . . trivial. Especially compared to the way Trick's been setting my blood on fire.

Trick passes in front of the stable windows, drawing my attention back to the present.

My phone rings and I jump. For a second, I hope it's Trick. But then I chastise myself. Number one, he doesn't have my number. Number two, why would he be calling me when he's a few hundred feet away? Number three, I shouldn't want it to be.

I look at the Caller ID; it's Jenna. She doesn't even give me time to answer. She starts talking the instant I hit the talk button.

"I'm plotting and I need your evil genius mind to help me work something out. You busy?"

"I guess I am now," I reply. She's the perfect thing to get my mind off Trick. "What's up?"

"I need you to get that lickable stable boy of yours to bring Rusty to your house. Can't you institute a bring-your-hot-friend-to-work day or something? I think it's a great idea. And who knows? It might catch on. It could take the nation by storm and earn you the Nobel Peace Prize or something."

"Have you been drinking?"

"No, but I can fix that if you need me to bring you a treat. You need some company?"

I look out the window again, at the light burning in the stable, as if beckoning to me. Yes, but her company isn't exactly what I have in mind.

"Nah, I'm kinda tired. But thanks."

"Well, you have to agree to help me before I'm letting you off this phone. So go ahead, tell me you're in."

"Jenna, what am I supposed to say to him? 'My crazy friend wants you to bring Rusty here so she can molest him. Yes, she has a boyfriend. Yes, he works with Rusty. Yes, this could cause a shit storm for all of us, but what the hell! Do it anyway.'"

There's silence on the other end of the line for a few seconds. "Do you think that would work?"

"Jenna!"

"I'm kidding. Of course you don't say that. You just tell him I'd like to meet Rusty. That's it. I'll take care of the rest."

"And if he happens to remember you have a boyfriend, which he probably will?"

"You can tell him the truth. We're seeing other people, too."

"What? When did this happen?"

"About an hour ago."

"And you're just now telling me? What the . . ."

"It's been coming. I told you I thought something was up, that I was losing him. Turns out, I was right. He wants to see other people."

"So you broke up?"

"No, I just suggested that we both see other people *as well as* each other and see how things go."

I pause to mull over what she said. "And you're okay with this?" This isn't like Jenna. She's very possessive.

"Hells yeah!"

"Is this because of Rusty?"

"Hells yeah!" she repeats.

"You really think it's a good idea to drag him into this?"

"I won't be doing any dragging. Um, did you not see the way he was looking at me?"

I can't argue. Because I did see it. I thought for sure pretty much everyone saw it. "That doesn't mean—"

"It means if he's interested, we'll talk about it. That's all. God, Cam, it's not like I'm setting out to ruin the guy's life or anything. I just want to meet him. Without Trevor around. That's it. And I'll even have a chaperone that's a thousand times worse than any parent."

"Uh, I am not!"

"You can be."

"Well, maybe I don't want to be the chaperone anymore. Maybe I want to be the one taking risks and doing crazy things."

"Then, by all means, go for it! I got your back, girl. You know that."

And I do. Jenna's like family. Crazy family, but family none-theless.

There's a long pause before she says anything else. "Wait, is there something you're not telling me?"

Yes! I want to say. But I don't. For the first time since the second grade, I don't tell Jenna every little thing that's going on inside my head. For some reason, it just feels like something she wouldn't understand. It feels like no one would. I'm not even sure I under-stand it myself. It just feels different. And private. And . . . real. In ways that nothing else ever has.

Before I start freaking myself out, I change the subject. "All right. I'll talk to him in the morning. But we'll have to be careful. You know how Daddy gets."

"You'll figure something out. I have faith."

"Thank you. For leaving all the heavy lifting up to me," I add facetiously.

"Anytime, sweetie. You know I love you."

And she's right. I do.

TWENTY-TWO: *Trick*

I sit on a hay bale, drinking a bottle of water, looking at the empty stable, listening to the late-morning quiet. It makes me miss Sooty a little. I'd give anything for some distraction.

I thought for sure rubbing down both horses after Cami left last night would've been enough to work off some frustration, but it wasn't. Not nearly. I'd spent the majority of the evening after that watching the house, hoping Cami would decide she needed some late-night lovin'.

That would've been a disaster, of course. But sometimes I wonder if this job is worth missing out on her. Because, damn! She's something else.

The rest of the night, I'd spent tossing and turning on the narrow bed in the loft, the one Sooty had labeled as my "area" when he was away. He has an actual apartment in the back of the stable, but I'm not allowed in there. And that's fine with me. I don't really want to be in his space. I think the biggest problem was that my bed was missing something. Not *something*, *someone*, someone soft and warm and excitable. Someone who smells like strawberries.

Even now, I feel the telltale stirring in my jeans just thinking about what I'd do to Cami if she ever came to visit me like that.

A shadow passes through the light streaming in the stable bay doors. As though my thoughts summoned her, Cami is standing in the opening, once more bathed in sunshine.

She's wearing shorts today—barely-there denim ones that have a ragged hem and show off her long, long legs—and cowboy boots. Couple that with the tank top that perfectly outlines every curve of her upper body and I'm fighting the urge to throw caution and responsibility to the wind.

She saunters up to me and stops not far away, smiling down into my face.

"Mornin'."

"Mornin'," I return.

"I'm sorry I left you with all the work untacking and taking care of the horses last night."

"It's my job. Don't worry about it. How are you feeling today?"

I watch her as she rolls her eyes to the right and tests the muscles of her back and shoulders, wiggling her body to check for sore spots.

"I'm fine. Just a couple of tender spots. I'll live."

"Good. Sleep okay?"

She shrugs. "Okay, I guess. You?"

"Like shit," I say honestly.

Her brow wrinkles in concern. "I'm sorry. Was it the bed? Because I could talk to Daddy—"

"The bed was fine, just . . . empty." I wink at her as I take a pull of my water. When she blushes, I remind myself that I'm playing with fire. Teasing her is only making my life more miserable. How freakin' stupid is it, then, to keep doing it?

Only I can't seem to stop. She's in my blood. Under my skin. *Dammit!*

She clears her throat and stares at the toes of her boots.

"I, um, I actually came to see if you wanted some lunch. Drogheda is making quesadillas. I told her to fix some extra. They're really good. She's a great cook."

Truth be told, Sooty didn't leave me much in the way of supplies in the fridge, so that would sound appealing even if it didn't have anything to do with Cami. Her serving it up, preferably on her flat stomach, would make it the best meal I've ever had, even if it sucked. But that's beside the point.

"Sounds good. Give me some time to clean up."

"Don't worry about it. I'll bring it down to you, if that's okay."

"Sounds good," I say again, draining my water.

"I'll be back down in half an hour, then."

"Sounds good."

She turns away like she's about to leave, but stops. She looks back at me over her shoulder. She's grinning and sexy as the day is long. "Are you always this agreeable in the mornings?"

"Oh, I can be much more agreeable than this."

Smiling broadly, she nods a couple of times, then walks away. The way her hips sway, I can't help but wonder if she knows my eyes are glued to her ass.

I go into the bathroom off the office and clean up, running damp hands through my hair to tame it. Well, as much as it can be tamed, anyway. It's getting a little long and the natural wave makes it stick up at weird angles. I guess I'm lucky this particular look is in style.

I clean off the small table that sits off to one side of the spacious office and get us both a drink from the fridge. Not two minutes later, she comes walking through the door, an enormous basket hooked over one forearm.

"Good God, how many people are eating down here?"

"I didn't know how hungry you'd be. Or what all you had down here, so I brought plates and drinks and stuff, too."

Her eyes go to the table, to the beers sitting there, condensation forming over the dark glass of the bottles.

"Let me just put these away, then," I say, grabbing the longnecks and sticking them back in the fridge.

"Isn't it a little early to be drinking?"

"It's never too early."

She smiles, but it doesn't reach her eyes. For just a second, I see the same odd expression that my mom wears a lot, but I brush it off as my imagination.

She sets the basket on the desk and starts pulling stuff out and setting the table. My mouth waters at the smells coming from inside.

"I hope you like sweet tea and lemonade," she says as she takes a thermos and two glasses out of the basket.

"It's fine. I'm not picky."

When the table is set and a platter of delicious-looking quesadillas is planted in the center, she moves to take a seat. I hold out a chair for her. She smiles up into my eyes and gives me a shy "Thank you."

Of course, it makes me want to brush everything off the table and throw her up onto it instead. But I don't. I just want to.

She says a quick grace before nodding toward the plate of food. "Dig in."

"Ladies first."

She grins again. I wonder if this delicate game of cat and mouse is charming her as much as it's driving me crazy. For some reason, I think it probably is. And it just makes me want to do it all the more.

She serves herself a quesadilla and I get mine. I'll admit that the first bite nearly made my eyes roll back in my head.

"Holy shit! You weren't kidding! These are amazing."

She smiles happily. "I'm glad you like them."

"If I'm ever on death row and get a last meal, I'm requesting some of these."

"So you think about prison a lot, do you?"

"Heh. Not *that* kind of prison." I want to add that there are all types of prisons, but I don't. "So, what are you up to today? No riding?"

"How'd you know?"

I lean to the side and glance down at her smooth legs. "Shorts."

"Oh, right. Yeah, no riding today. I've been cooped up in the office all morning looking at pedigrees."

"Exciting stuff."

"You have no idea."

She says it so dryly, I chuckle.

Her eyes dart up to me a couple times, and I get the feeling she has something on her mind. Rather than pressing her, I just sit quietly and wait for her to get around to it.

"So, um, your friend, Rusty, what's his deal? Does he have a girl-friend?"

Of all the things I might've expected her to say, that was nowhere in the mix. In fact, it was light-years away from the furthest thing from my mind. And I would've thought it would be the same for her. But I'd have been wrong.

It annoys me that her question stings. Bitterly. Somewhere deep in my chest.

"No, no girlfriend. Why? Are you looking for a hookup?"

I smile and try to be nonchalant. I hope it's more convincing than I imagine it to be.

Her mouth falls open a little and she looks at me blankly for a few seconds. Then her eyes widen. "What? Me? No!"

"Oh," I say, more relieved than I care to admit. "Who then?"

"My friend Jenna."

"The one whose boyfriend is getting Rus to fix his car?"

She wrinkles her nose and cringes. "Yeah, that one."

"Wow. Um, okay."

"It's not what you think. They aren't exclusive. They have agreed to date other people, too."

"And how is he gonna feel about one of those 'other people' being the guy that's working on his car?"

She shrugs. "I don't know. I'm just the messenger."

"What's the message?"

"She wants me to have you bring him out here one night so we can all hang out and she can get to know him."

Talk about your golden opportunities! Dangerous ones, too. Red flags start popping up all over the place, but I completely ignore them. The only thing on my mind is spending an evening with Cami.

"What did you have in mind?"

"Well, I thought maybe we could hang out down here. Maybe have a beer and play some cards or something. I don't know. Nothing too . . ."

"Too what?"

"Too . . . intimate or date-ish."

"Date-ish?" I ask, smiling. There's something so cute and adorable about the way she says things sometimes.

"Yeah, date-ish. I have a fondness for nonwords. You got a problem with that?" she teases with mock bravado.

"No, ma'am," I say, holding up my hands in surrender.

"Good, so, you know, something casual and fun. That's it."

"And what's your father going to say about this?" I ask, leaning back in my chair and crossing my arms over my chest.

"Well, here's the thing. He'll be out of town for a couple days, going up north to check on a couple horses before those buyers come down. I thought we could do it then. He wouldn't even have to know."

"Hiding things from Daddy? Oooh, I like it. Sounds dirty. And forbidden."

It makes me think of sneaking into her room in the middle of the night, when the house is still and she's asleep. Waking her up with a kiss and peeling whatever she sleeps in off her body. Unless she sleeps in the nude . . .

I don't mean to groan out loud. It just slips out.

"What's the matter?"

"Oh, uh, nothing. Sorry. Just thinking. Um, that sounds fine. I'm sure Rus will be fine with it. I think everyone but her boyfriend saw him drooling over her."

She laughs. "Yeah, I think so." We both get quiet, and she finally clears her throat and asks, "So how about Sunday night?"

"You know Sooty might be back by then, right?"

"Well, if he is, he'll be in his apartment. What time does he usually turn in?"

I shrug. "I don't know. I'm not usually here at night. I think he tries to finish up by six or so every evening."

"That works. We could just come down about eight or so."

"Okay, we'll give it a shot."

"Here's the thing, though. Can you just tell Rusty that you want him to come hang out? Jenna doesn't want him to think he's being, like, set up or anything."

"I can do that."

"You think he'll come?"

"For free beer? Oh, hell yeah. Rusty's a cheap date."

"How 'bout you? Are you a cheap date?"

"I'm even cheaper than that. I've been known to work for kisses before."

She leans back in her chair, too. A smile plays around the edges of her mouth. "Really?"

"No, I never work for kisses. But I'd be willing to make an exception."

TWENTY-THREE: *Cami*

I know why I'm so nervous. Somehow—and I'm still not sure whose willpower I'm using—I've managed to stay away from the stable for two whole days. Of course, it helped knowing that I had definite plans to see Trick tonight with Jenna and Rusty. Now, the time is at hand and I'm not sure my stomach can take it. I think it must've tied itself in at least a dozen knots already.

Daddy has been keeping me super busy, so that helped me stay put. I have no doubt he's doing it on purpose, too. But he's gone now. Left earlier this evening. Now there's no one to keep tabs on me. Or on the stable.

I turn away from the mirror when I hear the knock at my door. As I suspect, it's Jenna. She's wearing short shorts and a huge grin.

"Have I told you how freakin' awesome you are? Because if not, I should totally be flogged."

I put a finger to my chin in thought. "Might have to go with the flogging, as I don't seem to remember hearing you go on and on about my awesomeness."

"Well, it'll have to wait. I might be doing some flogging of my own tonight. What what!"

"Just gonna jump right in there, huh?"

"If the temperature's right, I just might."

I roll my eyes heavenward.

"Don't roll those eyes at me. I'm just doing what you're too afraid to do."

"And what's that?"

"Go out there and get what I want."

"Yeah, but only since Trevor was already heading in the let's-see-other-people direction."

"Cam, let me tell you something. I think I would've done it anyway. This guy . . . I don't know. He does something to me. For days now I've been like 'Trevor who?'"

"Suuuuure."

"I'm serious. There's something different about him. About the way he makes me feel."

"And you know this after meeting him once for a few minutes?"

"Don't be a hater. I know it sounds crazy, but can't you just go with it? God, you're such a Debbie Downer."

"I'm sorry, Jen. I don't mean to be. I'm just . . ."

"I know. I know exactly what you are. You're nuts about Trick and you're being a stubborn jackass. And now you're making yourself miserable. Is that about it?"

I look at Jenna, standing in the center of my room in her Daisy Dukes with her hand on her hip and a smug look on her face, and I've never loved her more. She just doesn't pull any punches.

"You know what? You're right. But my situation is a bit more complicated than yours. At least give me that."

"Daddy issues are not exclusive to you, Cami."

"It's not just about him. Well, not like you're thinking. Trick really needs this job. I mean he *needs* it. What if I mess that up for him?"

"He's a big boy. Maybe he thinks you're worth the risk. If he doesn't, then *he's* not worth the risk."

"Maybe I'm not."

"Of course you are! Look at you." Jenna walks over to me and puts her hands on my shoulders to turn me around toward the mirror. She stands behind me, a good bit taller than me. "You're gorgeous. You're smart. You're sweet. You're funny. You've got legs that go for miles and an ass I'd kill for. Any man in his right mind would risk death for you!"

"And I'm sure you're not the least bit biased. Or jacked up on caffeine."

"One Red Bull hardly counts as 'jacked up,'" she says, giving me a "look."

"I guess we'd better get going, then, before it wears off."

She smiles brightly. "That's more like it."

I return her smile and let Jenna drag me out of my bedroom and down the stairs. As soon as we step outside onto the patio, my stomach clenches.

"Don't be nervous," Jenna whispers, patting my hand like a little old lady.

"I'm not nervous. I'm just . . ."

"I know. You're nervous."

I laugh. There's just no talking to Jenna.

When we get closer to the stable, I can hear music drifting out from the open bay doors. When we round the corner and step into the light, Trick and Rusty are sitting in two folding chairs pulled just outside the office door. Rusty is playing air guitar on his leg with a beer in one hand. Trick is looking on, laughing, pounding out a beat on invisible drums.

"Just in time to see the band," Jenna says, bringing both guys to a comical midair halt. "Don't stop on our account. I've always wanted to kiss a rock star."

Ohmigod! She's coy and brazen at the same time! How does she do that?

Rusty grins from ear to ear. "Then, baby, you're about to have the night of your life."

Jenna giggles attractively, and I glance at Trick. He's not watching them. He's watching me. I feel my cheeks get hot, and his lips quirk at the edges. He turns his head and looks at me from the corner of his narrowed eyes, as if he's debating whether I blush on purpose. I shrug, assuring him it's beyond my control. He shakes his head and a slow grin spreads across his face. Without taking his eyes off mine, he raises his beer to his lips and takes a long drink. I can't help but watch his mouth, where his lips are pursed against the bottle. And then the action of his throat as he swallows.

I'm pretty sure my knees have turned to butter.

Trick stands. "Here, take my seat. I'm sure there are a couple more chairs around here somewhere."

Jenna slides quickly into Trick's empty seat and smiles her brightest smile up at me. "Cam, you know this place inside and out. Why don't you help him find some? I'll wait here with Rusty."

She turns her smile on Rusty, and he is appropriately dazzled. There's a look in his eye, though, that makes me think he's not going to be the docile prey Jenna is used to. She might just have her hands full with him.

I smother a grin with the back of my hand. Serves her right! Every man-eater meets her match eventually.

"Come on," Trick says, tipping his head toward the dark night outside. "I think there might be a couple in the storage shed."

I nod at him and turn to Jenna. "We'll be right back."

"Take your time," she says, widening her eyes meaningfully.

I smile at her, then smile at Rusty, who is grinning like the Cheshire cat. I wonder if Trick really didn't tell him Jenna and I were coming. He seems genuinely surprised. Thrilled, but surprised.

I follow Trick out and around the corner, leaving the rectangle of light from the open stable door behind us. It gets darker and darker as we cross the yard to the shed that sits behind the round pen.

The moon is huge and bright overhead, illuminating the tiny white flowers that sprinkle the lush grass at my feet. I pause to pick one, twirling it in my fidgety fingers. A lightly sweet, floral scent drifts up to my nose. I inhale deeply, letting the aroma sooth my jangling nerves.

"You like flowers?"

"Some of them. Why?" He nods toward my fingers. "Oh. Yeah, Drogheda used to braid these into my hair when I was younger. They have long stems that are perfect for that. I don't know if I liked them before then, but I know I've loved them ever since."

"How long has she been with you?"

"Since I was eleven or twelve, I guess. Something like that. A long time. She's like family now."

"Did you have a different housekeeper before her?"

"No. That's when the business sort of took off, I guess. Life changed a lot after that."

"How do you mean?"

"Well, before that, we lived closer to Greenfield. Our house was much smaller, and we only had one car. I went to public school and got to play at the playground. Daddy was home more, and Mom was just . . . happier, I guess. I don't know. It seems like everything changed all of a sudden. Not that it was all bad. Don't get me wrong. But Drogheda was definitely one of the good things to come out of it."

"So you're saying you were happier when you were poor?"

I laugh. Even to my own ears, it sounds a little bitter. "Would that be so strange?"

Trick shrugs. "Maybe. Money solves a lot of problems."

"For adults, that's probably true. But for kids, sometimes it just creates them. I didn't care that we didn't have a lot of money. I was happy. And, let me tell you, there are a lot fewer expectations when you're poor, too. Well, not even poor. Just not . . . wealthy."

"Poor little princess, is that it?"

I whip my head around to look at him, immediately taking exception to what he's insinuating. But I see his playful grin and my anger dies. I smile. "Sounds like it, doesn't it? Poor me?"

"Nah, you're not the type. I knew that after talking to you for two minutes."

"You did?" This should not please me as much as it does. I try to suppress my wide smile.

"Yep. I knew you were a phone sex operator right off the bat. And I've never met a snobby phone sex operator in my life."

I laugh. "And just how many have you met?"

Trick tilts his head back and starts counting on his fingers. I watch him tick off ten and then start again.

"Um. One," he says anticlimactically, grinning. "Just you."

"Well, I hate to disappoint, but . . ."

"You never disappoint. I don't think you have it in you. In fact, I might go so far as to say that you strive *not* to disappoint."

"What's that supposed to mean?"

"It just seems that way, like maybe your father has everything all planned out for you and you're going right along with it."

I want to argue, but he's hit a nerve that feels all too raw and real. I've wondered the same thing a thousand times, especially lately.

"You left your dream behind. How is that so different? You're not going after what you want, either."

"I think it's very different. My choices have been out of necessity and responsibility. And I haven't left anything behind. I'll still get what I want out of life. It will just have to wait a little longer."

"Some things don't wait."

"The things that are worth it do."

We reach the storage shed and Trick unlocks the door and opens it, flicking on the light switch to the right. I stand off to the side as he looks for the chairs. The hot, still air feels suffocating, and a light sheen of moisture breaks out on my skin. I lift my heavy hair off my neck and fan my face.

I see Trick move a big piece of plywood. Behind it is a stack of six or seven folding chairs with padded seats. He grabs two and backs out to close and lock the door behind him.

When he turns to me, he stops. Just stops and stares at me. He leans the chairs up against the shed and steps toward me.

"You know what would make this picture perfect?"

"What?" I ask, breathlessly hoping he'll kiss me, even though I know it's wrong.

He takes the little white flower from my fingers and tucks it behind my ear. "With your hair piled on top of your head like that, all you need to be a Southern belle is a flower."

His fingers trail down my cheek and neck as he drags his hand away. Without meaning to, I sway toward him, wanting to prolong the moment, the feel of him touching me.

I let my hair fall and Trick reaches out to steady me, his hands strong on my upper arms. He's so close I can feel his warm breath tickling my cheeks.

"Are you okay? Is the heat too much for you?"

Good God, what a loaded question!

"I'm fine," I manage to say.

We stand like that, staring into each other's eyes, until Trick releases me and looks away.

"I guess we'd better get back before the kids get into trouble," he says with a lopsided grin.

"Yeah, we can't have that, now can we?"

I wish I could recover as fast as Trick. My knees still feel weak and I'm more than a little disappointed that there hasn't been another attempt at kissing me since the field party.

It's for the best, it's for the best, it's for the best.

That's my mantra all the way back to the stable.

When we arrive, Jenna is sitting in Rusty's lap and he's helping her place her fingers in the right position on the neck of a guitar.

I glance at Trick, and he smiles at me and shakes his head. "Crazy kids," he mutters under his breath. I laugh. Sometimes I do feel like the adult in my relationship with Jenna. I think it's funny that apparently Trick feels that way with Rusty, at least part of the time, anyway.

Jenna spots me. "You're back! Rusty and I were just talking. We think a trip to the pool is in order since it's still so hot."

Trick in swim trunks and nothing else? Um, yes please!

"Okay."

"Yay!" Jenna squeals. "I told you she'd be down."

"You forgot to mention the best part, though," Rusty says, playfully pinching her side and making her giggle.

"Oh, yeah. To be more specific, Rusty and I think we ought to go *skinny-dipping* in your pool."

Thoughts of seeing Trick in the buff makes my cheeks flame and my stomach flutter with excitement. But that won't be happening tonight.

"Jenna, we can't. You forget that Drogheda is still here."

"So? You know she sleeps like the dead."

"She'd kill me, Jenna. We can't take that chance."

Jenna sighs heavily, like she's so put upon. "Fine. Skivvies then. I didn't bring a suit, and neither did Rusty."

I arch one brow. That's a pretty convenient excuse. I turn to Trick. He holds his hands up.

"Don't look at me. As long as your dad doesn't find out, I don't care either way. I don't have trunks regardless."

My mouth goes dry thinking about seeing Trick standing on the edge of my pool, water dripping off his body, his underwear plastered to his body. In some ways, that picture is far more appealing, partly because I can't really imagine what he looks like naked. I'm sure it's glorious, though. Not that I've been looking, but his jeans fit pretty snugly in the crotch.

I look back at Jenna. Her eyes are sparkling with excitement, and she's nodding her head in encouragement.

"Come on, Cam! Live a little."

"Fine, but we have to be quiet. Not a lot of splashing, okay? We'll just cool off a little and then come back down here."

Everyone agrees and, although I'm concerned about Drogheda finding us, I know deep down that she'd never do anything to hurt me. My secrets are always safe with her.

TWENTY-FOUR: *Trick*

I can't help but be a little worried that my dick is making decisions I really shouldn't be going along with. Even as we're walking up to the main house, I'm telling myself this is a mistake, that if we get caught and Jack finds out, I'll be out on my ass. And that would be a disaster. But still, I follow Cami through the wrought-iron gate that surrounds the pool.

She walks around the pool to the shallow end and stops. I stop beside her, and we wait for Jenna and Rusty to catch up. They're giggling and whispering the whole way.

From the corner of my eye, I see Cami fidget. At first, it appears to be a nervous thing. But when I glance at her, she looks at me and smiles. It's a bright smile. Bright and . . . excited, which makes me think it's not all *bad* nerves. In fact, it makes me twitch a little in my jeans, which is never a good thing when I'm getting ready to strip down in front of mixed company.

Without even pausing, Jenna pulls her shirt over her head, then reaches for Rusty's. While they're all wrapped up in removing each other's clothes, I turn more toward Cami.

"Are you sure you're up for this?"

She takes a deep breath and grins at me. "Yep. You?"

I nod. "Yep."

She puts one small hand on my arm and looks me in the eye. "It'll be fine, you know. Drogheda would never tell on me, so you don't need to worry, okay?"

She's worrying about *me* worrying? Now I feel bad for telling her how important this job is.

"I'm not worried," I assure her. "I trust you."

Her smile is sweet and pleased and it makes me want to kiss her. Hell, everything she *does* makes me want to kiss her.

"Good. You should."

As if she's making her point, Cami takes a few steps back and pulls her shirt over her head. She does it quickly and then holds it in front of her and waits. That's my cue to shed a piece of clothing, too.

In the brightness of the full moon, I can see her eyes twinkling devilishly. She's so coy. So damned adorably coy.

God, it would be so much fun to have her all to myself for one night. Just one night. Maybe that would be enough to get her out of my system.

"All right then, Mr. Rock-Hard Abs, show me what you got," she demands teasingly.

She doesn't have to ask me twice! Grabbing a handful of shirt behind my neck, I pull it over my head. But *I* throw *mine* on one of the white lounge chairs, upping the ante a little. Her eyes flicker down my chest and stomach. My muscles tighten. I see her gaze drop lower, then hurry back to my face. She's curious. She wants to look, she wants to see what's under my jeans, but she's trying not to show it. I bite back a groan.

What I wouldn't give to carry her off to someplace more private . . .

Slowly, she pulls her arms away from her chest and holds her shirt out by her fingertips, then drops it onto a chair. I have to clamp my lips shut to keep my mouth from dropping open when I see the little purple scrap of lace that's covering the most perfectly firm flesh I think I've ever seen. I can even see the outline of her nipples. The fact that they're hard makes me want to squirm.

When I look up at her face, she isn't smiling anymore. Her expression *looks* like I *feel*—hot and bothered and about as close as I've ever come to ripping someone's clothes off.

She isn't moving. She's just staring at me. Like, right at me. Her eyes aren't leaving mine. And there's something about the intensity of her look that makes me feel like some kind of animal.

Just to tease her, I bend down and pull off my boots, kicking them to the side. My socks follow. I see her lips curve and she kicks off her own shoes and gives them a nudge. Then she's watching me again, all serious and . . . hungry. It's like we both know we're getting down to business. And that excites me.

I reach for the button of my jeans and I pop it loose. Her eyes drop to my hands and I slowly slide the zipper down. My jeans hang a little on my hips, so when I let them go, they fall into a heap around my ankles. I step out of them and straighten to watch her look me over.

Her eyes start at my bare feet and move slowly up my calves and thighs. My balls tighten when she gets to my crotch. Her eyes stay there for a lot longer than what they should. It makes my pulse pick up speed.

Holy shit, that's hot!

"I guess it's a good thing I wore underwear today," I say glibly, anything to break the tension. I'm not sure how much more I can take of Cami's teasing torture and still act like a responsible adult.

Her eyes fly to my face and her mouth drops open. "You don't normally?"

I shake my head. Even in the silvery light of the moon, I can see her cheeks darken. I know she's blushing.

"Tonight is not a good night for you to be doing stuff like that."

"Stuff like what?" she asks, a little breathlessly, which also turns me on.

Dammit!

"Stuff like looking me over as if you wanna lick every square inch of me and then blushing about it. It's taking every bit of willpower I have and then some not to come over there and kiss you."

"But you don't want to do that." I don't know if it's a statement or a question.

"Hell yeah, I want to! But I can't. I shouldn't."

"I know. And I admire you for your . . . restraint."

Before she even finishes the sentence, she's biting her lip and tugging on the zipper to her shorts. She wiggles her thumbs under the waistband and shimmies her hips back and forth. But slowly, like she's actually doing a striptease. My mouth goes completely dry as I watch the material make its way down her slim legs.

When her shorts are pooled around her ankles, she steps out of them and flings them away. I notice she jacks her chin up a notch, like she's not used to being on display but she's determined to be cool about it. That makes it even sexier in my opinion.

The triangle of lace between her legs matches her bra. I don't really much care either way. I'm as much a fan of white cotton as I am of sexy lingerie. I don't pay any of it a lot of attention. I'm much more interested in what's underneath.

Cami is built perfectly. At first I'm surprised that, with a body like that—long legs, tight stomach, curvy hips, narrow waist, awesome rack—she doesn't wear more revealing clothes. But then, when I think of her personality, of what she's really like, I'm not surprised at all. I'd say she's picky about who sees her like this, and the fact that she saves it for a few select people makes me want her that much more.

"You do realize you're perfect, right?"

She looks down, letting her hair fall forward to hide her face. But not before I see the smile of pure pleasure pulling at her lips. I can't help but wonder what things are like with that boyfriend of hers. Doesn't he tell her how beautiful she is? Doesn't he know how lucky he is to have a girl like this? To touch her whenever he wants to, probably with her daddy's blessing?

Those thoughts bring an unwelcome dark cloud to the night, so I put them out of my mind and make a point to keep things light. For both our sakes.

"Now, are you getting in or am I gonna have to throw you in?"

She looks confused at first, but then I see her face light up when she captures the mischief of the night.

That's more like it.

Although it works to relieve the tension, in my head I know all she has to do is move the *wrong* way or touch me the *right* way and my rock-hard willpower will crumble like day-old bread.

TWENTY-FIVE: *Cami*

We play in the pool for a while. Believe it or not, Jenna and Rusty are fairly social, although I can tell they'd like nothing more than to be alone.

We talk about old cars and Rusty's garage. We talk about horses, and Rusty jokes about Trick being like the Horse Whisperer. We talk about the band and the fact that Trick can sing as well as play the guitar and the drums. That makes more sense now when I think about stumbling upon them playing make-believe instruments with Trick being the drummer.

"Did you tell her about your big dream?" Rusty asks Trick.

"Why do I ever tell you anything?"

"What? Was it a secret? You gotta tell me these things, man! How am I supposed to know?"

Trick rolls his eyes, but he's still smiling. Now I'm intrigued and have to ask, "So, what is it? I thought you wanted to be a veterinarian."

"I do. And I plan to. What Rusty's talking about is more of a stretch than being a vet."

When he doesn't continue, I prompt him. "Well? Are you gonna make me beg?"

Trick raises one brow and my heart stutters in my chest. I wonder if he knows I'm almost to that point already. Only it has nothing to do with hearing his dream and everything to do with him kissing me.

"Not tonight," he says softly.

I hear Jenna make a noise that's a cross between a gasp and a snicker. I know which side she's on. She'd love nothing more than for me to cut loose with Trick. I'm beginning to think I would, too.

"It has to do with a small herd of wild horses up around the Outer Banks."

"Wild horses?"

"Yeah, some of them are from the original Spanish Mustang bloodline. They'd be incredible racers if they could be broken."

I put two and two together. "And what? You want to try to *break one*?"

"You don't have to sound so confident," he teases.

"It's not that, it's just . . . well, I mean, has it ever been done? Has anyone ever broken one of the wild horses?"

"I've heard of it, but I don't think anyone's ever tried to race one."

"And you think you could do it?"

Trick looks right at me, his smile slow and assured. "Yeah, I really do. Some even say the wild ones are the best."

I think of how far he's come with Highland Runner, who was too wild even for Sooty. I've heard tales of people who have a special gift, a special connection to horses, so much so that they can ride and train almost any horse. Maybe Trick has . . . whatever it is. If he could do it, and if the horse raced well, he'd make an instant name for himself in the horse racing world.

I return his smile. "You know, as crazy as it sounds, I really don't doubt it."

His smile widens and he winks. "Smart girl. You should never doubt me."

"That's true, unless you're doubting he'd steal your virtue," Rusty says with a laugh. "He's wilder than any of those damn horses."

"You're such a liar." Trick punches Rusty in the arm. It's playful, but I see him glare in a way that seems like a warning. In my head, there is definitely a warning there, and it's duly noted. He turns to me. "He's exaggerating. He exaggerates *everything*!"

"What's that supposed to mean?" Rusty asks.

"Nothing. I just want the ladies to know how to do anti-Rus math. Take any length he gives you, divide by two and subtract an inch. That's much more accurate."

Rusty flings himself out of the water and tackles Trick, shoving his head under the water. They both laugh, as do Jenna and I, but the unease is still with me. Is he really nothing more than a player? After only one thing?

Shortly after that, we get out of the water and head back down to the stable. Jenna is still teasing Rusty about his exaggerations.

"You don't believe me, but when this guy used to play regularly with the band, the chicks would go wild! He was like a rock star."

"You're so full of shit," Trick mutters with a chuckle.

"You know it's true, man. This dude can pick. More than just the other night in the field, I'm tellin' ya. Makes the ladies' panties fall right off."

We all laugh. Trick looks at me and rolls his eyes. "Don't believe a word he says."

"I'm not even playin'! I've got the acoustic in my trunk. Play something and see if panties don't drop. Just not these panties," he says, hugging Jenna playfully. "Hers, you can have." He grins at me and winks.

Rusty really is an adorable guy. And pretty hot, too. Jenna has a good eye. His hair is a dark red and his eyes are bright blue. They pop in his face. He's got a great physique, and his grin is contagious. In my opinion, though, his best feature is his personality. Of course, I'm a little biased, though.

I look at Trick, who is watching me. A bit of a smile still lingers on his perfect lips. "Do you want to hear me play? I promise your panties are safe."

All warnings instantly forgotten, I think to myself that I don't want my panties to be safe from him. I want him to tear them off. With his teeth!

Just the thought of that makes me blush. His smile widens again. "You're really gonna have to quit doing that."

"That's it. I'm getting my guitar. Maybe I can speed things along a little for you two."

"Ignore him," Trick says quickly.

The funny thing is, Trick seems more determined to keep me at arm's length than I do. And that's so backward! I should be the one reminding us both that I have a boyfriend. But I'm not. If he said he wanted to be with me, that he was ready to go for it, I'd break up with Brent in a heartbeat. I'd do that because I'd never cheat on Brent. The thing is, sometimes the way I respond to Trick makes me feel as though I already have. And that doesn't sit well with me.

I'm gonna have to do something about this. It's so wrong! I need to really look at my feelings for Brent, figure out what they are. And where they're going.

Rusty comes back with his guitar. He takes it out of the case and hands it to Trick with a pick.

"Show 'em what you got, Trick." Rusty sits in one of the four chairs and pulls Jenna onto his lap. "I'm keeping this one close just in case it works on her, too." He winks at Jenna, and she giggles. She's eating it up.

Trick takes a chair, and I choose the one across from him. He puts the leather strap over his shoulder and settles the instrument across his body. He plucks the strings a few times to make sure it's in tune, makes a couple of adjustments, and then starts picking out notes.

My father is a fan of classic rock, so it doesn't take long for me to recognize what he's playing. He hums along at first, his voice adding depth to the acoustic sounds. And then he starts singing. I become every bit as mesmerized as Rusty promised I would.

The song is "Wonderful Tonight" by Eric Clapton. His voice is perfect for it—a little scratchy and gruff, hauntingly soft and sexy.

After the first few lines, he looks up at me, singing every word and playing every note as if I'm the only person in the room. His eyes never leave mine.

I barely notice when Jenna and Rusty get up and walk away. My only thought is, *Please don't let him stop playing!*

When he strums the last note, we sit and stare at each other in complete silence for what feels like a short forever. His lips are curved the tiniest bit, but there's something so sad and melancholy about his expression, it gives me a pang somewhere around the vicinity of my heart. I can't help but wonder what he's thinking.

He doesn't leave me wondering long.

"Tonight was a mistake."

Of all the things I don't expect to hear, that has to be way up near the top of the list. And I'm confused by it.

"Why? I think it seems like they're getting along fine."

"That's not what I mean, and you know it."

I suppose I do. I just didn't want to think that's what he meant.

"Why? We're not doing anything wrong."

"You shouldn't even be here. You have a boyfriend."

I'm instantly irritated. And defensive. And hurt.

"Me? Well, what about you? Who was that girl you were snuggled up to at Lucky's the other night? She certainly didn't look like just a friend!"

To my utter distress, I feel tears sting the backs of my eyes like pinpricks of humiliation.

Trick laughs, a short bitter kind of laugh that almost says, *Ha!*

"She was . . . heh, she was not nearly enough. That's who she was."

"Not nearly enough for what?"

Trick's eyes burn holes into mine. I think at first he's not going to answer me. And when he does, I almost wish he hadn't.

"Not nearly enough to make me stop thinking about you."

I don't know what to say to that. I don't know what to say to any of it, partly because it's true. I *do* have a boyfriend, and I *shouldn't* be here.

But I want to be. More than I want to be anywhere else.

As if on cue, as if he somehow picked the very worst (or very best) time in the history of the world to call, my phone rings. I dig it out of my pocket and see Brent's face dominating the lighted screen.

I look at Trick. He looks at me. Now I know why his smile seemed sad and bitter.

"Go," he says, tipping his head toward the house.

Not knowing what to say or what to do, I get up and walk away, clicking the talk button as I leave.

TWENTY-SIX: *Trick*

feel like shit. I never would've thought it would be that hard to watch Cami walk away like she did. But it was. God, it was!

I sat there for at least ten minutes after she left, just to make sure she wasn't coming back. When it became obvious she wasn't, I left Rusty's guitar on one of the chairs and headed for Sooty's hidden stash of "painkillers." His tastes are limited and all I could find was bourbon, but it did the trick. All I wanted it to do was drown Cami from my thoughts, and I knew any form of alcohol could accomplish that if I drank enough of it.

In the last year, it seems the thing I was constantly trying to drown out was my bitterness at having to leave school to work at a thankless job. That and anger at my father for leaving us the way he did. I'm not sure I'll ever be able to get over that.

But the last few times I've sought solace in the bottom of a bottle has been because of a redheaded devil who seems bound and determined to torture me.

The bad thing about bourbon, at least for me, is that the hangover is absolute hell. All morning, my head has suffered with every thump of the horses, every bright ray of sunshine, and every plaguing thought of Cami.

I hear a familiar voice and look up the small hill at the main house. It irritates me that I hope to see Cami walking toward the stable and that I'm disappointed when I see she's not.

You'll never learn, will you?

Instead, she's walking around the pool. She's wearing a bikini, but her bottom half is wrapped in some sort of skirt-type thing. Of course, she looks edible in it. She looks edible in everything.

She hollers something else, something I can't understand, and I see a short, older woman come to the door and ask her a question. I figure it must be Drogheda, the housekeeper.

Cami answers and then settles onto a lounge chair, turning her face up to the sun. Purposely, I turn away—away from the house, away from the temptation, away from her. It can't happen, and that's that. Might as well get over it and move on.

I'm still telling myself that when I hear voices again, and one of them is much lower. I look back over my shoulder and see her douche of a boyfriend making his way around the pool to her.

With an intimacy that hits me like a sucker punch to the gut, I watch him bend down and kiss Cami. And it's not a little peck, either. Even from a distance, I can see that he wants to devour her. Of course, it makes me furious, but I can't really blame the guy. I want to devour her, too.

When she pulls away, he taps her back and she scoots forward. He swings a leg over the back of the chair and sits behind Cami. Pulling her hair over one shoulder, he leans down and kisses her neck before he starts massaging it.

I see him whisper something in her ear. She nods and says something in response. Like watching a train wreck, I can't look away from the scene. I've never been so jealous of someone else in my entire life. I've been fortunate in that there have been few things I've ever wanted that I couldn't have. And none of those things were girls.

Until Cami.

I reason to myself that's why I want her so badly. It's a matter of wanting her so much simply *because* I shouldn't, because I can't really have her. But even as that part of my brain works to try to convince the rest of me, I know it's not true. It has nothing to do with something so superficial. I want Cami for other reasons, reasons I'm not quite willing to admit yet because they come with consequences. Nasty ones.

An engine starts up and I see a station wagon backing out of the garage. Must be the housekeeper again. Everyone else is gone.

I look back to the couple and see that Brent the douche is also watching the car drive away. It must've been what he was waiting for. He wastes no time in taking full advantage of the alone time.

Fury boils in my blood when I see him pull one strap of Cami's suit off her shoulder as he kisses her neck a little more aggressively. Cami shrugs that shoulder, a clear indication she's not into it, but he doesn't take the hint. He reaches around and slips his hand underneath her bikini top. It's all I can do not to run up there and kick his ass.

I grit my teeth. I know I should stop watching them, but I can't.

Cami grabs his hand and pulls it away, but rather than giving up, he moves it down to where her wrap is tied at her waist. She moves it again and he stops kissing her.

He leans back and it's easy to see by his body language that he's not happy. But neither am I. I still want to rip off his arms.

Cami says something to him and he leans back, crossing his

arms over his chest. She turns and continues to talk. She moves her hands animatedly. I'm beginning to learn her body language, and I've never seen this before. I wonder if it means she's upset. That's the impression I get.

After a few seconds, the douche of a boyfriend flings his hands and stands up. He walks off, and Cami pushes her fingers into her hair. I get the feeling she wants to pull it in frustration. But she doesn't. Instead, she gets up and stalks off, too.

I'm a little disappointed that she's chasing after him. I'm still chastising myself when I hear someone tearing down the driveway. I know it must be him. Another minute or two later, I hear a door slam. I look back toward the main house, and Cami's walking back to her chair by the pool. She's carrying some kind of little square kit that has handles. Curious, I let my focus shift completely to her again.

She sits down and unzips the kit, then angrily pulls her foot toward her. She takes a bottle out of the kit, pours something on what looks like a cotton ball and then starts swiping at her toes. My only guess is that she's giving herself a pedicure, or whatever it's called. For some reason, watching her do something so girly and intimate is fascinating. And very alluring.

I glance at her face. Her brows are drawn down tight over her eyes and she's muttering. Whatever happened with the douche, she's not happy about it.

When she's finished swiping at all ten toes, she rifles through the kit again and brings out a bottle of red polish. I could see it a mile away, it's so bright. She shakes it angrily before unscrewing the cap. She leans over to carefully brush some on one toe. She must've messed up, though, because she gets the piece of cotton again and wipes it off. She holds her hands out and looks at them before she closes the bottle and lays her head on her bent knees.

She's absolutely motionless. In my head, I can almost hear the soft sounds of her crying and, even though she's crying over a douche, it still bothers me. A lot. Before I can even begin to think of how stupid it is to go to her, I'm already halfway to the pool.

As quietly as I can, I open the wrought-iron gate we used last night and close it behind me. Cami doesn't budge. She's perfectly still and perfectly quiet, not even making the soft crying sounds I'd imagined she would be. When I stop in front of her, she slowly lifts her head. Her eyes meet mine. They're dry and she doesn't look away.

Without saying a word, I bend down and lift her legs, pulling them across my lap as I sit down.

"Here," I say, holding my hand out for the little bottle she's still clutching. She frowns, but she hands it over, anyway. I shake the bottle again, like I've seen women do before, and then I unscrew the cap. "Talk to me," I urge as I bend down to paint a bright red streak on her first toe.

"There's nothing to say."

Bullshit!

"You're upset. Now talk to me. Tell me what happened. Maybe I can help." She snorts and I look back at her. "What? You think just because I'm not a Harvard grad I'm not smart enough to give a little good advice?"

"Don't be ridiculous! You're every bit as smart as Brent, maybe even smarter."

Something about the way she said it, the expression on her face, makes me think she actually believes that. I clear my throat and swallow the smile that's pulling at my lips. It bugs me that what she thinks of me matters. It shouldn't. But it does.

"Well then, spill it."

I return to painting her toenails. In the quiet before she starts talking, I am berating myself for being a complete imbecile. I need to stay away from this girl, so what do I do? I go and get myself all wrapped up in her. Literally. Every nerve and hormone in my body is locked in on her warm body so close to mine and the knowledge that all I'd have to do is pull her into my lap and . . .

"Talk!" I bark, a little more sharply than I'd intended. She has to say something, to talk about that douche boyfriend of hers or she'll soon have something else to rest her legs on. Or any other body part she might want to rest on it.

"All right, all right. Geez!" She pauses for a minute before I hear her sigh. "I don't know what's wrong with me. Things are just different between Brent and me lately. I don't feel as . . . certain about him as I used to."

"Certain?"

"Yeah. You know, like he's the one. Like *the* one."

I can't help but turn and look at her. "Is that what you're looking for? *The* one?"

She looks down at her toes and shrugs. "No, not specifically. It's just that he's perfect in every way. It just seems smart."

I return to painting.

"Smart? To what? Marry him because he looks good on paper? That's not smart. That's incredibly stupid. And you're anything but stupid."

"How do you know?"

"Because I know you."

"No, you don't."

I turn and look at her again. "Yes. I do. At least in all the ways that count." I pause. My better judgment is telling me I shouldn't flirt, but I punch it right in the mouth and say what I'm thinking, anyway. "Well, minus the way that's the most fun."

I wink at her, and she blushes. I watch her white teeth sink into the flesh of her lower lip. I shift under her legs and turn to look at her feet. They're the only body part I don't want to get naked and rub myself all over.

"So, what's the problem? Why are you suddenly not so sure?"

"I don't know. Things just feel . . . different. It's hard to explain."

"Try."

She sighs again. I can tell she's not exactly comfortable talking to me about this, but not so much so that she won't. I just have to pry a little. Why it's important to me to help her or to find out the answers is something I don't want to think about.

"I don't know. It's like . . . like . . ." She trails off and I make myself *not* turn to look at her. Her face is expressive and I know it would tell me more, but looking at her only blurs that line I'm having such trouble with.

Her voice drops to something a little louder than a whisper, but not much. "I know it when he touches me, when he kisses me. It doesn't feel right anymore."

"And why is that?"

"I don't know. I just don't feel that way about him anymore. I don't want him that way."

"Then what do you want?"

What I meant was, what does she want from him, but the way it came out didn't sound like that, even to my ears. Painting the last stroke on her left foot, I pick it up and bring it to my mouth, blowing on the wet polish. I don't even realize I'm rubbing her arch with my thumb until I feel the chills break out on her calf. Lowering her leg, I turn to look at her. Her lips are parted a tiny bit and her eyes are sharply focused on me. On my mouth specifically. I watch her pink tongue slip out to wet her lips and I feel an ache deep down in my stomach.

Without looking away, she tugs her foot from my hand. I let it go and she carefully tucks it behind my back and scoots forward, putting me squarely between her legs.

Oh shit! Stop her now or you won't stop at all!

"Do you really want to know what I want?"

God, yes!

That's what I want to say, right before I lay her down on the lounge chair and peel her bikini off. But my sensible side speaks up this time. Fast and loud.

"More than you can imagine, but we both know it's not a good idea."

I see the fire in her eyes die. It's like I doused it with the cold water of rejection. I wounded her, the last thing in the world I wanted to do.

"Cami, I—"

Drawing up her legs, she turns to the side and stands. "You don't have to explain. I understand. Completely. Thanks for listening. I appreciate it."

Without even taking her little kit with her, she turns and walks away. And doesn't look back.

TWENTY-SEVEN: *Cami*

"Cami, you haven't been out of the house in almost a week. You're coming with me tonight whether you like it or not."

"I'm not really up to it tonight, Jenna. Maybe later in the week."

"Don't make me come over there and toss your gorgeous butt in the shower. You know I'll do it."

"I know what you're trying to do. And I really appreciate it, but I'm just not in the mood, Jenna."

She's quiet for a second. "Is this about Brent?"

"No, it's not. We're fine."

Jenna snorts. "Yeah, right. You and Brent haven't been 'fine' since you met Trick."

"Jenna, I—"

"I know, I know," she interrupts quickly. "I'm not saying another word. Look, Cami, just come out with me. For a little while. When you're ready to leave, we'll leave. Do it for me. I'm worried about you."

I know by her voice and from being her friend for a zillion years that she really is worried about me. That's what makes me cave.

I don't bother to hide my reluctance. "Fine. But I don't want to stay long. And if Trick shows up, we're leaving!"

"I told you, he won't be there. He and Rusty have other plans."

She'd said as much earlier but didn't elaborate. It makes my heart hurt to think of what (or who) those other plans might be.

"How are things going with you two, by the way?"

I can hear her smile when she answers. "Awesome! He's just . . . he's just . . . It's awesome."

"Sounds to me like you like him. At least a little," I tease.

"Shut up, smart-ass. Don't be a hater just because you're too afraid to take the leap."

My laugh is bitter, even to my own ears. "It's not a matter of fear anymore, Jenna. I told you what happened. He chose. That's it. The end."

"God, Cami! He didn't choose. He had to *have you* to be able to choose something else over you, silly. And he never had you. You never let Brent go long enough to see where it would go. Me? I can't blame the guy. I'm sure he took one look at you and knew you were a heartbreaker."

"I've told you—"

"I know, I know," she says again as she interrupts. "Let's not talk about this again. Get ready. I'll be there to pick you up in an hour. Tonight, Lucky won't know what hit him."

She's referring to the namesake of the bar. "Lucky was a horse, Jenna."

"I know."

"A female horse."

"Oh," she says, deadpan. "That bitch won't know what hit her," she corrects.

I laugh. "Much better."

* * *

Jenna grins at me over the top of her mug as she gulps down swallows of cold beer. "Aaaaaaaaaaah," she growls heartily as she fake-wipes her mouth with the back of her hand. "Love me some beer." She acts like a burly cowboy who's been out on the range for a month.

"It's a good thing I'm used to your incredible femininity, or else I might be in shock right now."

"It's pretty stunning, right?" she asks, giggling and looking around the crowd of country-lovin' folks at Lucky's. "Look. They're all dancing again. They've recovered just fine."

She's referring to our dance floor disruption. Jenna gets a kick out of dragging me onto the dance floor from time to time to dance freestyle while everyone else line dances. To say that it causes a stir would be a tragic understatement.

As I scan the myriad faces around the room, I see that they're still throwing strange and slightly irritated looks our way. All except the men, of course. They loved the show.

"I don't know how you talk me into these things."

"Um, because they're fun and you like fun and you need fun and I can give you fun. That's how."

I grin. "I guess." And she's right. Jenna and a night of goofy, carefree fun are exactly what I need.

"What the eff?" she says suddenly, looking at something over my shoulder. I turn to see what caught her attention. Brent is standing near the entrance, scanning the crowd. I have a feeling I know who he's looking for. "How the hell did he know where we were?"

I sigh. "Drogheda."

"I thought she didn't like Brent."

I shrug. "She thinks I can do better, I guess. But she still won't lie to him."

He spots me and smiles. Instantly, I recognize a difference. Things have been strained between us lately, and his smiles have been as tight as mine have felt. But not this one. This one is full of all the charm that first attracted me to him so long ago.

I'm immediately suspicious.

I smile as he approaches. "What are you doing here?"

"I've come a-courtin'," he says in a thick accent.

"A-courtin'?"

His smile widens. "Yep. Isn't that what they call it?"

"Who's *they*?"

"The locals."

"Oh," I snort derisively. "You live, what, like an hour away and now we're suddenly hicks down here?"

I can't help the prickliness in my tone. He's as much of a snob as my father. And neither of them has any right to be, as far as I'm concerned.

"I'm just teasing you, Cam. Geez, take it easy." He reaches for my hand and tugs. "Dance with me."

He's smiling down at me, his eyes twinkling and playful, and I think to myself that maybe I ought to give it one last try, give myself one last shot to feel what I thought I once felt. So I let him lead me onto the dance floor.

As if on cue, the DJ switches to the set of slow songs he plays each half hour. It's kind of a thing at Lucky's—every thirty minutes, the DJ plays two ballads back to back.

Brent pulls me into the crowd and then into his arms. He holds me tight against him, much tighter than I would've liked, and I wind my arms around his neck. He buries his face in my neck and I feel his lips as he kisses the skin beneath my ear.

I want to feel desire. I want to enjoy the close contact and the way our bodies sway to the music, but it just doesn't feel like it used to. It's as though there's space between us, even when there *is* none. Yes, there's something between us. Or more like some*one*.

I squeeze my eyes shut against the image of Trick as it tumbles into my mind. I know I wouldn't be having these thoughts if I were in Trick's arms. Therein lies the problem. I can't have Trick. Or rather, Trick doesn't *want* me. At least not enough. So why am I still hanging on? Why can't I move on? Why can't I return the love of the guy who *does* want me?

Turning my head to lay my cheek against Brent's shoulder, I concentrate on the lyrics and try to clear my mind of everything but Brent and the moment. I focus on my breathing and the feel of his muscular chest and arms. But no matter how much I want to be in the moment, I'm not. Not with Brent.

I open my eyes.

Damn! Wouldn't you know . . .

They collide with the intense greenish-gray ones I can't forget. No matter how much I wish I could.

He's watching me, his expression unfathomable. I lift my head, my eyes locked on his, and we stare at each other. He takes one step toward me and stops. My stomach twitters and my heart flutters in my chest. It's in that second, in that very moment, that I realize Brent will never be enough. He never has been. He's never made me feel this way. No one has. No one but Trick.

No doubt sensing the change in my body language, Brent lifts his head and looks down at me. He's smiling lazily at first, but it dies pretty quickly when he sees my expression.

Like a fish out of water, my mouth is working its way open and closed as I struggle to find the words. I know I have to end it, but I never expected it would be so hard.

I've been waiting, putting it off. I've been hoping on some level that things would change, that either my feelings for Brent would strengthen or my feelings for Trick would fade or . . . something. And something has happened. I'm in love with Trick and I can't keep trying to make something out of nothing with Brent. No matter how much I wish it and my father wishes it and Brent wishes it, it's just not happening. It's time to do the right thing, the thing I feel in my heart. And even though I wouldn't cheat on Brent, it's starting to feel like I already am. Even when I'm with him, it's not where I want to be. I'd rather be with Trick. Always. And even if Trick never gives us a chance, I can't pretend my life will ever be the same again. Because it won't. I'm all in, whether he is or not.

Brent frowns and shakes his head slightly, as if he's trying to understand the unspoken conversation between us. But then he looks up, looks in the direction I was looking. I know the instant he spots Trick.

He turns narrowed eyes on me and his lips thin into a bitter smirk. "So that's how it's gonna be?"

"Brent, I . . . I'm sorry, but I can't do this anymore. It's just . . ."

I don't even know what to say. I can't tell him I'm leaving him for someone else. Trick's not mine. He may not ever be. And even though that reality twists my stomach into a sick knot, I know I can't string Brent along when my heart is with someone else, even if there's a chance I may never have that someone else. I can't ignore it any longer.

Brent flings my arms from around his neck and hisses, "Don't bother." He turns around and stalks away, weaving through the crush of bodies on the dance floor, leaving me standing by myself as the song winds down.

I don't really know what to do with myself, so I just stand there in the middle of all the happy, dancing couples. The notes of another song begin, and I tell myself that I need to move. But I don't. Still, I just stand there, wondering what has become of my life. I'd started the summer with a plan—learn the business side of the ranch, spend some time with Brent, go to a few parties, maybe feel a little more solid about where my life is going. But now, nothing is simple or certain. And, in a way, none of that other stuff even matters. The only thing that seems to register on my radar is Trick. Always. Trick.

As if my thoughts have the power to conjure, Trick appears in my line of sight. He stops a few feet away and just stares at me.

I'm not a fan of country music, but the lyrics to the song perfectly define the moment. "Glass" is what it's called and, right now, I feel like glass—thin, unstable, transparent. Vulnerable.

Trick doesn't say a word as he approaches. He walks to within a couple inches of me and looks down into my face. I'm caught in his eyes. They're like a spiderweb and I'm entangled. I can't seem to fight my way free of him. Then again, I don't want to. Not really. I just want him. Whatever he'll give me. For however long he'll give it. I know, at this point, I'm all in. Whatever it takes.

With his eyes holding mine, he reaches down and grasps my hands in his. He raises first one to his lips, then the other, kissing the backs of my fingers, sending chills up my arms. Lowering them, he tugs my hands, pulling me forward. Closer.

All the people, all the sounds, all the world fades. Our thighs are touching and his chest is brushing mine. I can smell his soap, even above the smoke in the room. He laces his fingers with mine and pulls our joined hands around to his lower back, bringing me closer still, our stomachs pressed together. He starts to sway to the music, his body rubbing gently against mine. The friction sets fire to every nerve beneath my skin.

My eyes are drawn to his mouth. I think I might die if he doesn't kiss me. His lips part and I hear the hiss of air as it's pulled between his gritted teeth.

He drops his head, his cheek pressed to mine, and he whispers in my ear. "If we go there, we can't come back. Not ever. Things will never be the same."

I lean into him, needing to feel every inch of him, wishing he could absorb me and put me out of my misery.

"I'm not perfect, Cami. I'm not a Thoroughbred like he is. I never will be."

I'm under his spell, but I hear what he's saying. And I don't care. I don't care about anything but having Trick, having him in my life, having as much as he can give me.

"I hear sometimes the wild ones are the best."

He says nothing at first, but I can almost hear his smile as he no doubt recognizes his own words.

"That may be. It's still a gamble, though. But it's *your* gamble. *Your* choice."

I pull away to look up into his face. "My choice? I thought—"

"So did I," he interrupts. "But I was wrong. It's always been your choice."

"What are you saying?"

I'm so breathless, my chest hurts. I don't want to misunderstand what he's getting at.

"I'm saying I'll be waiting for you." His eyes are deep and serious as he watches me. Pulling my hands from behind him, he releases them and drags his fingers up my arms to my shoulders and winds them around my neck. His thumbs tip my chin up and for one heart-stopping second, I think he's going to kiss me. "Make your choice, Cami."

And then he turns and walks away.

I watch him until I can't see him anymore, until the crowd has swallowed him up. There is no question what my answer is, what my choice is.

Immediately, I make my way back to Jenna. She's laughing at something Rusty is saying. When she sees me, her smile fades and she scoots off her bar stool.

"What is it? What's wrong?"

"I need your keys."

"What? Why?"

"I just need them, Jenna. I need to go."

"Go where?"

"Home," I answer. Jenna's eyes search mine. When I smile, I know she knows I don't mean home, as in my house. I mean home, as in Trick. Where I belong.

Her face splits into a stunning smile and she reaches into the back pocket of her jeans. She dangles the keys in front of me, and after I take them from her fingers, she grabs me in a spontaneous hug. When she pulls back, her eyes are a little shinier than usual.

"Go get him, Cam."

I give her a quick smile, then wink at Rusty, who is just looking on with a satisfied grin, and I run for the door. For the first time I can remember, I'm going to chase after what I want. With everything that's in me.

I know where Trick will be. Sooty is still gone, so he'll be at the stable. Hopefully waiting.

My muscles are coiled like a rattlesnake by the time I get home. I don't park at the house; I park at the stable. Trick's car is there. I don't stop to fully appreciate the rare and valuable classic; I don't care about the car. I care about the driver.

There are no lights on in the stable. The big doors are open just a crack. I push on one side until I can step through. It takes my eyes a second to adjust, but then I see Trick leaning against the office doorjamb, facing me, his arms crossed over his chest.

It's so quiet I can hear my heart hammering against my ribs. When he speaks, his words pour over me like rain over flower petals. And I blossom under them just the same.

He straightens. "God, I hope you're sure."

I take a step toward him. "I've never been surer of anything. Ever."

There is a slight pause, during which my heart stops beating, but then I'm in his arms, crushed against his hard chest, burning up in the heat of what's between us.

His lips take mine in a kiss I feel like I've been waiting for all my life. They're wild and passionate, everything I remembered, everything I'd imagined, and more.

His hands dive into my hair and he tilts my head to the side. His tongue slips into my mouth and I taste the most delicious flavor in the world—Trick. Unbridled. Unreserved. Unfettered.

All I can think of is how much I want him—want his skin against me, want his hands all over me, want his body inside me. I am ravenous and the only thing that can satisfy me is Trick.

Before I know it, my hands are fisted in his T-shirt, pulling it up and rubbing over the smooth skin of his back. He pauses long enough to yank it over his head and then his lips are back on mine.

I feel his fingers at my waist, working the buttons of my blouse loose, making their way toward my chest. I'm lost in the moment. I don't care where we are, who might walk in, or who might find out. I don't care about anything but the here and the now, and finally getting what I want most.

Trick pushes my shirt from my shoulders, and I let it slide down my arms and fall to the floor. Grabbing me under my butt, he lifts me up and carries me into the office. I hear the clatter of things falling to the floor and then the cool of the wooden table beneath my butt where my skirt has been pushed up.

I reach forward to work the button and zipper loose on Trick's jeans. His fingers are tugging at my panties, pulling them down and out from under me.

Running my fingers along Trick's waistband, I push his jeans past his hips. They fall easily to the floor. My hands are met with nothing but warm skin. He's not wearing any underwear.

Suddenly, I'm inflamed beyond the point that I can think clearly. All I can do is feel and taste and crave. And all of it comes back to Trick. My entire being is centered on him.

Grabbing my hips, Trick scoots me to the end of the table. Automatically, my legs come up and around his hips. The intimate contact is enough to steal my breath.

Trick leans back and looks into my face. I can see that he's struggling to retain some kind of sense in the situation. I can also see that he's barely succeeding. The knowledge makes it that much harder to wait.

"Condom," he pants, bending to dig one out of his pocket.

"Hurry," I whisper.

I hear the rattling of foil and then Trick is standing. I watch him as he quickly rolls down the latex. A shiver runs through me when I see what's coming. There isn't one disappointing inch on Trick's entire body!

When he's finished, he cups my face in his hands. "Are you sure this is what you want?"

"I want it more than anything. I want *you* more than anything."

I see the white flash of teeth in his tanned face. "Then come here, baby," he says, pulling me forward again and covering my lips with his own.

As his tongue invades my mouth, I can feel the tip of him pressing against me. More than I can ever remember wanting anything, I want him inside me. Now.

In a way, I'm glad I'm not a virgin. I don't want anything to ruin this perfect moment, certainly not pain.

Trick's lips blaze a trail down my neck and chest to my breast. He reaches up to pull one bra strap down, lowering the cup enough to pull one aching nipple into his mouth.

His tongue is hot and wet as it flicks the sensitive flesh. He draws it into his mouth and sucks. I feel like I might come apart at the seams.

As he treats my other nipple to the same delicious worship, his hand slips between my legs to find my core. With one fingertip, he slides between my folds to make slow, rhythmic circles over my clitoris. His tongue moves at the same pace over my nipple until I feel the familiar tension of an orgasm building.

My fingers fist in his hair and my breath is coming in short pants. Trick lifts his head, his face even with mine and only a few inches away, and he watches me as he replaces his fingers with his thick tip.

He pauses at my entrance. Passion and . . . something else is shining from his face. Instinctively, I know there will be few more poignant moments in my life.

Slowly, purposefully, inch by breathtaking inch, he pushes into me. His eyes never leave mine. He exhales on a moan, burying himself inside me as far as he can go. Still he watches me, refusing to look away.

He slides one hand into my hair and pulls my face to his. With his mouth on mine and his body in mine, I've never felt more connected to another human being. He's a part of me and I'm a part of him. And not just physically, but soul deep. We're perfectly matched, divinely fitted. Joined. I can feel it.

Expertly, Trick moves inside me while he continues to tease me with his hands, his lips, and his tongue. And just before I topple over the edge, he leans back to look at me again. With his smoky greenish-gray eyes, he watches me intently as I explode all around him, squeezing him with spasms of the most life-changing, earth-shattering sex I've ever had.

TWENTY-EIGHT: *Trick*

I'm sitting on the floor, in the dark office, with my arms wrapped around Cami. She's between my legs with her back against my chest. I can feel her breathing returning to normal.

It's surreal, the whole thing—the way it happened, the fact that it *did* happen. I couldn't have planned it any better if I'd tried. Don't think I'd even have wanted to. There's no way I could've made it any better. In my wildest dreams, I never anticipated it would be like this.

She's just as hot and fiery as her hair, but she's sweet and sincere, too. The perfect combination. Or maybe just perfect. I don't know. I have yet to see any flaws, physical or otherwise. Unless it might be that she cares too much what her dad thinks. Of course, if that were the case, she wouldn't be lying half naked in my arms.

I hear her say something, but it's too low for me to make out. I lean my head down and cock my ear toward her mouth. "What did you say?"

"I asked why you changed your mind."

"Why I changed my mind?"

"Yeah. About this, about us."

"I don't think I did." I feel her jerk, as if she's going to sit up. I tighten my hold and grin. Yeah, she's fiery all right. "What I meant by that is I think I knew all along that it was inevitable. I wanted you too much to let anything stand in my way. I guess I was just trying to convince myself that I was stronger than that, more responsible."

She gets very quiet and I can't help but be concerned that she's drawing all the wrong conclusions.

"We can't let my dad find out. I'd never forgive myself if you lost this job and your family had to suffer for it."

I can almost feel the guilt rolling off her in waves and bunching up her muscles. "This is not the only job in the world. Don't worry about it. We'll be fine. I wanted this. Wanted you."

She leans to the side and turns to look back at me. She grins, and I feel relieved that she's not having second thoughts. Or regrets.

"That's nice to hear."

"What? That I want you?"

She nods.

"I thought that would've been fairly obvious by now."

She laughs, a sort of husky sound that has my lower body parts stirring again.

"Oh, you made it pretty clear, but it's still nice to hear."

"Ahhh, you're one of *those* girls, the kind that likes to know what I'm thinking, aren't you?"

She shrugs. "I suppose. I think all girls like to hear nice things, heartfelt things."

I bend my head to kiss her cheek, then her ear. "Like you're the most beautiful woman I've ever seen?"

"Mmm," she moans, tilting her head to the side to give me better access to her neck.

"Or that you captivated me with your beer-soaked T-shirt?"

I pull her bra strap down and kiss the curve of her shoulder. She reaches up and runs her fingers through my hair. I'm already thinking about round two when I hear soft sounds coming from next door, from the stall that shares a wall with the office.

I listen closely and hear what seems like scuffling sounds. Cami notices my distraction. "What is it?" she whispers.

"I'm not sure," I reply, still listening. "Mint is next door. Let me check on her real quick." Cami leans forward and I slide out from behind her. I bend to brush my lips over hers. "And then I'll come back and 'check on' you. But it won't be quick." I growl playfully, and she giggles.

"Then hurry up!"

I'm smiling as I zip my jeans. The summer has taken an unexpected turn for the better. Much, much better!

I'm surprised and a little alarmed when I peek into Mint's stall and see her lying down. I open it and go inside. She's groaning.

Although we all knew she was close, she hasn't given any sign that she'd be delivering tonight, which concerns me. I turn on the light and go around to her tail to check her. When I see the red, velvety sac protruding from her, I spring into action.

"Cami, bring the foaling kit from under the table! Now!"

I didn't put my T-shirt back on, which means that my clothes won't get bloody. Unfortunately, that means that *I* will. But there's no time for considerations like that. Mint and her foal are in danger.

When Cami arrives with the kit, I can see the concern on her face. "What can I do?" she asks, out of breath as she maneuvers the plastic trunk of supplies.

"Call the vet. Tell him Mint has placenta previa."

Cami rushes away and I hear her on the phone in the office, talking to Dr. Flannery. I open the kit and pull out everything I'll need. There's no time for doubts; only time to rush through and remember everything I've witnessed at the two other red-bag births I've assisted with during practicums in school. When Cami returns, I've already gotten everything into position, the light set up near Mint's tail and the long palpation gloves stretched up my arms.

I meet her wide eyes. "Oh God! What's wrong?"

I put as much calm as I can manage into my voice when I speak. "Cami, Mint's placenta detached prematurely, and I have to deliver the foal right this minute or it could die. You're just gonna have to trust that I know what I'm doing, because we can't wait for the vet."

Mutely, she nods. I search her eyes. I don't see doubt or indecision in them, only fear for the horses as her eyes dart from mine to Mint and back again.

I nod once, then turn my full attention to the horses. I mutter soothingly to the distressed Mint as I use the knife from the foaling kit to cut into the red bag surrounding the foal. Immediately, I reach in to see if I can feel the foal's feet. I suppress my sigh of relief when I do and feel that they're facing down. At least the foal is in the correct position.

I tug on the foal's legs, but there is no give. Getting a better grip, I pull harder, but still I don't feel the foal move.

"Trick?" Cami's voice holds all kinds of concern. And it's warranted.

"Cami, are there calving chains here? Do you know?" Again, I pull, even harder.

"I . . . I don't know. Where would they be?"

There's no time to have her go look. The foal is in danger of brain damage from oxygen deprivation or even death with every second that passes.

"That's fine. There's no time to look. Get the other pair of gloves on, Cami. I need you to help." While Cami is stretching the gloves over her hands and up her arms, I'm pulling as hard as I can on the foal's legs. Bracing my feet forward, I lean away from Mint, pushing with my legs. I feel the foal shift toward me, then fall back into the birth canal.

"Is he gonna make it?" Cami's voice is trembling, but still she moves to my side to help.

"I'm not letting this horse die, Cami. Come around on my other side and grab his leg." Cami does as I ask, grabbing the leg that is most forward, indicating it is the foal's leading shoulder. I grab the deeper leg, hoping it's where my strength can be most effective. "This has caused a delay in Mint's contractions. She may be a little help, but not enough to birth the foal. We have to pull him out. Now. When I say pull, plant your feet and pull down and out as hard as you can, okay?"

I barely hear Cami's whispered, "Okay."

"On three. One, two, three!"

We both pull as hard as we can and, just before I think we won't be able to get the foal out, the lead shoulder pops free and the foal's nose and head become quickly visible.

Mint's sluggish uterine contractions are able to push the remainder of the foal free. I place him immediately into the towels to clean and stimulate him, suctioning his nostrils with the bulb. Still, he's not breathing.

Standing, I hold the foal upside down, my heart stuck in my throat like a cold stone. Thoughts of Cami's asshole of a father are nowhere in my head, only the foal. The foal I want to see alive and well when the sun rises.

Fluid drips from its nose and, much to my relief, I see its chest expand with its first breath. Gently, I lay the foal back down on the towels. As I finish cleaning him off, I look up at Cami. Tears are streaming down her face.

"He's fine, baby. He's breathing. It's okay."

She nods and swallows hard, but the tears still come.

And that's how Dr. Flannery finds us when he arrives.

He says nothing, but rather puts on latex gloves and moves into the stall to take over, examining first the foal and then Mint. I move to the back wall, behind Dr. Flannery, while Cami edges her way toward the stall door to watch from an unobtrusive distance. Each time I look up at her, she's watching Dr. Flannery. But each time, almost as if she can feel my eyes on her, she looks over at me and smiles. A beautiful smile. One that says she knows she just witnessed a miracle. And I'm even more thankful I didn't let her down.

I'm not sure what I expected, but the only person who manages to surprise me is Dr. Flannery. When he finishes assessing the two horses, he stands, peels his gloves off, and offers me his hand. I take it and he pumps it in two short bursts.

"Good job, son. You saved the foal and probably the mare. It's a good thing you were close. Just a few more minutes and . . ." He trails off, raising his eyebrows and shaking his head. He doesn't need to finish. I know what would've happened. We'd have two dead horses.

Unfortunately Jack Hines isn't nearly as happy when he arrives.

I'd already resigned myself to being seen as the "help" at the ranch, even though I've got enough training and education to dispute it. My age doesn't make matters any better, either. Men like Jack Hines will always be biased based on that fact alone. It doesn't help that I still haven't graduated, despite the fact that I'm only a few courses shy. But even without a degree, all that I've done in school is still deserving of a higher designation than the "help."

But on a night like tonight, when I'd already stabilized both horses and the situation long before any of the "real" professionals arrived, it's particularly hard to swallow when Jack comes in treating me like a liability rather than the person who saved his horses.

"Why didn't you call me sooner?" he asks, instantly on the attack.

"Sir, I was working to save the foal. I had little time for much of anything."

"You should've called me when you called Dr. Flannery."

"I apologize. I was only thinking of the horses."

I wait for him to make a comment about Cami calling the vet, but he doesn't. Maybe he just doesn't know. Maybe Dr. Flannery didn't tell him. The latter is confirmed when he turns to Cami.

"What are you doing down here?"

"I, uh, I came to get Jenna's car and saw the lights on. I just came in to see what was going on," she explains.

"What was her car doing down here?"

"She met me here earlier to ride, but we ended up going out instead."

"With whom?"

"Another one of her friends. Why the fifth degree?"

I curb my desire to smile when she fires back. Damn, she's feisty! Jack frowns and looks from Cami to me and back again. When he nods, I take that as an indication that he believes her.

"Daddy, Trick saved Mint and the foal. Aren't you even going to thank him?"

I cringe. Although I know her heart's in the right place, I don't want her fighting my battles. Or guilting anyone into appreciating me. Jack Hines is an ass, but he's great at what he does. He's also Cami's father. That makes me want to *earn* his respect, not have someone badger it out of him.

Jack turns his stern expression on me. It doesn't soften, but for just a second I see a flash of something that looks dangerously close to gratitude flitter across his face. The sad thing is, it's gone before I can even really identify it.

Asshole!

"Thank you for your hard work. Although I don't appreciate you taking such reckless chances with my horses, it panned out this time. Just don't let it happen in the future. If you're to continue working here, I expect you to be more prepared next time."

My mouth wants to drop open and curse words want to fly out. But instead, I clamp my teeth together and nod curtly.

"Yes, sir."

"Daddy, how—"

"If you two will excuse me," I interrupt, shooting Cami a quick and meaningful look, "I'd like to go check in on Mint."

Without waiting for a response, I walk away.

My fists are clenched so tight, my knuckles ache.

TWENTY-NINE: *Cami*

Like it is every day, the first thought to enter my mind when I wake is of Trick—the way he smells, the way his eyes sparkle when he laughs, the way his lips feel on mine. I'm determined today is going to be *the day* I get to see him again.

It's been almost two weeks since Mint Julep gave birth to Lucky Star. I haven't seen Trick or the foal since that night.

My father let me name the new horse. Considering what had happened before Mint went into labor, I still had Trick on the brain big-time, so all my thoughts were centered on him. As usual. Of course, naming the horse something obvious like Trickster or Trickery was out of the question, so I went with Lucky, for the place I first met Trick. It's well hidden inside Lucky Star, which is a play on the expression *thank your lucky stars* and just sounds like the foal is lucky to be alive. But for me, the name and the horse will always remind me of meeting Trick and of the first night I spent in his arms.

I can't help but wonder if Daddy knows there's something

between Trick and me. He has gone out of his way to make sure I don't have time to ride or even to pay a visit to the stable. He's insisted I accompany him on two trips, and when we're home, he seems to be down at the stable talking to Sooty, who came back to work the night after the birth. I'm getting to the point now, though, where I'm desperate to even *see* Trick, much less spend some alone time with him. A couple of short texts and some missed phone calls between us isn't nearly enough. Not nearly!

It was bad before, the constant desire to see him and be near him, but now? A thousand times worse! I feel like my life both started and stopped when Trick made love to me. Everything changed. And Trick was right—there's no going back.

I've already made up my mind that no one, not even the great Jack Hines, is going to keep me from the stable today. Throwing back the covers, I hurry to brush my teeth and wash my face and get dressed. The sooner I can see Trick, the better.

As I make my way through the quiet house, I realize it's so early not even Drogheda expects me to be up. I don't smell anything cooking, and she hasn't yet started banging around to wake me up. Mom is no doubt at the club, and Daddy's probably locked away in his office plotting world domination.

I slip out the back door and practically run down the small incline that leads to the stable. I'm extremely disappointed when I don't see Trick's Mustang parked out back.

Good grief! You really are desperate! You've beat even the early risers down here!

I push open one of the bay doors and head through the stable toward Mint Julep's stall. It's empty. I walk on to where the two main aisles of the stable cross, forming a T-shaped intersection, and I turn left, heading to the other end of the stable and the doors on that side.

I see a tall, skinny man in jeans and a plaid shirt leaning up against a post in the small pen off the north field. He's watching Mint and Lucky. She's standing perfectly still as her young male offspring romps and plays around her.

Before I can duck back inside, Sooty turns. I know he spotted me. Even in the shadow of his cowboy hat, I can see his sharp eyes focus on me from inside his tanned, leathery face. He nods once and then straightens to walk toward me. I lean against the door frame and wait.

Sooty stops beside me and turns to back up against the side of the stable to where both of us are looking out into the paddock. "He's lookin' pretty good, huh?"

"He looks great! I'm sure Daddy's pleased."

"Yep. He might just have himself another winner with this one."

"Nothing would make him happier."

There's a short pause. "You know, if Trick hadn't been here, Lucky probably wouldn't have made it. Doc Flannery says it's a miracle the foal didn't die."

"That's probably true, but Daddy will never see it that way. You know how he is."

"He's a tough sell, that's for sure, but that kid's got something. Never seen anything like it. All he needs is someone to believe in him and the sky's the limit."

I look over at Sooty. He turns his head and narrows his eyes on me, then nods. Just once.

"You think?"

"I know."

"I just wish Daddy could see that."

"Your daddy's not the one I'm talking about."

Sooty eyes me for a couple of tense seconds before he tips his hat and walks back to where he was at the edge of the paddock.

Although I'm still standing where he left me, facing Mint and Lucky, I don't really see them. I don't really see anything. My thoughts are turned totally inward, running over Sooty's words as they rearrange the pieces of what I thought I knew my life would be.

The throaty rumble of a muscle car is unmistakable, especially to a girl who's grown up around them. This one holds a particular thrill because I know it's Trick. It has to be.

The sound reverberates across the tall ceiling of the stable, and I follow it to the doors closest the parking area out back. From inside the shadowy interior of the stable, I watch Trick as he gets out of his car.

His shaggy hair is damp and he's wearing aviator sunglasses. His wide shoulders are bare in a white wife-beater tank top that shows off his trim waist. And, as always, his lower half looks delicious in faded blue jeans that hang just perfectly on his hips. Looking at him makes my stomach feel like it's full of hot, melted butter.

He starts to walk in my direction but stops and takes off his glasses, tossing them through the open car window onto the seat. When he turns to head toward the stable, he runs his fingers through his hair. It looks rumpled, and my fingers itch to dive into it and pull his lips down to mine.

My smile is way too full and bright by the time Trick can see me standing inside the stable. It only gets wider when he stops and grins that sexy half smile of his. "Hi," he says, shifting his weight onto one foot while his eyes rake me from head to toe and back again. I can almost feel them, like he's touching me everywhere at once.

"Hi," I say in return, suddenly feeling nervous and fidgety.

He starts walking toward me again. It's such a pleasure to watch, too. He has a strut that's just cocky enough to make my knees weak.

When he gets close to me, he looks left and right to make sure no one is around, and then, with lightning speed, he takes my hand and jerks me into the empty stall behind him.

Trick flattens me against the wall and presses his body into mine. "I've missed you," he growls. Then he kisses me. And what a kiss it is! I feel it everywhere—in the hands that are holding mine above my head, in the knee that's wedged between mine, in the tongue that's teasing me into a hot mess.

When he lifts his head, I'm totally breathless and ready for him to drag me off to some dark corner and finish what he started.

"This day's already the best one I've had all week and it just started." He winks at me, pecks me on the lips, and steps back. I miss him instantly. "Guess I'd better not get caught manhandling the youngest Hines or I might find myself in trouble."

He's teasing, I know, but it still makes me feel guilty, like he risked so much more than I did to be with me. He takes my hand and leads me back out into the main stable area.

"So, what brings your mouthwatering self down here so early?"

I shrug, not having thought about how to explain that I crave him like I crave air and water and food. Maybe more.

"Haven't been down in a while. Thought I'd come see Lucky and check on the horses. You know . . ." I trail off, willing myself to stop kicking the dirt with my boot like a huge nerd.

Trick smiles. Broadly. A smile that says he sees right through me. "Damn! And here I thought you might've missed me."

He winks, knowing good and well that's exactly why I'm here. I can't help but return his smile. "You are the devil, you know that, right?"

Trick squeezes my hand. "So I've heard."

We walk hand in hand to the doorway I'd left not too long ago and stop to watch Mint and Lucky. Trick doesn't bother to let my hand go. He seems content to hold it, even though we could get busted at any minute.

"What kind of plans do you have for the weekend?"

"Not many. I'm setting my foot down about spending so much time with my father. One more trip and I might stab him on the airplane."

Trick chuckles. "Don't hold back. Tell me how you really feel."

I grin. "*You* go with him then! See how *you* like it."

"Oh no! I don't think I'd get the same treatment as you, so I *know* I wouldn't like it."

And he's right. He wouldn't.

I look for a change of subject. "Why do you ask? About my plans, I mean."

"I was thinking about heading up to the Outer Banks to look for a horse. There's one in particular I've seen up there before, one I think I could really work with. I thought you might like to come."

A weekend? With Trick? Alone? In a Southern paradise? Um, yes please!

Before I jump at the chance, the logistics of it occur to me. I chew my lip as I think of how best to address it. Thank God, Trick saves me the trouble.

"Rusty wants to bring Jenna, too."

"Oh, that's perfect!"

"I thought Jenna could pick you up and we could all meet at my house. Rusty and Jenna are gonna follow us up in Rusty's car. He just finished rebuilding the engine and he's dying to get it out on the road."

I can't stop my smile. It really is perfect. I don't have to worry about making up some kind of elaborate lie to tell my father.

"A road trip? With you? In that sweet car? I'm all over it."

Trick tugs my hand, pulling me closer to his side. "If by 'it' you mean 'me,' then that's just the answer I was hoping for." He arches one brow suggestively, and I feel the heat of a blush break out in my cheeks.

He opens his mouth, no doubt to comment on my rosy face, when a gasp makes us both jump. Reflexively, I jerk my hand out of his and spring away. When I see the dark red head standing behind us, I breathe out a sigh of relief. Even if she noticed us holding hands, which I doubt she did, Mom would never frown on someone I'm interested in, and she certainly wouldn't tell Daddy. I doubt they ever talk about such mundane things anymore. My father is far too busy with his business.

"Mom! You scared the crap out of me. What are you doing down here?"

Since Mom spends most of her days fulfilling her social butterfly duties as the wife of *the* Jack Hines, she doesn't visit the stables much. In fact, I can't remember the last time I saw her here.

When she doesn't immediately answer, I take note of her stricken expression. Her skin is paler than normal, her lips even looking a little washed out, and her bright blue eyes are wide with shock. The thing I find odd is that she's staring at Trick.

"Mom?"

Her eyes flicker to me, but go straight back to Trick. Her mouth falls open a little and her lips tremble like she's trying to say something, but can't get it out.

"Mom!" I try again. Still, no response.

I walk toward her. It's not until I'm almost right on top of her that she really looks at me, and even then, she appears to be a little addled.

"What's wrong?"

We are exactly the same height, so I can look her right in the eye. Some would say it's like looking at a mirror image of myself, only a few years down the road. I can see small differences, like the shade of her eyes and the thinner lips that grace her face, but otherwise I must admit that we very closely resemble each other.

Finally, she seems to overcome whatever she was mentally tripping over and she smiles. She shakes her head and stammers, "Oh, sorry, I . . . um . . . I, uh . . . Drogheda . . ."

"Drogheda what?"

"She's made breakfast for you. Come and eat before it gets cold."

I see her eyes dart over my shoulder, to where Trick is standing. Maybe she did see us holding hands, but I don't think so. If anything, she seems to be more shocked by Trick's presence *at all*. Even if she did see us, though, it doesn't explain why she's acting so weird. Mom couldn't care less who I date as long as I'm happy. She's the female in the family who's burdened with upholding the Hines name, not me.

"Okay, I'll be right up."

She gives me a shaky smile and reluctantly turns to walk away. I get the feeling she wants to look back, but doesn't.

When she's out of sight, Trick appears at my side. "What was that all about?"

"That was my mother. I don't know what her problem was. Maybe she saw us holding hands. I haven't told her about Brent yet." Even though I don't really believe she did see us.

"Hmmm. Maybe."

"Weird."

"So, breakfast time, huh?"

I roll my eyes. "Yes. Drogheda would kill me if I skipped breakfast. She goes to so much trouble because she knows it's my favorite meal." I pause. "Well, second favorite."

"What's first then?"

"Dessert!" I say, licking my lips dramatically.

"Mmm, do that again," Trick growls, his eyes locked on my lips.

"What? This?" Slowly, I drag my tongue along my top lip. Trick's pupils dilate, swallowing the beautiful pale green of his irises. I feel his reaction deep in my stomach, in that place he can touch without even trying, it seems.

When I finish, his eyes move up to mine. In them, I see everything that I'm feeling, eating away at him like it is at me. "Oh, you'll pay for that."

"You think?"

"No, I *know*. You'll be at my mercy all weekend. All I can say is you'd better bring your game face, because it is on!"

"Is that a threat?"

"No, it's a promise. A promise I very much look forward to keeping."

His gaze heats up and it's all I can do to remember my name, let alone that I'm supposed to be up at the house eating Drogheda's delicious breakfast. If I had my way, I'd be somewhere enjoying some delicious Trick instead.

"You'd better head up to the house before I forget my manners and lure you off somewhere to ravish you."

I laugh, not because it's funny but because there's nothing I'd like more. Damn him and his control!

"Breakfast," he says, tipping his head toward the main stable doors. "Go while you can."

"Are you hungry? Can I bring you something to eat?" I ask, my wits and my manners finally returning to me, albeit slowly.

I really didn't mean to be provocative, although Trick would probably never believe that.

"Good God, woman! You're killing me!" He runs his fingers

through his hair and turns to walk away. When he gets a few feet from me, he turns around and walks backward. "Don't get too satisfied. Save some of that appetite for this weekend."

He smiles and winks at me before disappearing around the corner. I think I might die from wanting him to come back.

THIRTY: *Trick*

I can only hope spending the weekend with Cami will curb my appetite for her. Surely it's a physical thing. Surely. I'm too young to fall in love with the wrong girl. I mean, hopefully I'll *always* be too young for the wrong girl. Not that Cami's really *wrong* in that sense. It's just that things with her would be so complicated. Her dad's a big deal, she comes from money, everyone expects her to marry into greatness. That's more drama than I'll ever need in my life! I've had my fair share already. I'm ready to get her out of my system and move on.

That's why I'm sure it's physical. That's the only explanation.

Right?

"So we get to meet your girlfriend?"

Grace is practically vibrating with excitement. She views any girl in my life as a potential playmate and big sister.

"She's not my girlfriend, Gracie."

Her grin is so big it shows off the twin dimples in her cheeks. "But you like her, right?"

"Yeah, I like her."

"Then maybe if you ask her nice enough, she'll be your girl-friend."

If only life were that simple. But rather than telling Grace about how cruel and twisted and complicated life really is, I scrub the top of her head. "Maybe she will. We'll see."

"Yay!" she exclaims, running off excitedly.

"She'll probably come back out in yet another dress," Mom says.

I laugh. "Probably. She wants to make a good impression. I feel like I'm hosting a princess."

"To Grace, you probably are," Mom says, shaking her head. Grace is full of all the life and love and hope our now-smaller family so desperately needs. "So, you haven't said much about this girl."

She's trying to be all casual, so I play along and shrug. "Not much to tell. She's just a girl. No big deal."

"Where did you meet her?"

"At Lucky's."

"Now, you know what I've told you about girls you meet in bars."

I look down at my tiny mother. She gets like this sometimes, all fiery. Her hands are on her hips and she's loaded for bear. It's easy to see the girl she once was, all full of piss and vinegar, the one my father fell in love with. I can't help but smile. "Yeah, I think you might've mentioned that a time or two."

"And yet you pay so little attention to it. Why is that?"

"Uh, because I'm a guy."

I can tell she wasn't expecting that answer. She rolls her eyes, but I see the corners of her mouth twitch. She's trying not to smile.

"They're here! They're here!" Grace squeals as she runs, Mach 1, into the kitchen, pulling a different dress over her head as she goes.

Mom looks at me and grins, straightening her short brown hair. "Do I look okay? I've never met a princess before."

It's my turn to roll my eyes. "You look fine. And don't ever ask me again why I don't bring many girls home. Just remember this."

She punches my arm and I wink at her. She's come a long way in the last few years. She's sporting a few more gray hairs as a result of all she's been through, but she's still smiling. That has to count for something.

I go to open the door, but Grace slides across in front of me. "Let me get it."

"Okay, but introduce yourself before you attack her, 'kay?"

"I will, I will."

I shake my head as I watch her dance from foot to foot. It can't be healthy to get this excited over having a visitor. Then again, we have so few, maybe *I* should be getting *more* excited.

But then, when I hear Cami talking quietly, I realize I'm plenty excited. I'm instantly thrown back in time to the little sounds she made and the words she whispered when her body was wrapped tightly around mine.

Yep, I'm plenty excited.

I readjust in my shorts and turn my mind to something else, like the horse I'll be looking for this weekend. Anything to take my mind off Cami and that incredible body of hers.

I hear Grace's gasp and know she sees Cami. That's kind of the way I felt when she looked up at me after I dumped beer down her shirt.

"You must be Cami," Grace says in her most grown-up voice. "It's so nice to meet you. I'm Grace, but you can call me Gracie."

"It's such a pleasure to meet you, Gracie. This is my friend, Jenna."

"Hi, Jenna."

When there's a long pause, I figure I should step in and help. "Why don't you invite them in, Grace?"

Grace doesn't even look in my direction. She doesn't stop smiling, either. Her focus is straight ahead and slightly up, on Cami's face.

She finally pushes the door open and I see Cami step through, followed closely by Jenna. Grace takes Cami's hand and leads her into the kitchen.

"This is my mom, Leena."

I watch as Cami smiles brightly and extends her hand. I don't really notice anything's amiss until Cami's smile fades a little and she starts to look uncomfortable. I glance over at my mom and she looks like she's seen a ghost.

"Mom, what's the matter?"

She says nothing at first, just stares at Cami like she's grown a second head. "Mom," I prompt. She jumps a little, like I scared her out of a daze or something.

"What?" She appears confused, but then she shakes her head, like she's snapping out of a spell. "Oh, I'm so sorry. I'm so happy to meet you, Cami. Please forgive me, I'm . . . I'm a bit out of sorts this morning. Late night. You know how that goes."

She relaxes into something closer to her normal self, but not quite. I doubt it's strange enough for Cami to notice, but I certainly do.

What the hell?

"What up, Gracie girl?" Rusty says as he busts through the door.

Grace squeals and leaves Cami to throw herself at Rusty. It gives me the perfect opportunity to break up our tense little party.

"So, let me get my bag and we'll head out."

Cami nods, her smile tighter than usual. I'm sure all sorts of crazy things are running around in her head. And I'd love to give her a rational explanation for my mother's bizarre behavior, but I've got nothing. I just hope she doesn't think I'm not telling her something. Because the truth is, I have no idea why my mother acted so strangely.

In record time, I'm back in the kitchen ushering Cami toward the door.

"Wrap it up, man," I say to Rusty, who's still wrestling with Grace. "We've got to get on the road."

With a little more prompting, I finally get everyone to the door. Grace runs to give me a hug and a kiss on the cheek, and then Mom follows suit.

"Bring me a horse," Grace says.

"Be careful, son," Mom says, her face now just . . . sad.

"You," I say to Grace, "not this time, but maybe I can find one for you soon. And you," I say, turning to Mom. "Of course. I'm always careful."

I start to walk away, but Mom grabs my arm. "I'll be working when you get home, but I'm leaving something on your bed for you. Tend to it first thing, will you?"

Well, that's cryptic.

I frown. I can't help it. She's acting really weird.

"Okay, I will."

She nods and smiles, and then both she and Grace say in unison, "Love you."

"I know," I return, just like I always do. "You, too."

I lead the way outside. I notice Cami is hanging back a little. Rusty and Jenna are talking about something, and Cami's walking quietly behind them. Getting a better grip on my duffel, I turn around and walk right up to Cami, surprising her when I bend down and throw her over my shoulder.

She squeals. "What are you doing?"

"This is all part of the VIP package. Didn't I tell you?"

"No. You must've left out a few details."

"Oh, well, I'll just tell you as we go then. No big deal."

I hear her laugh again. It soothes me, possibly more than it does her.

I carry her to Rusty's car first. "Where'd you put her stuff?" I ask him.

"It's in the trunk."

"Let me get it out."

"We're going to the same place, man. Just leave it."

"Nope. I'm taking no chances. You jokers could get lost or something and I'd be stuck with a woman who has nothing to wear but my T-shirts. She'd seduce me and I'd let her because I'd be helpless against her charms. Then I'd build us a hut on the beach and we'd never leave. Grace would be devastated and Mom would kill me. You see how ugly this could get?"

"Hey!" Cami exclaims. I grin when I feel her muscles clench with her chuckle.

"I'm just telling the truth. You can barely keep your hands off me. You know it's true." She slaps me on the butt. "See? But it's nothing to be ashamed of. I'm irresistible. It's my curse."

"Poor guy! Born irresistible. What a nightmare," she teases.

"We all have our burdens to bear."

"Here," Rusty says as he pushes two huge bags at me. "Take her shit and go. I can't stand to listen to your constant self-deprecation for one more minute. Good God, man! Have some faith in yourself."

Jenna and Cami laugh. Rusty shoots me an evil grin and I cart Cami back to my car, letting her down at the passenger-side door. After stowing our stuff in my trunk, I open her door and usher her in with a flourish. "You're riding in style, today, Miss Hines. Not one, but five hundred horses will be delivering you to your destination. So mount up!"

With a smile, she slides onto the original vinyl seat. I shut the door behind her. As I skirt the hood, I look in and see her smiling at me through the windshield. Watching me. There's something just . . . right about seeing her in my car.

I push the thought away.

THIRTY-ONE: *Cami*

I listen to Trick talk about the horse he hopes to find, one he's seen on two other occasions and is hoping to adopt when the town thins the population. It's strange because as he talks about his dreams for "one day," I realize I've never felt so . . . invested in someone else's dreams before, in their plans or ambitions. But when Trick paints the picture of his future, of what he wants out of life, I find I'm in the dangerous position of putting myself into the empty space beside him in all those visions.

But that won't be easy.

First of all, Trick has never given me any reason to think he wants me there. He's never talked about anything permanent with me. Actually, he's never really talked about his feelings much at all. At this point, I'm only hoping there's more between us than just sex. Really great sex.

But the fact is, *if anything*, Trick has tried to keep me *out* of his life in any romantic way. Not pull me into it. Until recently, that is.

Since meeting Trick, I've acted like some lovesick schoolgirl—thinking about him all the time, pining away for him. All I lack is writing his name all over my fourth-grade social studies notebook. But we're not kids. This isn't play. Our choices have real consequences. For both of us. And I don't know if either of us is ready for that, if what we have is even worth it.

Even as the thought goes through my head, I look over at Trick and my heart screams so loud it makes my eyes water.

Yes, he's worth it! You're in love with him!

After we stop for lunch and I get my belly full of carbs, my eyelids start getting heavy. A Lizards CD is playing softly in the background and Trick is humming along with it in his silky voice, lulling me right to sleep. I turn in my seat, and Trick looks over at me. He smiles and reaches for my hand. He laces his fingers with mine and whispers, "Go to sleep. I'll wake you up when we get there."

So I do.

Something brushing my neck wakes me. Before I even open my eyes, I smell his soap. It's Trick. It has to be.

I'm lying on my side in the front seat and he must be leaning over me. I don't stir. I lie perfectly still to see what he'll do next.

I feel his lips. He rubs them back and forth over the bare skin of my shoulder. I want to turn over and kiss him. But I don't. Quietly, I wait.

"Rise and shine," he whispers, now close to my ear. Chills break out down my arms, but I remain still.

His hand pushes my hair to the side, away from my cheek. He's so close I feel his breath on my lips when he speaks. "I know you're awake. The question is, how long can you keep quiet? Stay still? Not make a sound? Not move an inch?"

I would've acknowledged him when he said he knew I was awake if he hadn't added the last part. But that changed everything. I warm to the game immediately, excitement tingling down my spine.

His lips graze mine and then slide across my cheek to my ear. "I hope you can hold out. This is gonna be fun." I feel his tongue as it draws the lobe of my ear into his mouth. He bites down lightly and then moves on to my shoulder. He kisses all the way down my arm, to where it's folded across my waist. Gently, he picks it up and straightens it, laying it along my hip.

I feel the warm air hit my belly when he pulls up my shirt. It's all I can do not to jump when he lightly bites the skin over my ribs, just below my bra line. I want to roll over and let him strip me down like a stolen car, but I don't. I can't. It's just too much fun to do it this way.

My breathing has picked up by at least a multiple of three and I'm pretty sure it goes up another notch when I feel Trick tug at the drawstring that's holding my shorts in place.

He loosens it and pulls my shorts down on one side, exposing that super sensitive patch of skin right beside my panty line. And that's where he puts his lips. Right there, no more than a few inches to the right of where I want them.

Desire pools low in my belly and heat shoots down my legs. His tongue sneaks out, wet and hot, and licks a path from where my legs are pressed together along my panty line to my hip bone. And he nips me again.

I'm just about to melt when I feel the fingers of one hand tickling their way up the crease of my thighs and sliding under the edge of my shorts.

Without thinking, acting on instinct and passion alone, I raise my top leg so he can find what his fingers are searching for. What I want them to find. But they stop. He doesn't move a single muscle.

"Damn, why couldn't you have waited just a couple more minutes?"

My eyes pop open and Trick is smiling down at me.

It takes me a minute to realize what he means, what he's doing. Or *not doing*, as it were.

"Are you serious?"

"I don't make the rules. I just work here."

"That's so mean!"

I'm almost trembling, I want him so badly. And knowing that he's not going to finish what he started only makes it that much worse.

"You'll thank me later," he promises, giving me a peck on my stunned lips and then reaching for my hand. "Come on. Let's go check in and get some supper."

I gripe as I let him pull me up. "Well, I'm gonna have to change clothes now."

"And why is that?"

"These seem to have gotten a little . . . damp," I tease with a wicked grin.

Trick throws back his head and laughs. I mean, really laughs. Like a belly laugh. "God, you really are awesome."

I blush but try to play it off. "I try."

When I'm on my feet, standing beside him in the V of the open car door, he takes my chin in his hand. There's still the ghost of a smile flirting around his lips. "No, you don't. You don't even have to."

After Trick checks us in, he carries our bags to the room. He lets me in first and then sets our stuff in the corner. When I turn to him, all

I can think about is finishing what we started. But there's a knock on the door that comes almost immediately.

Trick slumps. Comically. The postural equivalent of *Damn!*

I smile. He winks. Then Jenna intrudes.

"Hey, you two, get your asses to this door and let me in!"

"Is she going to be interrupting us all weekend?" Trick asks quietly.

I laugh. "Probably. And I blame you."

"Me?" he whispers indignantly.

"Yes, you. It wasn't *my* idea to bring them."

"She's *your* friend!"

"Doesn't matter. I didn't ask you to invite her."

"Oh, so that's how it's gonna be. Throw me under the bus."

"Yep. All the way."

"You know what I do to people who throw me under the bus?" he asks, walking toward me like a predator stalking prey.

"Wave with your good arm?"

He stops and hangs his head. Then he laughs. "I give up. Let's go." With a grin, he grabs my hand and says in a louder voice, "Coming!"

"Ew! I didn't need to know that," Jenna replies.

"Jenna!" I cry.

"Hurry it up, girl. We got some freak to get on."

The four of us go to eat at a little seafood restaurant with a great ocean view. I think it's strange when Trick asks to sit beside Rusty, across from me.

"I want to watch you eat," he says by way of explanation.

"No, that's not going to make me nervous at all," I tease. But I'm not teasing. Every sip of water I take, every bite of bread I nibble, I'm aware of him watching me.

When the food arrives, it becomes obvious why he did it. I

ordered crab legs. He did the same. As we crack and eat them, stuffing tiny pieces of meat into our mouths and licking lemon butter from our fingers, I realize how erotic it is to watch Trick eat, especially something so messy. Rusty and Jenna talk the whole time. Neither Trick nor I say much at all. We simply gaze at each other across the table, over our hands, from behind our napkins. We hold an entire conversation without ever saying a word.

The food is probably the best I've ever had, but I'm sure it has much more to do with the company than anything I actually ate.

I'm ready to go back to the room right away, but Jenna starts begging us to come dancing with them for just a little while. I really want to say no, but I reluctantly agree. She *is* my best friend, after all. And she'd probably do it for me.

Probably.

So we go.

The bar is not much more than a loud, smoky hole in the wall. Like most establishments of its kind, it has a dark interior and throbbing music. We find a table, and a busty blond, gum-popping waitress in a teeny-tiny top comes to take our order. We all smile at each other, each of us probably thinking the same thing—*Ohmigod, we've stumbled into a cheesy porno!*

Jenna speaks up before anyone else has a chance.

"Four shots of Patrón."

"You got some ID, sweetie?" she asks in her Betty Boop voice.

I know none of us, Jenna and I especially, look twenty-one, which is fine. One day I'll appreciate that, like when I'm eighty and still look sixty.

We all produce our licenses and she glances at each of them. I'm pretty sure she can't do the math without kicking off her stilettos, but at least she asked, which no doubt makes the manager very happy.

"You want salt and lemon?"

"Yes, please."

Her eyes make their way around the table, but she nods and winks at Jenna, watching her for several seconds before walking off to get our tequila.

"Ohmigod, have we stumbled into a cheesy porno? I totally thought she was gonna offer me a lap dance or something," Jenna says.

I laugh at her voicing my thoughts almost verbatim.

"I could never be that lucky," Rusty retorts. Jenna playfully pokes him in the ribs.

"Watch it, buddy. You've got your hands full now, but that can change in a hurry."

"Why don't we go see what you can put in my hands to fill 'em up?"

Jenna giggles and they start whispering presumably naughty things in each other's ear. When the waitress returns with the shots, we all lick and salt the backs of our hands. Jenna grabs her tiny glass and holds it up for a toast.

"To a wild weekend filled with wild horses and wild rides."

The guys heartily clink their glass to hers. I roll my eyes. Jenna winks at me. She's a mess.

She eyes my glass until I raise it as well. "To a wild weekend filled with wild horses and wild rides," I repeat obligingly.

Jenna whoops and we all toast, lick our hands, down our shot then suck on a lemon slice.

"Another round," she calls to the waitress.

Five shots later, Jenna raises her hand to get the waitress's attention and I have to say uncle.

"Jenna, I won't be able to walk if I do another shot. Just water for me."

She tips her head toward Trick. "I have a feeling I know someone who would gladly carry you to your room and take advantage of that."

The room spins lazily as I whip my head around to Trick and back to Jenna. "Dude! Are you teeing me up?"

"I'm totally teeing you up. And Trick," she says, turning a wink on him, "you're welcome."

"I don't want her drunk. I want her lucid." He looks at me, his smoky eyes dark in the low light. "I want her to remember everything."

A pocket of lava bursts inside my stomach and releases heat throughout my lower body. His eyes, his words are like a touch. And I crave that touch. Once was not enough. I don't know how many times it will take for me to feel satisfied.

Trick stands and holds out his hand. "Let's go dance off some of that alcohol."

I slide my fingers over his palm and he grips them lightly. He leads me to the small yet crowded dance floor, where people are bumping and gyrating to the bass-laden club music. When he finds us a spot, he twirls me slowly, then pulls me to him.

As I watch him move, as I feel his body shifting against mine, I realize something that makes Trick even hotter, something I really didn't think was possible.

He has rhythm. Trick can actually dance.

It's not that he's doing anything elaborate. He's not Chris Browning on the floor or anything. Nevertheless, I can see it in the way he moves. It's fluid and in perfect time with the beat. And it's hot.

Very hot!

The music morphs into a slower, more sensual song and Trick steps closer. Pulling my body tight against his, he buries his face in my neck and we sway together. His hands roam my back and hips in long languid ovals. My head spins lightly and desire rushes through me.

As if sensing where my thoughts are going, Trick jerks away and turns me around, my back to his chest. He drags his hands up my sides and pulls my arms up as he goes, trailing his fingertips along the sides of my boobs. He winds my hands around his neck, leaving my body completely open to his roving hands.

With his hands now at my hips, he snugs me up against him. I feel his hardness as he grinds against my butt. Chills break out across my chest and I feel my nipples tighten.

Losing myself to the music and the man at my back, I spare one quick look around us and find that no one is paying any attention. Everyone else is involved in their own bubble, their own seduction. That makes it easy to close my eyes and let go when I hear Trick whisper into my ear.

THIRTY-TWO: *Trick*

"Do you know what I want to do to you right now?"

I'm so close to Cami, I can hear the purr vibrate in the back of her throat. I'm weaving a spell for her, but she's taking me under with her. I can't stop it. And I'm not sure I'd even want to.

"If we were alone," I say, running my hands back down her arms and sides, "I'd peel this shirt off you and watch your nipples pucker in the cool air."

Cami relaxes her head onto my shoulder, her fingers fisting in my hair. Her eyes are closed and I wonder if she can imagine the scene as clearly as I can. When I look down her body, I can plainly see the outline of her nipples as they push against her shirt. Blood rushes to my little head, leaving my big head as second in command.

I let my hands slide a little farther down, to her waist. "Then I'd pull this string," I explain, tugging on the ties of her shorts for emphasis, "and I'd ease you out of these so I could check to see if your clothes are still . . . damp."

I feel her breathing pick up and my pulse starts racing. The music doesn't seem as loud as the buzz of electricity between us, and the only people in the world are Cami and me. We are the only ones that matter. And all we can do is *feel*.

"And if they're not, I'd have to take measures to fix that."

She rubs her butt up against me and I grit my teeth. It's a testament to my self-control that I don't do something wildly inappropriate. I mean, we are in a public place. And Cami's not the kind of girl that's down with stuff like that, I'm sure. She's classy. Not stuffy, just classy.

But damn, I almost wish she weren't. Just for tonight.

She takes her hands out of my hair and lowers her arms. She surprises me by reaching around behind me and grabbing my butt, right at the same time she grinds her hips into mine.

A growl escapes and I feel almost violent when I sink my teeth into her shoulder. She gasps, but when I lean up and look at her face, she looks like she's enjoying it, which just turns me on that much more.

"Cami," I say, my tone louder and more serious.

Her eyes pop open and meet mine. They're dark with desire, but they seem lucid. "Are you sober?"

Her smile is slow. Super slow. And catlike. "Sober enough. Let's get out of here."

Without even pausing, I take her hand and pull her off the dance floor. Jenna is sitting in Rusty's lap trying to swallow his face when we get to the table.

"We're leaving. You can either come with us or find another way back," I say as I dump enough bills on the table to cover our tab and a big tip.

Rusty looks up at me and grins. He knows exactly what I'm talking about. And he couldn't agree more. Without a word from anybody, Jenna scoots off his lap and we all make our way out the door. We can't get to the hotel fast enough.

I'm practically running through the lobby to punch the elevator button. Thank God, it arrives quickly and we all four board the car. I don't feel like talking. No one else must, either.

The first stop is on the third floor to drop off Rusty and Jenna. They exit with mumbles of seeing us at breakfast. Jenna grins at Cami and Rusty gives me a peace sign as the doors close. As soon as we're on the move again, I pull Cami into my arms and kiss her. She melts against me and my mind is filled with thoughts of stabbing the emergency stop button, pushing her up against the walls of the small car, and slaking the hunger that's riding me like a prize bull.

A soft *ding* signals our arrival on the sixth floor. Reluctantly, I drag my lips from Cami's. The look on her face is soft and dreamy and full of promise. Impulsively I scoop her up and carry her to our room. When I stop in front of the door, rather than let her down, I tell her, "The key's in my back right pocket."

She squeezes her hand beneath my arm and wiggles her fingers into my pocket. She moves them around, probably more than she needs to in order to find the credit card–looking thing. I know that for sure when I see her devilish grin.

"Hurry up or I'm going to embarrass us both out here."

She chuckles and pulls the key out. I bend enough for her to work it into the lock. The light turns green and she hits the handle. I push the door open and let it fall shut behind us. I walk straight to the bed and stop.

The room is quiet around us. Cami is smiling up at me, something sweet and warm and sexy in her eyes. My heart is thumping in anticipation. We're finally alone. I have her all to myself, like I've wanted since pretty much the first moment I saw her.

She's mine.

I watch her smile slowly fade. We stare at each other for a long time.

I have no idea what I'm thinking. Or if I'm really thinking at all. And I certainly don't know what Cami's thinking.

I bend my head and brush my lips over hers. I feel them tremble. Not in passion. It's not that kind of kiss. I don't know what it says; I just know it's something I want to say.

When I lean back and look into her eyes, they're violet pools that hold some allure I've never encountered before. I feel like a mariner who, after months at sea, spots the bright flash of the lighthouse. I don't want to think of anything past that. Because there can *be* nothing past that.

Until she speaks. And changes everything.

"I love you."

THIRTY-THREE: *Cami*

W hen I see Trick's entire body freeze, I realize what I've done. Desperate to ease the uncomfortable tension, I pull his lips to mine and kiss away the awkwardness. It's quickly replaced by that fire that always burns between us.

His lips turn ravenous and he lets my legs drop onto the mattress. When I stand, I am above him, his head even with my throat.

His hands splay over my ribs as he watches me, wordlessly weaving a sensual spell around me. I thread my fingers into his hair as his palms skate to my waist and down over my hips. I wish there were no clothes between us.

As if reading my mind, Trick curls his fingers into the hem of my shirt and leans back, just enough to pull it up. Obligingly, I raise my arms and let him drag it over my head.

His eyes fall to my chest, my nipples furling into tight buds as if he's actually touching them. Light as a feather, he brushes his palms over the peaks, causing me to gasp, then gently runs his hands around my back to release the clasp of my bra.

When he pulls the straps down my arms, he tosses the material to the side and pulls me toward him, his hot tongue unerringly finding my nipple. As he draws it into his mouth and sucks, his fingers work loose the drawstring of my pants and push them down my legs. My panties quickly follow and, when he leans back, I step out of them.

Leaving me standing, naked, on the bed, Trick kisses a trail down my stomach, stopping to slide his tongue into my belly button then, lower, to nip the skin over my hip bone. He drops to his knees and glides his hands up the outsides of my thighs to cup my cheeks as he buries his face between my legs.

Shifting, I part my legs, I feel the hot tip of his tongue like a bolt of electricity. I fist my fingers in his hair to hold on. Or to hold him to me. I'm not sure which. I just know I don't want him to stop.

As his mouth devours me, I feel one hand move around and up the inside of my thigh, one finger slipping slowly inside me. He moves it in and out in perfect rhythm with his tongue, driving me closer and closer to the edge of insanity. A second finger joins the first and he penetrates me harder and faster as his face moves against me.

Then the world flies apart into a thousand tiny points of light. There's one word on my tongue, one name that I cry out into the quiet of the room. Trick. My world is centered on him. As it always seems to be.

When my knees can no longer hold me up, Trick wraps his arms around my hips and lowers me gently to the bed. As my body pulses with heat and breath comes back to my chest, I hear him rattling a package just before I feel his weight on the bed between my spread legs.

I don't even open my eyes when I feel his fingers again. But I do when I feel something larger, thicker, heavier replace them. When I look up, he's poised over me, staring down into my face.

He brushes his thumb over my bottom lip and whispers, "I'm nowhere near done with you yet." And then he thrusts into me, stealing my breath and waking my body to the pleasure only he can give.

My head is fuzzy, but I know where I'm at. And who I'm with. And it makes the morning bright and full of promise, even before I open my eyes.

I smile to myself as I think of Trick, of how awesome he is, how charming and handsome and—

An uncomfortable thought intrudes on the pleasure of the moment, like maybe something that was a part of a dream, but I can't be sure.

After a second, it begins to feel less like a dream.

And becomes alarming instead.

Holy shit! Did I tell Trick I love him?

I squeeze my eyes shut against the thought that I'd done something so stupid.

Maybe I dreamed it. Or maybe I imagined it. I had a crapload of tequila, after all.

I start praying desperately.

Please God, don't let me have told him I love him! Please God!

Then, when I realize it's a little late for that, I try another tactic.

Please God, don't let him remember it. Please God, let me have mumbled. Let me have stuttered. Let me have slurred. Anything!

As hard as I can, I try to focus on the details of the night. A warm flush sweeps through me as I think of the more intimate things, the things that are much, much clearer. Trick is amazing! And I mean a-mazing!

But I probably screwed it all up by telling him I love him.

The longer I lie here thinking about it, the more certain I am that I didn't dream the horrific deed. Or imagine it. I think it's real. I think it really happened.

Finally, when I'm in a near panic, I get the courage to turn over and look for Trick. The way he's acting will tell me all I need to know, probably. And I'm a big girl. It's time to face the music.

Slowly, I lean up a little and turn my head on the pillow. To my surprise, disappointment, and consternation, the bed is empty. But there's a note. I reach over and grab it from his pillow.

It reads:

Good morning, gorgeous. I'm getting coffee. BRB—

Trick

I feel the huge smile spread over my face. That doesn't sound like the note of someone freaked out by the premature launching of the L-word. Maybe I didn't say it after all.

Suddenly feeling light and gleeful, I grab his pillow, pull it over my face, and inhale. It smells just like him.

I lie there for a second until I realize what an idiot I'm being, and then I put the pillow back. Scooting quickly out of bed, I head for the bathroom to clean up before Trick gets back.

I brush my teeth and try to freshen up last night's makeup. I put on my clothes and spray some perfume on them. They still smell like smoke.

After a couple of minutes, I realize I still stink like a stale barmaid, so I turn on the shower. I might as well do it up right. If Trick gets back too soon, he can just come join me.

That thought alone makes me take my sweet time in the shower.

I get out and dress. Then put my makeup on. Then do my hair. Then undress and put lotion on and dress again. After all that, still no Trick.

Now I'm worried.

Surely he wouldn't get freaked and bail. Surely not . . .

I'm perched on the edge of the bed, looking out at the perfect morning sky, when I hear the lock click on the door. Trick creeps in and closes it silently behind himself. He's carrying a bag and a tray of coffee cups. When he sees me, he stops and smiles.

"I don't guess I need to worry about waking you."

"No, I've been up for a while."

He walks to the dresser and sets down his load, then turns to the bed. He plants his fists on either side of my hips and leans in. "I can see that." He sniffs my neck, giving me cold chills. "And smell that. You smell . . . edible."

The way he says *edible*—his voice low, his drawl evident—brings back flashes of the night. Late. Very late. After we'd both dozed off. He woke me up kissing my stomach.

My pulse flutters with remembered excitement.

"I do?"

"Mmm," he mumbles, kissing the corner of my mouth.

I'm torn between nervousness and desire, but nervousness wins out. I clear my throat. "So, you brought coffee?"

He leans back and I see that he's smiling. Wryly. Another good sign.

"I brought breakfast, too. Those two losers downstairs were still sleeping, so I got us a little something. That way we can eat and head on over to the horses."

"Perfect!" I exclaim. "I'm starving." I squeeze past him and go for the brown paper bag.

"Wait! I'll get it," he says, but he's not fast enough. I've already opened the bag. On top is a box of condoms. "Please don't be insulted."

I turn to him. "Why would I be insulted?"

He shrugs. "I don't know. It might come across as . . . presumptuous."

I smile. "After last night, I don't think that's possible."

He laughs. "Well, I usually keep one on me for emergencies. Because, you know, nowadays you have to boil people. But these are for you."

"For me? What do you mean?"

He cups my face in his hands. "I mean I wouldn't use anything if it were up to me. I'm clean. And I'm pretty sure you're clean. I think you'd have told me otherwise. I trust you that much. And I'd give anything to feel you. Really feel you. All of you. Wrapped around me. But I'll wait until you're ready for that. That's what I mean. These are for you."

As I look up into his eyes, into the beautiful collage of pale greens and grays swirling together, those three little words bubble to my lips again.

Of course, now, being sober, I shut them in. It does make me realize, though, that it's highly likely I really said them aloud last night. It also makes me realize that I don't remember him saying them back.

I want to die as I think of how uncomfortable my little bomb must've made him feel. The only way I can go forward is lightly, as if nothing happened and I'm not "there" yet. Prematurely.

"And for me so that I don't get pregnant, you mean."

"Oh," he says, clearly stunned. "Of course. I guess . . . I thought . . . I just assumed you were on the pill, since you and . . ."

"Brent," I supply.

"I know his name," he declares with a wry smile. "I met him, remember?"

"Right."

"I'm sorry. I'm really doing a shit job of waking you up this morning. Can I just go out and come back in? Let's try that."

Releasing me, Trick grabs the box of condoms, stuffs them in the top drawer of the dresser, and takes the bag and the coffee back out into the hall. After a few seconds of silence, I hear the lock click again and the door swings open.

Much as he did before, Trick silently lets the door fall closed behind him, but this time he doesn't stop when he sees me. He goes straight to the dresser, deposits our breakfast, takes me in his arms, and dips me like Fred might dip Ginger.

"Good morning," he whispers, grinning down at me. And then kisses me. Like, really kisses me. By the time he's done, I'm holding on to his shoulders for dear life, thinking I might melt into a puddle and ooze out of his arms if I don't.

He pulls me upright and says, "I brought you breakfast because you need nourishment after the thorough ravishing I gave you last night." I stare at him, mainly because I'm still thinking about where I wanted that kiss to go. "I'm pretending I left you exhausted and weak. Just go with it."

I smile, warming to his playful humor. "Oh, my! Just what I needed. I'm famished," I say in my best Southern drawl. Wide-eyed, I continue as an innocent belle might. "It's like I was ridden by a beast with great stamina last night. But surely it was only a dream."

Trick is smiling when he hands me a cup of coffee. "Now that's what I'm talkin' about. A beast with great stamina. Yeahhhhh." He takes the lid off his own cup and taps his coffee cup to mine. "Here's to long, steamy nights. May there be many more where that came from."

I say nothing, only smile, but in my head I'm thinking, *Hell yeah!*

I watch him as he looks at me over the top of his cup. I'm thoroughly captivated by his charm and that sexy way he has about him. It's a potent cocktail. He winks at me, and my stomach flips over. I smile again, even as I ignore the small part of my brain that's throwing off warnings about getting too close. I'm pretty sure it's too late for that.

On the way to Trick's preferred spot to watch the wild Mustangs, I learn that North Carolina, as well as most other states that host a population of the rare and endangered species, has a plan for keeping the numbers of wild horses at a manageable level. Among several other options, they allow for adoption at certain times throughout the year. Trick is hoping to be able to make his dream of owning a quarter horse a reality by adopting a particular black stallion he's had his eye on.

"I've watched him for almost a year now. I'm hoping no one has adopted him. I've talked to a guy with the Currituck Preservation Society a couple times about this horse. If Rags is still here, I think I'll be able to get close to him this time. And if I can, he's as good as mine."

"Rags?"

"That's his name. Rags and Apples."

"You've already named him?"

Trick grins sheepishly. "Yeah. I told you, he's already mine. It's just not official yet."

"Where'd you get the name?"

Trick's smile is nostalgic. "My dad used to say, 'You take care of a horse with rags and you make them love you with apples.'"

It's ridiculous how touched I am by that simple and sweet story, and by Trick's sentimentality.

"And just what do you plan to do with Rags once you get him? *If* you can get him."

"The place my father used to stable his horses, the one I was telling you about before, has a couple open stalls. The owner remembered my father and gave me a great deal on the space until I can get a couple races under my belt."

"So, you'll stable him there while you train him to race?"

"Yep."

"And then?"

"Well, after he wins a couple races, I'll use some of the winnings to invest in a broodmare and look into studs. I can get at least one foal out of them before I need my own place. Then I'll have a broodmare, a stud, one foal, and a winner. It'll just be a matter of working with what I've got until I can get another quarter horse trained or sold. Rinse and repeat until Rags is ready for stud. By then, I hope to have a stable full of viable horseflesh."

I nod. "That's actually a really good plan. Provided that Rags is a winner, of course." I hate to be the wet blanket, but the business side of me realizes the reality of the situation.

"Oh, Rags is a winner. I know it."

"That's pretty confident for a guy who's never trained a winner before."

"It is, but there's a good chance I'll have trained a winner once Runner starts to race. Sooty thinks he's got definite potential."

I can't hide my surprise. "He does?"

Trick's smile is smug. And thrilled. "Yep. He rode Highland Runner for the first time a couple days after he got back. Says he's got something special. For sure."

"Does Daddy know?"

Trick nods, his smile widening. "Yep."

"Wow. I bet that was quite the conversation."

"Oh, it was. And so worth the seven stalls worth of shit I had to shovel to listen in on it."

I laugh. "I guess that's one way of doing it."

"I wouldn't have missed that little talk for all the money in the world. Or all the clean boots."

I find it suspicious that my father didn't mention it. At all. Even if she *had* seen us holding hands, which I still don't think she did, I don't think Mom would tell Daddy. But she might not need to; my father is a very perceptive man. I just wish I knew. If he ever gets it in his head to fire Trick, I need to know. I need to be able to act. No matter what, I can't let Trick lose his job. "That's pretty awesome, you know?"

"Yeah, I know."

"Seems like your dad was right. You do have a natural gift with horses."

Trick's smile turns a little sad.

"I don't doubt it. If there's one thing that man knew, it was horses."

When we arrive at the long stretch of beach, Trick parks the car and comes around to let me out. I can't help but smile at the gentlemanly gesture.

"What?" he asks.

"What what?"

"What are you smiling at?"

"The fact that chivalry isn't dead after all."

"Well, if you're more comfortable operating under the assumption that it is, I can start treating you like I do Rusty."

"Do you kiss Rusty?"

"Hell no!"

"Then no. Let's go with chivalry."

Taking my hand, Trick leads me along a paver path between two tall sand dunes and out onto the beach. We walk to the surf and Trick stops. We look left and right, and I'm amazed to see the clusters of horses that dot the beach as far as the eye can see in each direction.

"About how many are there?"

"I think about a hundred and fifty total, but it's my understanding that they like to keep the population down to around a hundred and twenty or thirty. Something like that."

"So how do you find Rags?"

"I walk the beach until I spot him."

"Well, then let's walk the beach. I want to see this already-famous horse."

"Don't mock my future greatness. Or his. We're both sensitive males."

"Easily bruised egos?"

"Is there any other kind?"

"Heh, I guess not."

Trick first leads me down the beach. As we approach each small grouping of horses, he veers farther inland, toward the dunes. There is a "safe distance" requirement and he respects it completely, even though there appears to be no one around to challenge him if he chooses to do otherwise. That's kind of cool, actually. He's a good guy, even when no one's looking.

I look over at him. His hair is ruffled by the breeze. His eyes are narrowed as he looks off into the distance. I'm sure I've never seen anything sexier. Well, maybe him actually *on* a horse, but other than that . . .

As I watch him, those three bothersome little words circle through my mind again. Relentlessly, I brush them aside with an industrial-sized broom and force my mind back to the horses.

The mustangs are predominantly chestnuts, brown with a brown mane and tail, and bays, brown with a black mane and tail. But there are a few solid black horses as well. They are by far the most beautiful. I can almost see proud Spaniards riding them along the beaches, patrolling the coast.

"There he is!" Trick gasps excitedly, squeezing my hand almost painfully in his as he points down the beach with his other.

I grimace a little, which he sees when he glances at me. He frowns for a second, then lessens his grip on my fingers. "Sorry," he says, cringing.

"It's okay. You didn't hurt me." I pause and add, for dramatic effect, "Much."

His attention turns completely to me, his expression morphing from excitement into concern. "Are you okay? Did I really hurt you?"

"No," I reassure him with a smile. "You didn't hurt me. I'm just teasing."

"Good. I'd never want to do that."

I think, *Then don't*, but I say nothing.

"Let's go check him out, then."

We set off down the beach a little ways farther, until we reach another small group of horses. There are four chestnut horses and one black one. Looking at the proud angle of his head, the massive hindquarters, and the perfect posture, I don't even have to ask which one is Rags and Apples. I know immediately. He has one vaguely star-shaped white mark on his nose to break up his inky coat, but it only makes him more beautiful. It's easy to see that he'll be as much a star as the shape on his nose. Now I can see why Trick is so excited.

"Stay here," he says quietly, motioning me to stay put as he walks toward the surf, toward the horses.

He approaches them slowly. Above the sounds of the ocean and the breeze humming in my ear, I can hear that he's murmuring something, something soothing and low. The horses' ears flicker and they roll their eyes toward him as he gets closer.

Taking care not to spook them with quick movements or by coming around behind them, Trick stays clearly visible to the others as he nears the back of the group, to where Rags is standing.

I hear the horse puff once through his nose, and his ears prick. Trick stops. From this angle, I can see his mouth moving as he speaks to the horse.

He takes another step closer. The horse shifts his weight but doesn't move away.

Trick takes another step, but it's a little too soon. The horse shakes his head, backs away two steps, then stops.

When Rags suddenly pins his ears back, Trick stops dead, doesn't move a muscle. I hold my breath. Horses are large, powerful creatures that can be very dangerous if not handled properly. And wild ones are even worse.

I watch, spellbound, as Rags takes a step forward and pauses. He and Trick stare each other down. I hear Trick speaking his soothing words, and I hear Rags snorting as he decides what to make of Trick. It appears they're at an impasse.

Trick stands perfectly still and waits. I think to myself that he should just give it up, that Rags isn't going to respond to him.

But then something surprising happens. He does.

My mouth drops open when the black beauty takes three slow steps forward and drops his nose in front of Trick's face.

I see Trick's lips purse as he blows gently in Rags's nostrils. The horse sniffs and blows back. Carefully, Trick raises his hand and lays it on the horse's nose. Neither moves for a second until Rags nudges his hand. Trick responds by stroking him soothingly from between his eyes down to his velvety snout.

With very slow and calculated movements, Trick shifts to one side and runs his hand along Rags's jaw and neck. He continues dragging his palm lightly down the horse's side, stopping before he gets to the dangerous end. Rags turns his head and watches Trick closely, but he doesn't show any signs of fear or aggression. Just caution.

Trick moves back to his head, taking the big face between his hands and speaking right to the animal. Rags blows again and then spontaneously backs up and takes off to join his herd.

It's over.

But he did it. Trick did it.

Trick stands and watches the horses for a few more minutes. I don't ruin the moment for him. I can only imagine what he's feeling. He touched a wild horse. And the horse let him.

I see Rags watching him as well. It's almost like there is an understanding between them, some silent communication taking place.

One other big male in the herd turns to run down the beach. The others follow suit. It's then that Trick turns and makes his way back to me.

The smile on his face is so beautiful, so perfectly happy and sanguine, I want to kiss him. Not in passion, but in . . . something else. Maybe the love I'm beginning to think I can't contain for much longer. I'm not sure. The feeling is foreign to me. It's like I experienced it *with him*. I was *that* invested in what he was doing, in what it would mean for him to communicate with Rags.

And he did it.

And it's huge.

There's no doubt Trick's future is with horses. I just wish I knew if his future is with me, too.

THIRTY-FOUR: *Trick*

Watching Jenna drive Cami away is more than a little unsettling. I feel whipped for not wanting to let her go, for wanting to keep her with me instead. I mean, I haven't known her that long and it was just one weekend.

But, man! What a weekend.

In a way, I feel like several pieces of my life, of my dreams fell into place all at once. Introducing Rags to human touch for the first time and having Cami there for the whole thing was just . . . sublime. I can't remember being any happier. Ever.

Cami's alcohol-induced admission flits through my head, like it has at least a hundred times since I heard it.

I love you.

Did she mean it? Or was she just drunk? I know a lot of people who get into the I-love-you-man stage when they drink. But does Cami?

For the first time, I find myself thinking of my future wife with a face. Cami's face. Which makes no sense. We're all wrong for each other. Except in all the ways we're so right for each other, so good together.

Damn! What a conundrum.

When I can no longer see Jenna's taillights, I take my bag back to my room. I don't relish the idea of spending the rest of the evening doing laundry, not when I'd much rather risk my job, something that was one of the most important things in my life just a few weeks ago, to go and find a way to sneak in to see Cami, to hold her and kiss her for just a few more minutes.

You sound like a girl!

I chide myself as I sort dirty clothes into two separate piles and carry them to the wash machine. I go into Mom's bathroom to see if she and Grace have any laundry that needs washing, but the hamper is empty. I don't know when Mom finds the time to do all that she does, but it gets done. Of course, she's aged so much since I left for college, she probably doesn't sleep anymore.

As it always does, guilt assails me.

I start a load of colored clothes and head back to my room. I zip my now-empty duffel and put it away. When I turn back to the bed, I see the thing that Mom left me, the thing she said she wanted me to tend to first when I got back.

It's a long wooden box with a brand burned into the top. It reminds me of a ranch symbol or something. It's a horseshoe with the letters P, B, and H inside it. My initials. Yet I've never seen the box.

One side is hinged. The opposite side has a latch closure. I flip it open and lift the lid.

The contents are covered in a dark red velvet cloth. An envelope sits on top of it. One word is scrawled across the front—*Trick*. It's my father's writing. Even after all this time, I recognize it.

I'm sad and excited and a little nervous as I rip open the envelope and take out the folded piece of paper. It's bittersweet to have something new from him after all this time. But what must it say, for my mother to have kept it from me all these years?

It reads:

Trick,

I know you don't understand how I could take my own life and leave the family that I love so much. And I would rather think you'd never have to know my shame, but I also know there might come a time when your mother feels like you should know, that you need to know. You're reading this, so now is obviously that time.

I've written her a much different letter, but one that explains what's inside this one. No words, no actions, no amount of regret can take back the pain I've caused. I can only hope that my absence will help those hurts to heal.

All my adult life, the only thing I've ever loved more than horses was you, your sister, and your mom. Everything I did, I did for you three. Except for one thing. One selfish thing, one mistake. But that's all it took. It's the one thing that has destroyed everything I've always tried to protect—my family.

You probably don't remember that I had a partner for my dreams of breeding Thoroughbreds. You never met him. When we met, he didn't know as much about horses as I did, but he was able to get the start-up money that I needed to make our dreams as a family come true. He's a good man. After reading the rest of what I have to say, you'll see that he's a much better man than I am.

I met Jack Hines at a horse show. He was there to learn more about the financial side of the racing and breeding industry, him being a business major and all, while I was there to look at the horses and dream of one day owning my own Thoroughbred farm. It just so happened that we lived in the same town, although we'd never met. I'm a few years older than him. Anyway, long story short, after several more chance encounters, we hit it off and decided to partner and make both our dreams come true—his to manage a successful breeding operation, mine to own, breed, and maybe even race champion horseflesh. And for a while, it looked like we were both going to get what we wanted.

Within the first two years, we had three horses. You probably remember them. You used to help me with them after school and during the summer. You'd rather have been at the stables with those horses than anywhere else. I hope your love for them never dies. It's part of who you are, who you're going to be. It's your destiny.

After being involved in a business together for going on three years, Jack and I finally decided to let people other than our families know of our plans, so we hosted a party to join our two worlds, friends and family. And that's when I met Cherlynn, Jack's wife.

She was beautiful and charming. She was cultured and sophisticated, all the things that might fascinate a simple man like me. I'd never really valued those things, but they were appealing in a way that . . . well, she seduced me without even trying. I'll just put it that way.

Trick, I've never loved anyone like I love your mother. I don't know what happened inside me that would ever make me betray her the way I did. But it did. It happened. And I broke her heart. I ruined the family I'd always worked so hard to provide for, the family that had always been front and center in my dreams. I also ruined any chance of my professional dreams coming true by betraying my partner.

Your mother found out by accident. I like to think I would've been a big enough man to come clean eventually, but I never got the chance. One day in September, she came to the stables looking for me and found me there with Cherlynn. Life was never the same after that. I'd betrayed her trust, our marriage, and our family.

I thought it might blow over, especially if I could stop seeing Cherlynn, but a few weeks later Leena went to Jack. He took it a lot better than I probably would have if I'd been in his shoes. But I'm sure you can imagine that our partnership was over. And the only way I had to settle up with him financially was to give him the rights to the horses. All of them. Then I had to explain it to your mother, how my mistake had cost us everything else, too. We were destitute and broken, fatally broken, and I couldn't see my way clear.

After that, the only thing I could think to do was to take out an additional insurance policy, one that didn't have very many restrictions and take the life that ruined ours. Mine.

I hope one day you can understand that I did it all for you, for my family. I also hope that one day you can forgive me. I'm just a man. And I made a mistake. Unfortunately, it was a colossal mistake, one that I couldn't find my way out of without hurting you three even more than I already had.

I had this box made to give you when you turned eighteen, the day I had hoped to give you a farrier's set of your own and a part of the company I'd had a hand in creating from the ground up. That will never happen now, but I pray you'll go on to do great things, that you'll have your own breeding operation and that you'll use these tools and remember how much I loved you and your mom and your sister. You really were my whole world. I just lost sight of that for a few irreparable seconds in life.

I love you, son. Please don't live in the past. Go on and have the kind of future that I wanted for you. And take care of your mom and your sister. There was a time when the four of us were going to turn the racing world on its ear and you'd all want for nothing. I can't make that happen now, but you can.

Go be a great man, Trick. Be the man I couldn't be.

With numb fingers, I set the letter aside and peel back the velvet cover. Beneath it is a leather case. I don't need to open it to know what kinds of things it contains. I've used many a farrier kit in my lifetime. The fact that my father bought this set for me makes all the difference in the world.

I'm still sitting on the bed, working out what I've learned and how I feel when Mom gets home. I hear her open the door. Her footsteps don't even pause until she's standing in my doorway.

She looks at me. I look at her. She puts her hands over her mouth and squeezes her eyes shut, and then her body folds like a house of cards and she drops to her knees.

I have questions. How? When? Why? Why didn't she tell me? Does this have something to do with the insurance company investigating his death? Why would they just now become suspicious? Dozens more cascade through my mind like a waterfall of missing information. But I know now's not the time to ask them, so I go to the woman who has held the job of two parents all these years and I wrap my arms around her.

She cries for I don't know how long. A long time, it feels like. Then, as if I don't have enough to think about and worry about and work through, she deals me another bomb. She asks me to make a promise I'm not sure I can keep. Or that I even want to.

She's sniffling, her breath hitching in her chest as she gulps air. "Patrick, promise me one thing."

"Anything," I say, and at the time, I mean it. Until she tells me what it is.

"Stay away from Jack's daughter. I don't ever want to see her again."

And just like that, she jerks the rug out from under me.

THIRTY-FIVE: *Cami*

Like my last thought before sleep, my first thought upon waking is Trick. He dominates the vast majority of my available brain space these days. And it's only getting worse with each passing second.

I think of my accidental admission and how much I want to say it for real—sober and intentionally—but how afraid I am that he won't say it back. Of course, living in fear is never a good decision to make, but this just feels too . . . scary to rush right in to, no matter how much I might want to.

But that can wait until tomorrow. Or the day after. Today, I just want to spend with Trick and the horses. I want to enjoy every second of the present before I do anything that might ruin what we have. I'm not nearly done with Trick yet.

I'm smiling when I throw back the covers and head for the shower. Today, I'm gonna knock his socks off!

After showering and shaving everything from my ankles to my

armpits—twice—I smooth on a thick layer of lotion that makes my skin look like shimmering caramel and set about putting on my most unsuspectingly sexy outfit. Snug, low-riding jeans with a ragged hem and a hole in one knee coupled with a white cap-sleeved shirt that ties just below my ribs. My boots are the finishing touch to put me in the right frame of mind to turn Trick's head. Rather than go with a hat, I dry my dark red locks and pile them on top of my head in a loose style that looks like I just rolled out of bed. And out from under Trick. I grin when I catch my reflection on my way out the door. I hope he likes what he sees.

I dance through the kitchen, kissing Drogheda on the cheek as I pass her. "No breakfast for me yet, Drogheda. I'm on my way to the stable."

"Dressed like that?" she asks, looking me up and down.

"What's wrong with the way I'm dressed?"

"Nothing. I'm just worried that Sooty will fall off a horse and break something when he sees you."

I smile. "That's exactly what I want to hear."

"That you could cause Sooty to get hurt?" She's clearly outraged, and rightly so. Even if she's being ridiculous.

"Yes, Drogheda. That's my goal in life. Didn't I tell you?"

She swats at me with her dish towel. "Make fun of an old woman, smart mouth, and she might surprise you."

"Oh, you know I'm teasing. Of course I don't want anyone to get hurt. But Sooty's not the one I'm thinking of."

I wink at Drogheda, and she narrows her eyes on me. "Is this still about the new boy?"

"You can't tell Daddy. Promise me."

She rolls her eyes. "You know I hate it when you ask me to do that."

"It's important. Daddy's being crazy and if Trick loses his job, his family will be in a lot of trouble."

Drogheda has a soft spot for stories like that, not having come from a wealthy family herself. She worked the first many years of her life to support her younger sisters until they were married and well cared for. By then, according to Drogheda, she was a spinster, so she decided to make her life keeping other people's families. And thank God she did. She's been like a mother to me for a long time.

"Is that his name? You didn't tell me before."

I nod.

"What kind of name is Trick?" she asks, a sour look on her face.

"It's a nickname. It's short for Patrick."

Her eyes light up. "Patrick is a good, strong name. I like him already. Do you love him?"

"Drogheda! I've only known him—"

"I didn't ask how long you've known him. I asked if you love him. I say yes, you do. I can see it in your eyes even if you can't."

There's no fooling Drogheda. I melt onto a bar stool across from her. "I do. I really do."

"Does he know?"

"I think he might. I may have accidentally said something to him over the weekend."

"I thought you were with Jenna."

"I was. But we weren't alone."

"Lying to your *papi* won't do you any favors, *mi Camille*."

"I know, but he's just so hardheaded when it comes to Trick. I don't know what's wrong with him."

"Maybe you should ask him. He's a smart man, *chica*. Give him the benefit of the doubt. He's your father and he loves you. He only wants what's best for you."

"Even if it's Brent?"

She screws up her face, and I know her answer before she gives it. "Well, let's just hope that's not his only choice."

"Promise me you won't tell him, Drogheda. Please!"

"I promise. But you need to do the right thing by the people you love, Cami. *All* the people you love."

I sigh. "I know. And I will. I'm just waiting for the right time."

We both turn our heads when a light knock sounds at the door behind us. My heart jumps up into my throat when I see Trick standing there with the tips of his fingers stuffed into his pockets. I smile brightly, even as I'm praying he didn't hear any of our conversation.

I walk to the door and open it. "Good morning."

He clears his throat and smiles tightly. "Mornin'. Can I, uh, can I talk to you?"

His eyes are darting everywhere, like he doesn't want to look directly at me. My stomach drops into my boots and I fight back the urge to run to the bathroom and hurl.

"Of course." I turn back and smile at Drogheda. I know it faltered when I see her face is lined with concern. "Don't worry about breakfast, Drogheda."

She nods but says nothing. I can feel empathy pouring off her like water off a cliff. I know without having to ask that she feels as apprehensive as I do. Trick wouldn't be here, visiting me at the main house where there's a possibility of being discovered, if it weren't important. And bad.

I follow Trick onto the patio out back. He walks to the railing and stops, turning to face me. He looks down at the toes of his boots, making me more and more nervous.

"All right, spit it out. Whatever it is. I'm a big girl. I can take it."

That draws his eyes upward. And they're filled with a thousand things, not one of them good.

"I don't really know how to say this."

"Just say it."

Why am I encouraging him?

But I know the answer to that. Because the suspense, dragging it out, feels like it's killing me.

"I found out some . . . things when I got back last night, things that have to do with my father."

Like a death row inmate might feel when the red phone rings, I feel a temporary reprieve.

"Oh. Okay. Tell me."

"The thing is," he begins, then pauses to run his fingers through his hair. My nerves are back again.

"What is it, Trick? You're starting to scare me."

And he is. I feel like there's something much worse than getting dumped on the horizon. But what could that possibly be?

He looks up and his eyes meet mine. In them is an overwhelming sadness that makes my chest feel tight.

"My father left me something, something that my mother apparently had decided not to give me. Until she met you."

Now I'm just confused. "Me?"

He nods. "He left me a farrier's kit he'd bought me years ago, along with a letter."

I wait for him to continue, to tell me what's in the letter. When he doesn't, I prompt him. It's that or reach out and choke him. "And?"

"I never really knew why my father killed himself. Until now."

"Did he tell you in the letter? Or did your mother tell you?"

"He explained it in the letter. I think I told you when he first started out in this business, he had a partner. Someone he trusted and had a pretty close relationship with. Until he started seeing the guy's wife."

The gasp slips from my lips before I can raise my fingers to stop it. "He cheated on your mother?"

He nods again.

"I don't mean to be callous, but stuff like that happens all the time. Why would he kill himself over that? I mean, it's terrible, but . . ."

"That's not the worst part." He pauses to consider. "Well, maybe it is, but it's not the *only* bad part."

He stops again and this time rubs his fingers over his eyes. Everything from his posture to the hang of his head shouts that he's in misery. I do the only thing I can and I go to him.

I approach him slowly, like he did with Rags over the weekend. He doesn't move away when I lay a hand on his arm. I mean only to comfort.

"Tell me the rest."

"When they were discovered, his partner wanted out, of course, and the only way my father could repay the financial investment was to sign over the horses. It left our family with nothing. We had no money, he had no job. All he and my mother had between them was hurt. And regret."

"So that's why he killed himself?"

"Well, guilt, yes. But also, he was able to spend his last chunk of money on an insurance policy with pretty much no restrictions. Upon his death, Mom would get enough money paid out annually to take care of us for a long time. And it did. Until the payments stopped and they started investigating the indemnity clauses of the policy. I don't know what happened to make them suspect something after all these years, but now I know there's a legitimate concern. He *meant* to do it."

"How did . . . how did he die?"

"Wet roads, no guardrail, and a very deep quarry."

"But that could've been an accident. Are you sure he . . ."

"He left my mother a letter. He planned the whole thing, knew exactly what he was doing."

"Ohmigod, Trick. I'm so sorry."

I just want to take him in my arms, but when he looks up at me, I see that there's more. And by the look on his face, the worst is yet to come.

"But that's not all?"

He shakes his head.

"Cami, his business partner was Jack Hines." He pauses, watching me closely, as if I'm supposed to have some reaction to that. When I say nothing, his eyebrows shoot up.

"Okay. What am I missing?" I ask.

"The person my dad was sleeping with was your mom."

Yes, that would make sense with the way he explained things, but there's no way that's accurate.

"There has to be some kind of mistake. I mean, my parents have been happily married for, like, forever."

"As far as you know."

"No, they have been. You don't think I'd have known if something like that happened? Stuff like that tears families apart. I'd have known. Trust me."

"Is there any chance you could be wrong?"

He's not accusing anybody of anything. He's not shouting and telling me I'm wrong or calling anyone names. He's just asking a question, a question that feels like it might have claws long enough to rip my heart out.

"Trick, what's this all about? Are you trying to push me away, because there are easier ways of going about it than this."

"Of course not! God, Cami, do you really think I could make something like this up?"

"I don't know. I don't know you all that well. I mean, it's been, what? A few weeks?"

"Yes, you do. You know me well enough to know I could never do something like that."

"No, I don't know that. Twenty-four hours ago, I wouldn't have imagined you could come to my house and tell me things like this. But guess what. I was wrong."

Trick reaches for me. "Cami, you have to believe me. I—"

I step back. Away from him. Away from what he's insinuating. Away from the pain of what he's telling me.

"No! I don't have to believe anything. And I don't want to hear any more!"

In sadness, he watches me. I watch him back. The longer I think about it, the angrier I get.

I curl my fingers into tight fists. I want to lash out, to call him a liar, to tell him I never want to see him again. The fact that none of it is true only makes it hurt that much more. It burns like acid in my stomach.

"Stop looking at me like that. You're wrong. You're wrong and your dad was a liar. It looks like you are, too. Do you honestly think my father wouldn't have recognized you? Wouldn't have known you, if any of this were true? Do you think he would've hired you if any of this were true?"

A tiny voice speaks in the back of my mind. It's the voice of reason, the voice of the devil's advocate. A voice I don't want to hear.

Maybe this is why he wants you to stay away from Trick.

"Cami, it's *why* he hired me. He did it as a favor to my mother. He knew she needed help and he wanted to give it. They were both innocent in all this."

"Innocent? You mean if you overlook the fact that your mother couldn't keep her man at home?"

I know I finally landed a blow to his unshakable cool when I see his lips tighten.

"That's not fair and you know it. Be careful, Cami. Be very careful."

"Why? Does the truth hurt?"

Trick makes a noise, a split between frustration and exasperation. I don't care that I'm being mean and unreasonable. I can't believe what he's telling me. I won't.

"If you're so sure none of this is true, why don't you just ask your dad if he knew Brad Henley. See what he says. If, after that, you want to talk, give me a call."

"You know you could get fired for something like this, right? Telling lies and spreading rumors about your employer."

"You can't fire someone who has already quit."

With one final look that pierces some soft spot deep inside my soul, Trick turns and walks away. For the first time, I notice that his car is parked at the front of the stable rather than out back. Sooty is standing in the round pen that faces the house, watching us. He nods once and turns back the other way.

A toxic brew of emotions is churning in my chest as I watch Trick walk down the path, say something to Sooty, then climb into his car and drive away. Of everything that I feel—anger, bitterness, disappointment, confusion, betrayal—the most painful part is seeing Trick leave. Not knowing whether I'll ever see him again. Not knowing if I want to.

But I do. I know I do. Behind all my anger and resentment, I love him. Still. Always.

I see Drogheda pass the door and look out at me several times over the course of the next hour, but she knows me well enough to understand I need space and time. I need to think. To hurt. I'm still standing in the exact same spot when my father comes out to go to the stable.

"What are you doing out here?" he asks.

I don't say anything at first. I just look up at the tall, handsome man who has dominated my world for so long, even if it's from behind the scenes.

Do I really know him at all? Beyond what he wants me to know?

"Daddy, can I ask you a question?"

He doesn't look the least bit hesitant. Curious maybe, but not hesitant. Or guilty.

"Of course. What is it?"

"Do you know Brad Henley?"

There's a pause, during which my heart stops as I wait. I don't know whether to hope he does or hope he doesn't. Before I can work it out, though, it becomes a moot point.

I see it. The telltale twitch of Daddy's left eye. Although it's the only outward sign, and only people who know him well realize what it means, I recognize his fury before he even opens his mouth.

I bury my face in my hands. "Ohmigod, it's true."

"Cami, let's go inside. This isn't the place for questions like that."

Daddy holds the back door open for me and I walk numbly through the house to his office. It has all the solitude he might need to destroy my world.

During the short trip, I'm nauseated with knowledge that I never wanted, never needed, and now can't escape. And on top of it all, I'd said awful things to Trick and now he's gone. The glow I woke up to is now nothing more than a dark, stormy cloud that's threatening to never let me see sunshine again.

Daddy walks around to sit in the chair behind his desk, the ever-in-control Jack Hines. I plop down in the chair across from him.

"Tell me what you've heard."

"Tell me what you know."

"No, I want to hear what you've heard. I'll tell you whether it's true."

"How about you just tell me the truth, the whole story? That way you don't have to worry about what anybody else said or knows."

"Cami, don't be—"

"Dad!" I snap. It gets his attention. Not only do I rarely take a tone with him, I never call him "Dad." "Just tell me. The truth. All of it."

He leans back in his chair and tents his fingers against his mouth, watching me over top of them. I know he's debating on how much to tell me, what to leave out, wondering how much I know.

"If you don't tell me everything, I'll just have to believe whatever else I find out. If you won't tell me, someone else will."

After a long pause, he speaks.

"Yes, I knew Brad Henley. We were business partners a long time ago."

Well, at least it's a start.

"What happened?"

He sighs angrily. "Cami—"

"Tell me. I deserve to hear the truth from you, my father. Not from someone else."

"Cami, it was a long time ago. Neither your mother nor I wanted to burden you with something like that. And, as you can imagine, it took us a while to work through it. It's not a time I like reliving."

A stab of guilt. Maybe that's why my father has changed so much since I was little. He's had a lot of disappointment to live with.

"I don't doubt that it's painful, Daddy, but it's something I would've liked to hear from you. I'm a part of this family, too, ya know."

He hangs his head and I feel even worse. But I have to know.

"I know. And I'll tell you about Brad. And about the horses, but the rest you need to hear from your mother. It's not my story to tell."

I listen quietly as my father validates everything Trick told me, everything I'd accused him of lying about, and obliterates the perfect childhood I'd always thought I'd had.

THIRTY-SIX: *Trick*

I can't drive far enough or fast enough to escape the hurt and the anger and the disgust I saw in Cami's eyes. Since I've known her, I've watched them go from curious to interested to passionate to what I believe was loving. But there was no sign of that this morning. And it's that marked absence that's killing me now.

I question myself over and over again. Did I really need to tell her? Would she ever have found out if I hadn't? Was it worth hurting her and losing her to tell her the truth? Could she have gone her whole life and been fine not knowing?

I feel like I could've. Gone the rest of my life without knowing, that is, which makes me suspect she could've, too. And that makes it even harder to swallow. How could I be so stupid?

But then, as they have a thousand times, Mom's words go through my mind. Looking at Cami is painful for her. It brings back too many bad memories. Cami looks almost exactly like her mother, only younger. More like what Cherlynn must've looked like when she tore my mother's world apart.

I push back the bitterness. It has no place in my present. It won't change anything. It will only taint what happiness there could be in my future. And it's not worth it. It's not worth what I feel like it's already cost me—Cami.

I force my thoughts back to the things I can control, the things I *must* control—my family and my responsibility to them. I feel it now more than ever. I'll be damned if I'll be the second man to betray them in life. There's no way in hell.

And, just like that, the decision is made. I know exactly what I have to do. Turning left at the next stop sign, I head north. Toward Rusty's.

THIRTY-SEVEN: *Cami*

I feel like a zombie after talking to my father. I'm almost halfway to the club before I realize that I can't approach my mother about something so sensitive there. I pull over and park in an empty space in a McDonald's lot and I dial her number on my cell phone. When she answers, I cut to the chase.

"Mom, I need to talk to you. And it can't wait. It's about Brad. Can I come pick you up?"

There is a long pause on the other end of the line. She's so quiet, I wonder if the connection got dropped. I pull the phone away from my ear to see if the seconds are still ticking by. And they are. She's just silent.

Finally she answers. "Of course. I'll be waiting out front. How long will you be?"

"Give me fifteen minutes."

Thirteen minutes later, I'm slowing to a stop in front of my mother, who's waiting patiently and demurely beneath the grand front entrance of the country club. I unlock the door and she gets in. She looks at me and smiles a small, sad smile. My lips are frozen. I've got no return smile for her. In a way, I feel like I don't even know her.

Glancing away, I shift into gear and focus on the road.

"Where are we going?"

"I thought we could grab some coffee and talk."

"Okay," she says slowly. "Do you want to ask me anything now?"

She's impatient. She's feeling the uncomfortable prickle of the situation and, being the nonconfrontational type of person she is, she wants to get it over with and move on. She hates drama.

But today, she's going to get it, anyway.

"No. I'll wait."

Let her squirm.

I don't rush. Perversely, I want to make her suffer a little. It seems like she's gotten off the hook with barely a scratch, and meanwhile practically everyone around her has suffered. Or is suffering. Or will suffer.

The more I think about it, the angrier I get, so much so that torturing her with a wait doesn't seem as important as the answers.

"How? How could you do that to Daddy? To us? Did we mean so little to you?"

I glance at her, more to make sure my barbs hit their mark than anything else. I see tears in her eyes. Some small part of me feels satisfied that I've been able to hurt her just a little bit.

"I swear to you, Cami, I didn't plan it. I never meant to hurt anyone, especially you. You've always been my world."

This is news to me.

"I fell in love. I didn't mean to. It just happened. I tried to ignore it and deny it, but . . ." She turns in her seat to face me, her expression a pleading one. "Surely you can understand. I saw you with Trick. What if you'd been married to Brent when you met him? Can you just put yourself in that position long enough to see that sometimes the heart has terrible timing?"

"But I'm *not* married, Mom. You were. And you had me. Whatever happened to 'just say no'?"

"I did. For almost two years. But it only got harder with time. I tried to stay away from him, to forget him, but the more I tried, the worse it got. I loved him, Cami. You have to understand that only the most powerful emotions in life could've made me betray your father."

"And me."

She lowers her head. "And you."

"Is that why you acted so funny when you met Trick?"

She turns to look out the window. "Sweet Lord, he looks so much like his father. I felt like someone knocked the breath out of me when I saw him standing there with you. It was like looking at a picture of us, together, all those years ago." During her long pause, I see her chin tremble. "I knew what Jack had done in hiring him. I knew why he needed to. He's always felt like we—or, more to the point, I—was responsible for all the hardships Leena faced after Brad killed himself. And he's right, of course. It was his way of helping her when no one else was around to do it. Over the years, he's offered her money and horses, help, anything, but she wouldn't take it. None of it. But she agreed to let Trick come and do what he loved, what his father had taught him to do, for a generous wage. She wanted to give him that experience, that good start in life."

When she's finished, I keep expecting her to say something else. But she doesn't. "And that makes it all better? That makes up for . . . everything? Everything that happened? Everything you've been hiding? All the lives you ruined?"

She turns her tortured expression on me. "Of course not. Nothing will. Nothing *can*." Mom leans her head back against the headrest. "No amount of regret or apologizing can undo what's been done. And, of course, nothing can ever bring Brad back. If I'd known how it would all turn out . . ."

"Well, what did you think would happen, Mom? Did you ever think for one second that it might end *well*?"

Her laugh is a short, bitter bark. "I didn't think that far ahead, Cami. I loved him. I wanted to be with him. I was willing to put life and reality on hold for as long as I could to be with him."

"Then what happened? Why did it end?"

"Leena found out. Nearly had a nervous breakdown. He promised her he'd stop seeing me, although he didn't. Not at first. We just couldn't stay away from each other. One day you'll know what it's like to love someone like that, to want to be with them every second of every day, to crave their company and their touch more than anyone else's. But Leena must've known that, too. After a few weeks, she went to Jack and told him. The day Brad told me what she'd done was the last day I saw him alive."

I can hear the devastation in her voice, and it pricks my heart. Just a little. I *do* know how she feels. I feel like that about Trick. Maybe there's some weakness for Henley men in our blood. Even as horrified as I am about what she did, I can still picture myself in her shoes, risking everything to be with Trick.

I pull into a parking spot in the strip mall lot, right outside the coffee shop. But I don't cut the engine. I don't feel like going in anymore. I feel like running to Trick and asking him to forgive me for not believing him, for being so nasty. For the part my parents played in the events that led to his father's suicide.

As backward as it sounds, love had nearly destroyed two complete families. I don't want to let the past ruin any more lives, any more futures. It would be like giving in to a curse if I let Trick go without a fight, without at least telling him I'm sorry and that I'm in love with him.

I back out of my parking space.

"Aren't we going in? Where are you going?"

"To find Trick. I'm not going to let this, let *you* and *your* mistakes ruin my life."

"I wouldn't want you to. That's why we never told you. I had hoped you'd never find out."

"Well, obviously the better choice would've been to be faithful to your marriage, to your family, but hey!"

From the corner of my eye I see her flinch, and I regret my sarcasm. I know she's had to live in a hell of sorts all these years, but that isn't making me feel better at the moment.

"You might never have met Trick, then. Would you trade him in order to undo the past?"

That's a question I can't answer.

Trick's car isn't in the driveway when I pull up. I debate whether I should just leave, but before I can back out, Leena, Trick's mother, steps out on the front porch of the tiny brick ranch and motions me inside.

I turn off the engine and pull the keys from the ignition. My heart stutters inside my chest, fear making me jittery. My hand is shaking as I reach for the door handle, but I make myself get out and walk to the door. If ever there was a time to be brave, it's now.

Before I reach her, she turns and walks inside. I take a deep breath and pull open the screen door, following her into the house. I can hear her talking in a hushed voice. The higher voice of a child responds. She's talking to Grace. When she returns to the kitchen, she stops right inside the door, leaning against the jamb like she's afraid to get close to me. Like I might be contagious. Or toxic.

"Trick's not here," she offers without preamble. "I don't know if he's coming back."

The bottom drops out of my stomach. "Where did he go?"

"I'm not sure. Probably to sell his car since he had to leave his job."

Clearly, she blames me for that.

"Him and his daddy worked on that car every weekend for months getting it restored. Trick finished it after Brad died. It's got to be worth a small fortune, but I made him promise me when he got back he wouldn't sell it. He said he'd hold off as long as he could. But now . . ."

More guilt piles on. "Maybe if I could find him and talk to him, he wouldn't—"

"Oh, honey, he doesn't want to talk to you. You had your chance, but fate took its course and gave him just enough time to realize what a mistake it would be. He came to his senses before it was too late, and for that I'm thankful. Our families have too much bad blood as it is. I don't want that tainting Trick's future. He's a good kid. Smart, handsome, funny, hardworking. He'll go places. As long as he can keep his head on straight and stick with the right kinds of people."

She's not pulling any punches about how she feels about me and my family. It hurts, but I understand where it's coming from.

"Is this your decision or Trick's?"

"Trick's a grown man. He makes his own decisions. He's smart enough to see the writing on the wall. That's why he's not coming back. Not for a long time. He'll go and make something of himself. He doesn't need Hines help for that. He's strong."

I feel tears burning at the backs of my eyes. "But if I could just—"

"He's gone. Let him go. Let our family heal. It's what he wants. Don't embarrass yourself."

A ten-inch knife to the heart couldn't hurt any worse. I feel like someone is cutting out my soul and setting fire to everything that makes me happy, to everything that ever *could* make me happy.

"Could you tell him . . ." I trail off. It's no use. If she even agreed to give him a message, which I doubt she would, there's no guarantee that she's wrong, that Trick would want to hear from me. No, if he wants me, he'll come back for me. He knows where to find me.

Without another word, I turn to the door and open the screen, stepping out onto the porch. Before I let it shut behind me, I look back at Leena Henley. She looks sad and broken and beaten. Just like I feel.

"If it matters at all, I'm sorry. I'm sorry for everything that I had nothing to do with and for all the pain my family has caused yours. But I can't be sorry for loving Trick. I feel bad for having a good life, but he's still the best thing to ever happen to me."

Although she looks unaffected, she nods once. Without having to ask, I know that's all I'll get from her. I let the door fall shut behind me and walk away.

THIRTY-EIGHT: *Trick*

"Are you sure this is what you wanna do, man?" Rusty asks.

I give his question some serious thought. I've asked myself the same thing a dozen times in the last week. But I always come to the same conclusion. "I have to. Besides, it doesn't mean what it used to."

"Whatever mistakes your dad made, this was still something good you two had together. He wanted you to have this car. And your mom wanted you to keep it. If you let it go, that's it."

I nod. "I know. But it just doesn't make sense to hold on to something like this when getting rid of it could make things so much easier."

"Dude, you make it sound like holding on to something you love is a bad thing."

"Sometimes it is."

"Are we still talking about the car?"

My eyes snap up to Rusty's sharp blue ones. He's so laid back, so

255

devil-may-care, I forget there's a really smart, perceptive, occasionally wise guy in there.

"I think so."

"Don't you think you ought to give it one more shot?"

"Rus, we need the money. This car can fix almost all my problems and help me get started in a business that can give Grace and Mom the stability they've needed since before Dad. I have to do it."

"I wasn't talking about the car."

"Oh," I say, deadpan. "She hates me. And I don't blame her. I shouldn't have told her. But it's done. If she wants me, she knows where to find me. I'm respecting her decision by staying away. I've hurt her enough."

"Does she know you love her?"

"What makes you think I love her?"

Rusty just looks at me. At first, he doesn't say a word. He doesn't have to.

"You and Cami are the only two who *don't* know you're in love with her. And she's in love with you. If you let stupid shit your parents did a hundred freakin' years ago come between you *now*, you both deserve to die alone. That's just idiotic."

I stare at him. He's right, of course. But it's not my decision to make. It's Cami's.

"Damn, Rus. Why don't you just let it out? Be honest and tell me the truth about how you feel?"

He grins. "I feel like the inmates are running the prison these days, Trick. You haven't been right since you met that girl. At least you were still okay, though. But now . . . this is crazy. Just go get her and get it over with."

"I can't do that. It's because I care about her that I'm leaving it up to her. She has to be willing to let it go, too. We'll never be able to have anything if either of us is living in the past, holding on to all that trash."

He shrugs. "Your loss, man. I still think you're stupid. Women love that grand gesture crap. You've seen enough movies to know."

"Because movies are definitely what men should use as their romantic decision-making paradigm."

"Decision-what-a-what?"

"Drop the act. You forget I *know you*. I know you're more than just a dumb grease monkey."

Rusty smiles.

"You're a *crazy, delusional* dumb grease monkey," I add.

"Awww, that's just wrong."

He feints left and punches me in the right shoulder. "Wanna go a couple rounds? You know, like we used to before you went and got yourself whipped?"

"I'm not whipped."

"Well, whatever you call it. What do you say? Got a brand-new bottle of Patrón, all wrapped up and waiting for just such an occasion."

"Nah. I don't really feel much like drinking."

Rusty straightens. "Dude! Since when? You've been partying less and less since you met her. Does she have your balls, too?"

Rusty's right. The urge to drown my troubles has been present much less often since I met Cami. Just another good thing about her that I'll be left to mourn.

"Shut up! You remember what happened last time we threw down in here, right?"

The last time we roughhoused in his garage, we'd knocked over two tool chests, busted the hose to his air compressor, dented a metal cabinet, spilled an oil pan, then sat in the pit and drained a fifth of Patrón.

"I'll take my chances, because this time, I'm gonna kick your ass. No more Mr. Nice Guy."

"Bring it, monkey boy."

THIRTY-NINE: *Cami*

Like I have every morning for three weeks, I get up first thing and go to the window to look down at the stable. And just like every morning for the past three weeks, today there is no sign of Trick. There never is.

When are you gonna get it through your thick head that he's gone and he's not coming back?

My chest hurts. Just saying those words to myself makes me feel like something inside me is shriveling up and dying. Deep down, I know I'll never find someone like Trick. I think I had my suspicions at the time, but I didn't really delve into them too much because it seemed too soon. But now, now I know that Trick was the one. He still is the one. He always will be.

But he's gone. So where does that leave me?

Jenna has called me at least twice every day. She's been trying anything and everything to get me out of the house, but I'm just not interested. The only thing I want is the only thing I can't have, so what's the point?

I watch Sooty take Highland Runner from the stable. He strokes his neck and talks to him as he moves toward his flank, toward the stirrup. Trick said Sooty had ridden Runner after he got back, but I haven't seen it. He swore he'd made all the necessary progress with the horse, progress that would make him a winner. Even then, I believed him, especially after seeing him with Rags. I believed him when no one else did.

Carefully, cautiously, Sooty swings up into the saddle, then sits perfectly still and straight, I guess still hesitant, still waiting for Runner to freak out. But he doesn't. He shifts his weight from foot to foot, anxious for a run, but his ears show no signs of upset.

I see Sooty's foot tap lightly against the powerful horse's side, and they move smoothly into a trot across the field, toward the gate. It makes my heart hurt to watch them. Trick was right. He was right about Runner. And he was right about being born to train horses.

But now I'll never get to see him work miracles with wild horses.

Hot tears burn wet streaks down my cheeks. I blew it. I blew my one chance at true happiness. And now I'm left to pick up the pieces of the future I thought I'd had all mapped out and make some kind of workable existence from them. I have no other choice.

I get dressed and head downstairs, bypassing the kitchen and going straight to my father's office. It's empty, but I don't let that stop me. I'll hunt him down if I have to. I'm going to throw myself into the business and the horses. I'm going to put love and Trick as far from my mind every single day as I possibly can, for as long as I can. And then, when I can't do it anymore . . . well, I'll worry about that when the time comes.

I search the entire house for Daddy, but he's nowhere to be found. As I pass the kitchen for the second time, Drogheda stops me.

"What are you doing, Cami?"

"Looking for my father. Have you seen him?"

"He's out in the garage."

"Oh." The only one of two places I haven't checked yet. "Thanks, Drogheda."

With every step I take toward the huge garage, I am more determined to build a life around work rather than love. It's when I round the corner and see what my father's working on that I realize such a feat will probably never be entirely possible. Trick will haunt me, in some way, for the rest of my life. I'll never be able to escape the longing I feel for him, never be able to escape the way my heart reacts to anything that reminds me of him.

I stop and quietly watch as Daddy drags a polishing rag across the top of the Mustang. It's a Boss 429 in gunmetal gray with a wide black stripe up the center of the hood. I'd recognize it anywhere, partly because it's so rare and partly because it's Trick's. At least it used to be.

I feel like someone has knocked the breath out of me. My chest feels tight and achy with an incredible loss. Seeing Trick's car here, without Trick, is like suffering a small death.

"Where did you get that?"

"I bought it," he answers, not even looking up from the tiny circles he's making on the hood of the car.

"And here I thought you stole it," I snap. "You know what I mean, Dad."

There it is again—Dad.

"You know I always keep my eye out for classics. When a car like this goes on the market, everyone hears."

"Does he know you bought it?"

That gets his attention. He straightens and looks me dead in the eye. "No."

I'm not sure if that's a good thing or not, or what my father's motives were. Maybe he just wanted the car. Well, I'm sure he did, actually. I know that much about him. But did it have anything to do with Trick and his family, about the guilt Daddy feels over what happened? I'll probably never know. Obviously, transparency isn't a top priority in my family. Neither is honesty.

"How much did you pay for it?"

"That's none of your business."

"Yes, it is. You said I could be a part of this operation. Well, the finances are a part of it."

"This purchase wasn't part of the business. It's a personal purchase."

"Daddy, please tell me. I need to know that they'll be okay."

His expression softens. "They'll be fine, Cami. For a long, long time."

I nod, looking down at my fidgeting fingers. "Will he, um, will he have enough to maybe get started with a horse or two? And stall space somewhere?"

He doesn't answer at first. I hear scuffling, but I don't dare look up. I don't want him to see in my eyes how much his answer matters to me.

When I see his feet and feel his hands on my upper arms, I still don't look up. I feel my chin tremble and my vision blurs. I blink quickly to clear away the tears.

"Sweetheart, he'll be fine. But he'll be better off without you, and you'll be better off without him. He's not right for you. I know you can't see that now, but you will. Eventually."

Obviously, there's no reason to try to hide it from him anymore. He knows.

My eyes swing up to his. "How long have you known?"

"What am I, blind? Come on, Cami, do you really think I'm that stupid?"

"Daddy, why do you think he's not good enough? Why can't you see that he makes me happy?"

"Is he making you happy now?"

"That's not fair. He—"

"I don't want you getting mixed up with anyone from that family."

"Is it because of Mom?"

"It's because he can never give you the life and the security and the fidelity you deserve."

"You can't hold his father's sins against him. Trick's not like that."

"And how do you know that?"

"I just know, Daddy."

"No, you don't. You can't."

I search his eyes. They are hard. Unyielding. Unforgiving.

"No, you're right. No one can know for sure. I'm sure you never expected Mom to do what she did. But some things are worth taking a chance on, Daddy, and Trick's one of them."

"Then where is he?"

And just like that, I'm crushed once again under the devastating weight of reality.

FORTY: *Trick*

I can hear the knocks in the transmission as I hit the gas pedal in the truck. I knew I'd need something to pull a trailer, but I didn't want to shell out a bunch of cash for something nice at this point, so I bought a used truck that Rusty's going to help me fix up. I just hope it'll hold together until then.

I probably shouldn't be bringing it out for trips like this. I probably shouldn't be making trips like this at all. It's not like I can really afford to unload so much for land right now, anyway. But I like to look. It makes me feel a little more in control and a lot more optimistic. The only bad part is that I always picture a house where Cami and I will be living, one that will someday hold a couple of kids and a dog. And who knows what else. Being the animal lover she is, Cami would probably be bringing home strays all the time.

The thought makes me smile.

But then I push it out of my head. There's no point in thinking about a future with her. She's made her choice. She hasn't tried to contact me at all. And as much as I want to go see her, I know I can't. I shouldn't. I won't. I have to respect her decision, no matter how much I hate it and how stupid I think she's being. Maybe what it all boils down to is that she didn't love me after all. Maybe she was just drunk after all.

I can still remember her face, though, and it didn't seem like the drink talking. She seemed sincere. It *felt* sincere. But maybe that's just because I wanted it to be sincere. Granted, at the time it freaked me out a little. It seemed too soon and too scary, especially when I was still under the idiotic impression that my attraction to her might be purely physical.

Jackass!

I thump the steering wheel. There's nothing I can do about any of it now. I think that makes it even harder. I had my chance. And I blew it. Damn it! I blew it!

I see the sign for the road coming up and I slow to make the turn. As I navigate the many potholes in the gravel drive, I picture what it would look like paved with the trees overhead trimmed and arching over it.

The drive ends in a circular patch of grass and weeds. I shift into park and turn off the engine. I can hear nothing but nature on the other side of my open window.

Some months ago, someone had cleared the land for a home site, but the bank foreclosed before they could build. I can see their vision, though. In my head, I picture a huge plantation-style house in solid white with big columns along the wraparound porch. I see Cami planting flowers along the walkway, even though I have no idea if she's into that sort of thing. She just seems like she would be.

Cami's all girl. And I love that about her. She's at home in the saddle and she can wear a kick-ass hat and boots with the best of 'em. But underneath, she's all soft and feminine, silk and satin.

I think of her stripping in front of me the night we went swimming, of seeing those lacy little things she was wearing. I can still see her body with perfect clarity. And I can still remember exactly what it feels like under my hands, under my lips, under my body. It starts making me hard so I have to resituate in my seat and think about something else.

I get out and walk past the clearing and through the woods beyond it to the first of several fields on the property. I imagine what the stables would look like sitting at the edge, and the round pen and the fencing. I can see Cami and me exercising the one-year-olds and stopping to go roll in the hay. Literally.

Shaking my head, I make my way back to the truck. If I'm ever gonna get over her, I have to stop picturing her in my life, as part of my future.

But damn, how do I do that?

FORTY-ONE: *Cami*

M om left my room over an hour ago, but her words and our conversation are still bumping around inside my head. I know now that, more than anything, I needed her to be sorry. I didn't need to hear excuses or explanations or qualifications. No, I just needed an apology. A deep, sincere, heartfelt apology for doing what she did and ruining the lives of so many people.

And I got it. Her words were simple. "Cami, I am so, so sorry. I never meant to hurt anyone, least of all you. But I did. And if I could take it all back, I would. I just want you to be happy."

And then she cried. And I cried. And I think we both healed a little bit. But still, I'm having trouble concentrating. Even now, my heart and my mind are all over the place.

"Are you listening to me?" Jenna asks.

"What?" I ask, forcing myself to concentrate on my friend.

"Cami, it's been almost two months. You can't hide out forever. Come out with me. It'll be fun. Just the two of us. We can go to

M. LEIGHTON

Lucky's and you can drown your sorrows in peace. I know for a fact they won't be there."

"How could you possibly know that?"

"I asked Rusty."

"What happened to his restriction on not talking about us, about not getting involved?"

"I used some very powerful tools of persuasion. One of which nearly gave me whiplash."

I have to laugh. "God, Jenna. You're such a freak."

"Yeah, pretty much. It's part of my charm."

And that's probably very true.

"I don't know. I just don't feel like going out, especially there."

"Look, Cami, it's kind of like having a massive hangover. Sometimes the only thing that'll take care of it is a little hair of the dog that bit you. Consider a trip to Lucky's some hair. And it's even highly likely that there will be quite a few dogs there, too. Just not the four-legged kind."

"If that's what you think, then why do you even want to go?"

"Well, I have Rusty, so I couldn't care less what the guys look like, as long as they keep buying me drinks. The main thing is to get you out of the freakin' house. I'm seriously afraid that you only shower once a week and that you haven't shaved your pits in, like, a month."

"Geez, Jenna. I'm not that pathetic. I shower twice a week."

"Holy wow, I hope you're kidding!"

I snicker. "Of course I'm kidding. How long have you known me?"

"Since Jesus was a baby."

"And how many days in my entire life have I not bathed?"

"Two," she says definitively.

"What?"

"I don't know. I was guessing. Not that it matters. What matters is that you need some fun. And some drink. And some hair of dogs and crap like that. And as your best friend, it's up to me to make sure you get it, even if I have to force-feed it to you. Either you can come quietly or I will have to start plotting. And you know how that usually turns out."

"Yes. With someone missing her eyebrows."

"Exactly, so just say you'll come and save me the embarrassment."

I sigh. "Fine. I'll come. What time will you be here?"

"Nine. And wear something hot. Your confidence needs the boost."

She hangs up, and I'm left wondering how she knows that.

I slide back onto my bar stool, pushing my hair away from my face. I wish I'd worn it up. Dancing makes me hot.

I signal the bartender for another beer just as Jenna settles in beside me.

"You're not done already?"

"Just for a few minutes. I'm burning up."

"One beer and then we're going back out there."

"What is this? Death by dancing?"

"Nope. It's called therapy. Jenna style."

She picks up my beer just as the bartender sets it down and takes a huge gulp.

She looks over my shoulder and her eyes widen a tad. Smiling innocently at me, she blurts, "I gotta pee. Be right back," and then she slides off her stool and takes off.

My heart starts pounding when I wonder who she saw behind me that made her react in such a way. Almost every part of my heart and soul, along with several body parts as well, are hoping and praying that it's Trick she spotted. Even though it will be so hard to see him, especially if he's with someone else, at this point, I just want to see him. Watch him walk, see him smile. Watch him drag his fingers through his hair in that way that he does.

Before I turn around, I close my eyes. I'm preparing myself, trying to stop the butterflies of nervous excitement from making me puke all over the bar. I'm convinced I'll see Trick.

But I don't.

The earth-shattering letdown, the crushing of that tiny seed of hope is almost more than I can take. My throat closes up around an invisible fist of disappointment. I try to swallow past it, but can't.

Brent is standing a few feet from my bar stool, staring at me. I try to offer up even a polite smile, but my lips tremble around it and I know it looks as pathetic as I feel.

"Excuse me," I mutter as I scoot off my stool. I head for the bathroom, but when I get there, I keep right on going. Right out to the parking lot, to Jenna's car. There's no hope of salvaging the night now.

I'd rather just die instead. Get it over with.

FORTY-TWO: *Trick*

It's coming up on three months. I think I've gotten up every day since I left Cami's house and thought to myself, *This is the day. This is the day she'll change her mind and give us another chance.*

Today, I wonder if she ever will. I wonder if I'll ever get the future that I'd begun seeing as reality more than fantasy.

Today, it feels less likely than ever before.

And I hate that feeling.

FORTY-THREE: *Cami*

Daddy's droning on and on about the purse for one of the larger state races coming up and what he plans to do with the money.

I know I should be paying closer attention, and I genuinely try to focus on him when he's talking. The problem is, I seem to have lost all interest in pretty much anything lately. I feel like I'm being sucked into a downward spiral that has no end in sight. Daylight and hope and happiness get further and further away with every sun that sets.

I think in some small way, I expected Trick to come back. I expected him to change his mind, to hear from his mom that I tried to talk to him and suddenly decide he can't live without me.

But it seems like that is never going to happen. And I'm left trying to make some kind of life for myself without him.

The thing is, I don't think I'm interested in a life without him. Sometime when I wasn't looking, Trick became everything I want out of my entire existence. Without him, I just don't know what's left.

FORTY-FOUR: *Trick*

When did nights get so long? Probably when I started waking up thinking about Cami. Every time it happens, which is more and more often lately, I can't go back to sleep because of this miserable ache that won't leave me alone. So I lie in bed and remember and wish and curse and get angry. Then I think about all the things I wish I'd said, all the things that might've made a difference. But even still, I can't go back to sleep. And then the cycle repeats itself.

I've thought several times about downing a fifth of something before bed, enough to drown out all thought, especially those of Cami. But for some reason I can't bring myself to do it. I think the problem is that I don't really *want* to drown her out. Memories and wishes are all I have left.

And I'm not ready to let them go yet. If I ever will be.

FORTY-FIVE: *Cami*

I wonder if I look as determined as I feel. I decide from the look on Sooty's face that I probably do. I march right past him, down the main aisle of the stable, and stop in front of Lucky's stall. I yank open the door and start to walk in. But then I stop.

Tears fill my eyes like they have every other time I've visited him. Leaning up against the wall, I give in to the urge to cry, just like I have every other time I've stopped by the stall. I can't seem to help it. And I've tried. Dozens of times. But all I can see, all I can think of and hear and feel and smell is Trick and the night we spent together when Lucky was born.

How can the best day of your life also be the worst? I'm tortured by the memory of Trick giving in to me, of what we shared, and yet I can't stop thinking about it. Not even long enough to visit Lucky without having a hysterical tear-fest.

FORTY-SIX: *Trick*

The weather is noticeably cooler as I put Rags through his paces. He's made even better progress than what I'd anticipated. And I'm pleased. Really pleased. But it seems a more hollow victory than I'd imagined it would be. I've been dreaming of this day for a long time—the day I'd be breaking and training my own horse, laying the groundwork for my own future, finally getting back some control of my own life. Why isn't it everything I'd dreamed it would be?

I didn't realize until I lost her how much I'd included Cami in my thoughts, my hopes, my plans. My happiest daydreams.

Although it didn't start out that way, it hadn't taken me long to think of her as being a part of this whole taming-a-wild-horse process, of her cheering me on and being continually amazed by my horse-whispering prowess. I smile as I think of her laughing and rolling her eyes over my humongous ego when it comes to my confidence in Rags.

That smile dies when the image of her fades away.

FORTY-SEVEN: *Cami*

I usually love it when summer starts melting into fall. I love the colors and the cooler air, the excitement of football season, which my father has always loved, too. There's always a break in the racing season if the ranch is racing a horse for the year and, if not, it's turning into buying season for people who want to make the following year's races.

Then come the holidays. Thanksgiving and Christmas, followed by the New Year. New plans, new horses. More training, more breeding. It's a cycle I've been through half my life.

And I've always looked forward to it.

Until this year. It seems like even the best, most exciting things about life have lost their luster. I can only hope it'll come back. One day.

FORTY-EIGHT: *Trick*

"I don't know why you didn't just let me drive. Even that piece of shit I'm working on now would be a better ride than this thing."

Rusty hasn't stopped complaining since we left his shop.

"So what you're saying, since *you* helped me fix this truck, is that you do crap work. Is that it?"

"I do great work. I'm just saying that . . . it's a truck. They can only be so comfortable. A car would be much better for a ride like this."

"A, it's not that far. And B, I'm getting the word out. Since I got the logo magnets for the doors, I'm like a driving advertisement for equestrian awesomeness."

After I sold the Mustang, I felt pretty guilty, like I'd betrayed Dad or let him down, even though he did it first. He did love that car and he wanted me to have it. But financially, I just couldn't justify keeping it when selling it would help so much.

I don't feel quite as bad now, though. I used the logo from the top of the farrier's kit, the one with the horseshoe and my initials, for my new venture, my new life. Even if I don't always feel like an official champion quarter horse breeder, at least I can start looking the part. All I'm lacking today is the horse trailer I bought. It's outfitted with the logo, too.

"It's gonna feel pretty damn far when I try to get out on numb legs and a cramped ass."

"God, you're worse than a woman. Stop your bitching and find us some good music to listen to."

Our barbed banter continues the rest of the one hundred twelve miles to the track. The race we're attending is one of the biggest before the Colonial Cup in November. I know that all the big names in Southern breeders have at least one horse in the mix. If I hope to get Rags in a race early next year, I need to check out the competition.

For the couple of hundred years that Thoroughbreds have even been in existence in this country, they've been bred with quarter horses in order to produce tougher, more athletic horses that are more suitable for racing and steeplechasing. Although wild horses are all quarter horses, their bloodlines date back to the Thoroughbreds that Spanish settlers brought to this continent. When this breed is found in the wild, as feral horses, they're called mustangs. In these wild horses, the champion stock is there, the winning bloodlines are there, if only they could be broken . . .

And that's where I hope to blaze my trail in the racing world. To my knowledge, no one has ever broken a wild horse and raced him. Ever.

But I'm about to change all that.

At the track, after we've parked, Rusty and I head for the stable area. I made sure we left in enough time to be able to mill around down there and check out the horseflesh, maybe pick up on a little something helpful or important. I hadn't planned on jumping into this blind. I guess I'd sort of figured I'd get to know a lot more about this stuff from Sooty and Jack, but . . .

I stop to introduce myself to several trainers along the way. They're polite enough, most of them not seeing me as any kind of competition. I have my age working for me in that way. They don't fear me or feel threatened by me, which means they're more likely to answer my questions and feel more relaxed in talking than they might otherwise. At least that's my theory. And it seems to be spot-on so far.

After talking to a trainer out of the more northern parts of the state, I see the familiar colors of Jack's operation—dark purplish-blue and deep brick red. Maybe it's because I haven't seen it in a while or maybe it's because I still can't get Cami out of my head, but the blue looks just like her eyes and the red isn't that far off from her hair. Could be my imagination, but I wonder if Cherlynn's looks had anything to do with Jack picking those colors for his horses. Maybe, like me, he was so in love with her, he saw her everywhere, saw her eyes and her hair in every blue and red around.

I turn back the other way. No sense making it harder than it has to be. No reason to torture myself. It's been months since I've seen Cami, but it hasn't gotten any easier. In fact, it might even be getting harder every day. I'm not sure. Sometimes it feels like it can't hurt any more. But the next day, it does.

Rusty grabs my arm. "Where you going, man? Don't you know him or something?"

I look around to see who Rusty's talking about. I see Sooty standing at the door of a stall, looking in my direction. Our eyes meet and he nods. I nod in return. He tips his head toward the stall and disappears inside. I debate whether to go talk to him.

Surely it can't hurt anything, right?

I turn around and walk back to where Sooty disappeared. In a way, I hope Cami is in there with him. Even though it would probably kill me to see her, I want to. Just one more time. Up close.

But he's alone in the stall. Just him and Highland Runner.

I know the shock registers on my face.

"Are you kidding me?"

Sooty smiles in that way he has. It's mischievous. And pleased.

"Nope. I told you, you were right about him. He's got something. He's a winner."

"Is this his first race?"

"Naw, we've had him in some smaller ones. Jack wasn't convinced too easy. But once he saw him run . . ."

Pride, and lots of it, bubbles up in me. I feel like laughing and whooping like a kid. But I don't. I just smile. It's probably a pretty big smile, though.

"Damn."

Sooty laughs. "That all you've got to say?"

"What else *should* I say?"

"I don't know, but I hope you're proud, son. Jack's been picking and breeding winners for a lot of years. I've never seen him wrong about a horse, never seen him misjudge talent. He's got a great eye. But you . . . you got something different, Trick. You were born to work these horses. It's in your blood."

I take a deep breath. There's a swell of emotion in there that I don't want to get the better of me. Not knowing what else to do, I stick out my hand. Sooty takes it.

"Thanks, Sooty. I just . . . I don't know . . . Thanks. It means a lot."

He winks at me. "I knew it would." Sooty leans back against the wall and tips his hat up. "What brings you 'round?"

"Just checking out the competition."

"Competition? Is that right?"

I nod. "Got a horse of my own now. I'm making a go of it. I don't know exactly how it'll turn out, but I have to try."

"You talking 'bout that wild horse? Did you finally get it?"

I can't remember ever telling Sooty about my plans for adopting Rags.

"Yeah, I did. A couple months ago. How'd you know?"

"Pretty little bird told me you had plans for one," he says with another wink. "Glad to hear you got him."

Cami was talking to Sooty about me? I'm not sure how I feel about that. Encouraged, for sure. Curious. Confused.

Damn! Don't give me hope after all this time.

But it's too late. It's already opening up in my gut—hope. Maybe she'd changed her mind somewhere along the way but just didn't have the nerve to come find me. After all, I never got to tell her how I feel, even after she'd accidentally told me she loved me. Maybe I should've. Maybe that would've made a difference.

Sooty and I talk shop for a little longer, but my mind is far, far from the conversation. All I can think about is Cami and if I should find a way to run into her, just to see if maybe she's having regrets, too. I wouldn't be disrespecting or pressuring her that way. I could make it casual, just enough of a run-in to gauge her reaction.

We say our good-byes and Rusty and I make our way to the stands to watch the race. I keep an eye out for Jack but don't see him.

When the race is about to start, it's no surprise that I'm already rooting for Highland Runner. I'm almost as invested in him as I am in Rags. I feel like they're both mine, my projects, my winners. My validation.

The gun goes off and the gates open. The race is on. I can't imagine being any more tense if my own horse were running. I feel like every muscle in my body is tight, on edge. And when Runner crosses the finish line a full head ahead of the next-closest horse, I'm on my feet raising all hell before I can even think twice.

"Dude, calm down. You act like that's your horse out there," Rusty says from beside me. "Are you forgetting *that's* the competition?"

I can't stop smiling. "No, I'm not forgetting. But this win is proof that I can do it, that I know what the hell I'm talking about. They all doubted me, but now they see." In my head, Cami's face on the beach at Currituck swims by. She didn't doubt me. I don't think she ever really did. "I can pick a winner, Rusty." I turn to him and grab both his arms. I have the ridiculous urge to hug him and slap him on the back. I don't, but in my excitement, I do thump his chest with my fist a couple times. I can't help it. "Whooo! Holy shit, I can actually pick the winners!"

I'm relieved. And excited. And relieved to *be* excited. That's been markedly absent since Cami. I'm so caught up in the thrill of the moment, I pay little attention to the people around me as we make our way toward the winner's circle. I have to congratulate Sooty. And maybe let Sooty congratulate me. That might be pretty cool. More than any of that, though, I want to look Jack Hines in the eye, even if it's from a distance, and let him see that I know. He needs to see that I know I was right. And that he was wrong.

The crowd gets denser the closer I get to the circle. Luckily I'm tall, so I can see above the majority of heads between me and the people I'm looking for.

I spot Sooty first. He's standing there like a proud father. Beside him is Jack Hines. His arm is over Sooty's shoulders like they're the best of friends. I snicker. I doubt Jack is anybody's friend. Jack looks out for Jack and nobody else. Except maybe Cami. And even that I'm not so sure of. He seems more concerned with her making a good match than just being happy.

I keep my gaze trained on him until he looks my way. His expression changes almost imperceptibly when our eyes meet. It could be my imagination, but I don't think so. It tells me all I need to know.

Jack Hines will never think I'm good enough; no matter the proof, Jack Hines will never approve of me—for his daughter, for his horses, for his respect. Jack Hines will always see my father when he looks at me. Jack Hines will always be distrustful and superior, hard to please and snobby.

But he's the father of the person I'm pretty sure I can't live without, the person I know I don't *want* to live without. So where does that leave me?

Maybe I should approach him, try to talk to him. Maybe that could be my way back into Cami's good graces.

I'm debating the best way to handle the situation, the best way to handle *him*, when I see a flash of red move behind Jack. It's a color I see everywhere and nowhere, a color that haunts my thoughts all day and my dreams all night.

Instantly, Jack is forgotten when he turns and pulls his daughter in between him and Sooty. She looks amazing in a dark purple shirt that brings out that hint of violet in her eyes. Her hair is pulled up in a sexy way with a few pieces waving around her face and neck. Makes me want to get her alone somewhere and run my fingers through it. Mess it up the fun way.

She turns her head to speak to someone, and I look behind her. It's that douche of a boyfriend I thought she'd dumped. Brent.

My stomach and every last drop of hope I had plummets through the pavement.

FORTY-NINE: *Cami*

Brent is asking me something, but I can't hear him over the crowd, so I ignore him. Since the breakup, we've been essentially forced into a friendship of sorts. At the behest of my father, he's still a fixture in our family. I'm not sure if it's because Daddy just wants him around or if it's because he's still gunning for a reconciliation. Either way, it's . . . strained. At least it is for me. Brent seems to have had zero problems adjusting. His behavior speaks to the intimacy we once shared, intimacy I'd rather forget. But it's clear that he would be more than happy to revisit it.

As it turns out, he wasn't any more attached to me than I was to him. Only his ego was bruised. And temporarily at that. I think I was just a piece of ass with tremendous potential for trophy wife. For that reason, when Brent saw that I'm not with Trick, he started acting familiar in a way that makes me uncomfortable.

Men!

Finally, when I feel his hand at my waist as he tries to get my attention, I realize he's not going to be ignored. I turn to address him.

"What is it, Brent?"

I hate my snippy tone, but he's pushing all my buttons for some reason. Probably because I've got Trick on the brain (as usual) and he's not Trick, which he can't help. But still . . .

His smile doesn't falter. "I just got a call and I have to head back. Why don't you ride back with me?"

I turn away from him, swallowing my frustration. I start to answer him, but my response dies on my lips when my eyes collide with the pale green ones that haunt my every waking minute. And many of my nonwaking ones, too.

It's Trick.

My heart flounders in my chest and I can't breathe for just a second as he watches me. A thousand scenarios run through my head, most of them worthy of a made-for-television movie or at the very least a soda commercial. They all involve us running into each other's arms in some way, shape, or form.

But then his expression darkens, as if he's not very happy to see me at all, and my dreamy visions drift away like smoke on the wind.

His lips thin and he turns and walks away. He doesn't acknowledge me in any other way. He doesn't bother with any kind of social nicety. He just gives me a dirty look and leaves.

I feel nauseated. And hopeless. And alone. Deeply alone. The kind of alone that says I will never find someone to take his place. That I will die missing him, wanting him, mourning him. And now I know there's nothing I can do about it. His mother was right. There was no misunderstanding. Trick washed his hands of me when he left my house that day. All this time, I've been holding on to a dream, to an idea that doesn't exist. I don't think it ever did. I made much more of our relationship than he did. I was drowning in him, in *us*, and he was . . . treading water until he started to swim again. Until he started to swim away. From me.

Through tear-filled eyes, I watch the back of Trick's head disappear into the crowd. Daddy leans his head down to speak into my ear. "Don't forget you're in the spotlight."

Point taken.

I blink quickly to clear my blurry vision, and I smile brightly for all those who are watching. I wait until all the camera bulbs have flashed and all the commotion has run its course and then I make my excuses. I push my way through the crush of bodies and walk to Brent's car as fast as I can. I have to get out of here. I don't know how much longer I can contain the volcano of misery that's churning just beneath the surface. It's only a matter of time before I explode and then melt away.

Taking my phone out, I text my father to let him know I'll be riding home with Brent. I know he'll be very happy about that little tidbit and it irks me. Almost as an afterthought, I text Brent.

Can I get that ride home with you after all? Just as a friend. As Jack's daughter. Nothing else.

Within a couple of minutes, I see him heading toward me. He's smiling. A smug smile. Probably a lot like the one Daddy's wearing. I don't have to see him to know it's there. I know my father very well.

When Brent reaches me, he hits the button to unlock the doors and I climb inside. He turns to me to speak, but I cut him off without even looking at him. I don't want him to see what's bothering me. I'll just let him think I'm mad about something else.

"Please don't ask questions, Brent. I can't do this right now. Just drive. Please."

I close my eyes and lean my head back, hoping the gesture will speak volumes and put an end to further conversation. And it does.

But I can still sense his displeasure. It just so happens that, at the moment, I don't give a rat's ass.

After having to chase Brent off when I get home, all I can think about is what was, what is, and what will never be.

The selfish mistakes of my mother. The cold reaction of my father. The things they hid from me and how it ruined my life with Trick. The time I've wasted listening to the people I thought I could trust, people I didn't really know at all. And, of course, the future I'll never have with the man I love.

That eats at me more than anything—the loss of Trick. The rest I can forgive. Forget. Move on from. But not that. Not Trick. He's my sticking point.

I roam aimlessly, restlessly through the house. Drogheda must be out, and Mom is still at the club. Or somewhere. Maybe hitting up another hottie for some afternoon delight. Who knows? So it's just me. And my thoughts. And all the things I can't fix and can't get rid of.

On my way out of my father's office, I pass the small bar stuffed in the corner of the room. There is a half-full bottle of Patrón on the first lacquered shelf. Trick's favorite.

I wonder if that would count as some of the hair of the dog that bit me?

Taking down the bottle and a lead crystal tumbler, I pour myself a drink. Just tequila. Nothing else. I take a sip. It burns all the way down. Just like I want it to. I hope it burns away thought and hope and pain and regret and . . . everything. And leaves nothing behind but impenetrable scars.

I finish the glass and have another. And another. Until my head is too fuzzy to think straight. But even still, it's not too fuzzy to think of Trick.

I'm sitting in the chair behind his desk, on my fourth or possibly fifth glass of tequila, when my father walks in.

"There's the asshole who's tried to control my entire life. And then ended up ruining it. Happy to see you, *Daddy*!"

He stops in the doorway and narrows his eyes on me. I struggle to my feet and sway so much I have to grab on to the edge of the desk to remain upright.

"What the hell are you doing?" he asks.

"Having a drink. Because I can. And there's nothing you can do about it. I'm old enough to make my own decisions. I don't have to listen to the great Jack Hines anymore."

Although he controls it perfectly, I see his temper flare. I see the telltale twitch in his left eye. "As long as you live under my roof, young lady—"

"Oh, stop! I don't want to hear your threats. You've done enough damage already. You're so cold and heartless, you ran your wife into another man's arms. Isn't that enough? Can't you just leave me alone? Let me find happiness? Does everything have to be your way? Under your control? Live up to your specifications, your expectations? Because that will never happen, Daddy. No one in your life will ever be good enough. But that's not true for the rest of us."

"Cami, what are you talking about?"

It infuriates me that my eyes start to water. Tears are always just beneath the surface. At least they have been since Trick left. "Trick, Daddy. You are the one who ran him off. First because you were so hard on him and then because you kept something so important from me. I made the terrible mistake of defending you and Mom. I never thought in a million years something like that could be true and me not know about it. I blamed him, Daddy! I blamed *him*! I practically called him a liar! And now he's gone and he's never coming back."

Saying the words out loud is like throwing gasoline on a match. Every delusion I'd had, every last bit of hope I'd harbored goes up in flames. And I'm on fire. My chest, my head, my soul—everything hurts from my skin in. I can't stand to be inside my own head for one more second.

I run from the room, desperate to get away—from memories, from people, from the inevitable. I pull out my cell phone and dial Jenna's number. She answers on the first ring. She's laughing.

"Cami!" she says exuberantly.

"Come and get me."

"What?"

"Come and get me."

She giggles. "I can't do that. Why don't you come here?"

"I can't drive, Jenna. Now come and get me."

She sobers somewhat. At least her voice does. "Seriously, Cam, I can't drive, either. I've been drinking all day. Is something wrong?"

I start crying. I can't help it. It's like my last bastion of hope for sympathy and distraction just disappeared. "I . . . I . . ." I'm crying so hard now I can't get the words out.

"Sit tight, Cami. We'll be there in ten minutes."

I don't ask questions. I'm just relieved that she's working out something. "Okay."

She hangs up and I go out to sit by the pool and wait. I see Trick there, grinning at me as he takes off his clothes. So I get up and walk. Toward the stable. I tell myself on the way down there not to go, that it will only make things worse. But I'm a glutton for punishment, apparently. If I'm going to wallow in Trick, I might as well do it up right.

I go straight to Lucky's stall. His head is just tall enough to clear the top rail. I stroke his velvety nose. And I bawl.

My breath is coming in hiccups and I can barely see. I'm letting it all pour out, everything I have left.

My body is shaking so badly I can't stand, so I let my knees fold and I crumble at the foot of the stall. It's there that Sooty finds me.

He puts one leathery hand on my shoulder and asks, "What's wrong, darlin'?"

I shake my head. I'm crying too hard to talk. He squats down beside me and puts his arm around me. I lean over against him and cry all the harder. If only I had a father who acted like this, who cared like this and who showed it like this, maybe I wouldn't be in this position.

I'm sitting on the dirty stable floor soaking Sooty's shirt when Jenna finds me. She rushes to my side.

"Ohmigod, Cami, are you okay?"

Her eyes are darting back and forth between Sooty and me. It would have been laughable if I weren't so miserable.

"Please just get me out of here," I plead.

She helps me up and I dust off my butt. Sooty stands, too, and I see the enormous wet spot on his shoulder.

I look him in the eye. I want to thank him and apologize, but the tears come again. Sooty smiles in that sweet way he has and he pinches my chin.

"Don't let anything get in the way of what you want. Not even pride."

I want to take exception and explain to him that I'm not standing in the way of what I want, that what I want simply doesn't want me, but Jenna starts tugging at my arm.

"Thanks for looking out for her until I could get here," she says, and starts leading me toward the back bay doors.

I look around for her car, but don't see it. "How did you get here?"

She nods to a place halfway between the house and the stable. There sits Rusty's car, idling, with Rusty watching us curiously through the windshield.

"I'm so sorry, Jenna! I know you wanted to stay out of this, you and Rusty. I'm so sorry."

The tears start to fall again.

"Shh, shh, shh," she whispers comfortingly. "No guy is gonna keep me from my bestie when she needs me. But he didn't even try. Not this time. He knew it was serious."

"He won't tell Trick, will he?"

"No. He doesn't talk to Trick about much of anything these days. Today's the first time they've really hung out in forever."

I stop. "He was with Trick today? At the race?"

Jenna nods. "Yeah, they came back early and Rusty surprised me."

"But he's . . ."

"No. You're fine. Come on. He's taking us to his garage for a while. Once I sober up, we can go to my house and you can spend the night."

"O-okay."

When we get to Rusty's car, this time something I think might be a GTO but can't positively identify in the low light, Jenna opens the passenger door. She pushes the seat up and I crawl into the back. Jenna flops down in the front seat and slams the door shut. When we don't move immediately, I start to wonder why, but then Rusty turns around in his seat.

The outdoor lights that surround the stable illuminate the car enough that I can see half his face. It lacks its normal fun-loving grin and relaxed brow. Now, it's wrinkled in concern.

He reaches back and palms my knee, wiggling my leg back and forth. "You okay, girl?"

Rusty's touch is in no way inappropriate or slimy; it's the equivalent of a gentle pat on the back. I have no doubt whatsoever that he's actually concerned about me. I know from this second on, he'll be permanently endeared to me. The brother I never had. And Jenna the sister.

I give him a watery smile and nod. My assurance is a total lie, but if I start talking to him about Trick, I'll lose it.

He sort of slaps my knee a couple times, nods, and turns back around to shift into reverse. No one talks on the way to the garage. The silence plus motion of the car and the soothing road noises are more than enough to put me straight to sleep.

Hushed voices stir me, but between the tequila and the emotional exhaustion, I don't even bother to open my eyes. I much prefer the peace and solitude of sleep. I prefer oblivion.

I can't tell if it's a few seconds, a few minutes, or a few hours later when I hear the voices again. This time they're followed by a click and a bright light shining in my eyes. I squeeze my lids shut and turn my face away. I want to cuss and fuss and scream that I want to be left alone, but I just don't have the energy. I'd much rather sleep.

That becomes practically impossible, however, when I feel fingers wiggling their way beneath my shoulders and knees. Then someone is folding me up like a napkin and dragging me from the backseat. Just when I'm about to make my displeasure known, in a very nasty way, I'm cradled in strong arms against a hard chest. Something in the back of my mind niggles for me to wake up and take notice. I ignore it to snuggle in deeper.

But then I smell his soap. It's unmistakable. Clean and lightly scented. It's Trick.

I open my bleary eyes and squint against the light. It's not bright light, but it's offensive nonetheless. I blink a couple times until I can focus. We stop moving when he looks down at me. His expression is blank. I can't decide if it hurts or not. Right now, I'm just too happy to be looking at him again, so close, and to be held by him. I never thought I'd feel his arms again.

"Trick," I say hoarsely.

"Shhh," he whispers as he starts walking again.

Regardless of everything else—all the pain, the disappointment, the doubt, the loss—I'm content to be with Trick, even in this situation. I don't think the circumstances would matter. I just want Trick. Period.

I wind my arms around his neck and lay my head against his shoulder. He pulls me in tighter for just a second. Like a hug.

Did that just happen? Or am I imagining things? Maybe he was just getting a better grip.

I like the next thought much better.

Or maybe he wasn't.

Drink makes me brave. It always has. So it's no surprise that I find the courage to pull my arms tighter around him and bury my face in his neck. I hear a noise. Like a hiss. Could be one of disgust. Or frustration. But it could also be one of something else. There's only one way to find out, so I press my lips to his skin.

"Where did you come from?" I ask, but I don't really care. I just think there's a part of me that believes this is a dream.

"I was at home. I came to get Rusty to look at my truck."

My head is still swimmy, but I notice when the light disappears. It's much quieter now and I smell some kind of citrusy cleaner.

"Your truck?"

"Yeah. I got a truck. Go back to sleep, Cami."

I open my eyes as Trick lowers me onto something soft. A couch or a cot of some sort. I can see his face in the low light, but just barely.

"Why did you carry me?"

"Because you can't sleep in the car."

That's not the answer I was hoping for.

"Why are you here?"

"I told you. I was looking for Rusty."

"Trick, I—"

He cuts me off. "Good night, Cami."

And with that, he walks out of the room and closes the door behind him.

FIFTY: *Trick*

I stand outside the closed door for a few seconds. As bad as it sounds, part of me wants to go back in there and take advantage of Cami's sweetly drunken state. Just to hold her one more time, to feel that warm body against mine.

"Dammit," I curse under my breath, pushing myself away from the door.

"What's the matter?" Rusty asks.

"Nothing. She'll go back to sleep. Thanks for letting her crash back there, man."

"It's no problem. You know that."

"I'm sure you had . . . other plans for the night," I say, eyeing Jenna where she's sitting on the hood of an old Ford, drinking a beer.

Rusty grins. "Hell yeah I did, but nothing I can't relocate. Are you sure she's gonna be all right?"

"Yeah, she'll be fine. She'll feel like shit in the morning, but she'll make it."

"Man, that girl is tore up!"

"What do you mean?"

"She was a wreck when she called. Still was when we got to her."

"About what?"

"What do you think, dickhead? About you!"

"Whatever's wrong with her has nothing to do with me. She's back with that douche of a boyfriend she had."

"No, she's not. Not according to Jenna."

My heart is thumping so hard, it feels like it might jump out of my chest.

"What'd she say?"

"She's got it bad for you, Trick. I thought you knew."

"*If* she ever did, she sure got over it fast enough."

"Or you just *think* she did."

"No offense, Rus, but you don't know what you're talking about here. Maybe it's best for you to just stay out of it."

"That's exactly what I told Jenna, but damn if that girl didn't convince me Cami's in love with you. She looks at me with those sexy eyes and I quit thinking with this head," he says with a grin, tapping his forehead.

"It's okay. I appreciate you trying to help, but it's over. It's just . . . it's over."

"It's a shame, dude. You two were good together."

His words, they're like a knife in the chest. I smile as best I can. "I know. But . . . whatever."

I wish I could actually *feel* that blasé about the whole thing. But I can't. It's tearing me up inside. I'm just pretty good at hiding it.

I turn and walk to the fridge that sits in the back corner of the garage. I see the unopened bottle of Patrón sitting on top and I consider it. But then I open the door and grab a cold beer instead.

Before I can take more than one drink, the door to the little room at the back comes flying open, revealing a seriously mad Cami standing in the doorway.

She looks adorable. And hot. Her hair is messed up, coming undone from whatever has been holding it up all day. Her shirt is wrinkled and hanging off one shoulder. Her chest is heaving. Her feet are bare. But the most mesmerizing thing is her face. Her gorgeous face. Her cheeks are flushed, like a permanent blush, and her eyes are sparkling with fury. I don't know what has her so fired up, but I'd like to shake its hand.

She looks around the interior of the garage, her gaze stopping on Rusty and Jenna first, then moving on. They stop when she spots me, and I swear I think she actually turns about three shades more beautiful.

Her lips part a little and for just a second, there's something other than anger in her eyes. It's almost like she's glad to see me but hates that she is.

Could Rusty and Jenna be right? Could I have so badly misjudged and misread the situation?

As we stare at each other, for the space of no more than a few seconds, I decide there's only one way to find out. Just as she starts to stomp toward me, I start walking in her direction. I think it confuses her a little because she stops and looks to Rusty and Jenna again before turning her attention back to me.

I don't stop until I'm practically right on top of her. I'm staring down at her, never wanting to kiss somebody so bad in all my life. She's looking up at me, her eyes wide and confused. She's sexy as hell and I really have no other choice.

So I kiss her.

FIFTY-ONE: *Cami*

Of all the things I expected when I stomped out of that little room, this was nowhere on the list.

Trick's hands are cupping my face and his mouth is devouring mine. My head is reeling from the mixture of cold beer and sweet mint on his tongue.

I'm shocked. And confused. And thrilled. And hopeful. All at once. It takes a few seconds for me to recover, for me to figure out what to do. But when I do, there's no question what my next move is.

I go with it.

I don't care about the answers I don't have or the doubts that I do. I care about Trick wanting me right now, in this moment. That's all that matters. Even if it's just this one last time, I'll take it.

Turning my head to the side, I deepen the kiss and lean into Trick. His groan vibrates along my tongue and tingles on my lips. Heat pools low in my stomach.

His hands slide into my hair and the kiss turns hungry. Like he feels the same desperate need I feel. Wrapping my arms around him, I let my fingers crawl up under his shirt where I can feel the smooth, warm skin of his back.

Trick's lips never leave mine when he sweeps me into his arms. My pulse races and I hold on tighter, not willing to ever let him go.

When he takes me back into the room I just left, he kicks the door shut and sets me on my feet. I kiss him harder, not wanting to give him a second to breathe or think or change his mind. I want him all emotion, all hunger, all raw need. I can't take the chance that he'll remember all the reasons why not.

I tug at his shirt and lean back only long enough to pull it over his head. He whips mine over my head and then we're kissing again. I can't get close enough to him, can't get enough of his skin on mine. I strain against him as I work the button on his jeans. His fingers brush mine aside and make quick work of the closure. He sheds his pants, then picks me up and carries me to the bed.

Like magic, he has me out of my clothes in a heartbeat. He's gone only for a moment while I hear the rattle of foil and then he's back with me. I thread my fingers through his hair and pull him to me, kissing him with all the love and passion I feel for him. I shiver when he stretches out on top of me, every inch of my body covered by his.

I wrap my legs around his hips and hold on tight, anticipation winding my muscles into coiled springs. I gasp when he pushes into me. Nothing has ever felt more like home. Words pour from my heart, from my lips without thought to consequences.

"I love you," I whisper.

Trick stills. His body buried deep inside me, he lifts his head and looks down into my face.

His eyes are pale even in the low light. I stare into them, committing them and this moment to memory. The fleeting nature of this perfect piece of happiness rushes in and chokes me. Tears fill my eyes and spill over, running into the hair at my temples. I squeeze them shut, not wanting him to see my heartbreak. Or ruin the poignancy of the scene.

"What did you say?"

His voice is so low, so quiet, I open my eyes to make sure I wasn't imagining things. His lips aren't moving.

"What did you say?" he repeats.

Heat floods my cheeks. It's one thing to confess something like that in the heat of the moment, not knowing rejection is waiting on the other side. It is quite another to do it in the face of such serious lucidity, like now.

But I tell him what he wants to know, partly because I don't want to regret *not* telling him how I feel, even though he doesn't feel the same. I'll treasure the time I have with Trick for the rest of my life. I might as well go balls-out.

"I said 'I love you.'"

His brow wrinkles. "But what about Brent? And your father? And . . . everything else?"

"I don't care about anyone else. Or any*thing* else. All I care about is you."

"So you're not back with Brent?"

"No."

"If you love me, why didn't you come to me? Why have you stayed away?"

It's my turn to frown. "I did come to you. I went to your house and talked to your mom. Didn't she tell you?"

Trick sighs and lowers his forehead to mine. "No, she didn't."

Something alarmingly close to hope unfurls in my chest. A question stands on the tip of my tongue. My heart pounds as I let it go. But I have to know. And I may not get another chance. "Would it have mattered?"

Trick looks at me. "Of course it would've mattered. Cami, I'm in love with you. I stayed away because I thought it was what you wanted."

I hear nothing past the part where he said he's in love with me. The tears flow faster.

"What's the matter?" he asks softly, catching a tear with his thumb as it slides from the corner of my eye. "Why are you crying?"

"I thought you were gone. Forever. I thought I'd lost you."

"I thought the same thing," he admits, kissing my eyelids and my cheeks. "God, Cami, I didn't know how I was gonna live the rest of my life without you."

I wrap my arms and legs tighter around Trick, a physical way of expressing that I'm never letting him go. Never.

The action causes him to move inside me and my body reflexively squeezes, drawing him even farther in. I hear the breath hiss through his teeth.

"Damn, can we talk about this later? I can barely think when you do that, much less talk."

I laugh. In my heart, in my head, in my soul, I laugh. "Yes, we'll talk later. I think we've already covered the most important things, anyway."

He pulls out and thrusts back into me. The sensation steals my breath. "I think there's one thing left that I need to 'cover,' if you don't mind."

He bites my chin playfully as he flexes his hips, sending fingers of sensation skittering through me.

"Do what you must," I say.

And the rest, as they say, is history.

FIFTY-TWO: *Trick*

I put the truck in park right at the edge of the clearing where the house will sit. At least I think that's where it will sit. My wife will have the final say. Provided that she says yes, of course.

I look over at Cami, sitting quietly beside me, all blindfolded and excited.

"Are you sure you're ready for this?"

"To see what you bought with all that money from the car? Hell yeah, I'm sure."

"I told you part of it went to Mom and some of it went into stabling Rags and getting him ready to race."

"But the rest you invested. You already told me. And now I get to see what the big secret is."

Cami rubs her hands together excitedly. Now I'm having second thoughts. She's obviously anxious to know what it is, but I wonder if she has some preconceived notion. What if she's disappointed?

I get out and walk around to her side of the truck. I help her down, but leave her blindfolded.

"Come on. I'll go slow. Just hold on to me."

Always game, Cami nods and lets me lead her into the clearing. In the distance, I can see where the stable I had built sits at the edge of the field. I hope Cami doesn't mind staying in the tiny apartment in the top half of it until the house is completed. Since Rags won his first two races, I had enough money to get her a ring plus some to spare for a down payment on a construction loan. All the bank needs is the house plan.

And all I need for that is Cami.

I grab her by the shoulders and position her facing the house site and the stable beyond. "Stay right here." I drop to one knee and dig the ring out of my pocket. After a deep breath, I tell her, "You can look."

I watch her face as she pulls off the tie I'd used to blindfold her and looks around. She scans the clearing first, and I see her eyes pause on the stable before they search for and find me, kneeling at her side.

When she understands what's going on, her hands fly to her face. She covers her mouth and turns to face me. My heart jumps up into my throat.

"I know how much you've sacrificed to be with me. Having to stay with Jenna because of your dad and having to put off your last year of school for a while, until we can both go back. And I promised you I'd make it up to you. This," I say, sweeping my arm out to encompass all the land that I now call mine, "is the first step. I want this to be our home. I want to build a life with you and a business around Rags that we can run together. I want to pick out carpet and curtains with you. I want to pick out new horses with you. I want to pick out baby furniture with you. I want to grow old with you. I want you. Forever. I'm hoping that if you can see that future, the future that I see, you can wait just a little while longer for all of it to come together. I'm working on it. Every day, I'm working on it. For you. For us. But until then," I pause, holding out the ring. "Cami, will you marry me?"

I'm pretty sure I can't breathe. My chest is so tight it feels like it might pop from the pressure.

Although she pauses for only a few seconds, it feels like an eternity. When she drops to her knees in front of me and takes my hands, I feel a relieved sigh rush out in a flood, taking with it all the last little bits of doubt I'd had.

I can see her answer in her eyes, before she even opens her mouth. And it makes me want to celebrate.

"Yes. To all of that. I don't have a life without you. I never did. I never could. You're everything to me. You're all I've ever wanted and all I'll ever need. I'm never letting you go."

When she brings her mouth to mine, I can't help but smile. Yes, I'm happy—so, so happy—with her answer. But that's not all. I get to make her even happier later when I tell her that I finally got her father's blessing.

About two weeks ago, when I bought Cami's ring, I made an impulsive detour on the way back from the jeweler's. I decided to stop by the Hines ranch. I knew Cami wouldn't be there; she'd already moved in with Jenna. What I didn't know was whether Jack would be there. I knew it would be worth a try, though. And it was a good gamble. Turns out he was there after all.

The housekeeper, Drogheda, had smiled when she answered the door. I liked her instantly. Something in her eyes welcomed me as the guy who would make Cami happy. I didn't realize how much I needed to see that from someone else. Someone who loves Cami almost as much as I do.

Without a word, she led me back to Jack's office. He was sitting behind his desk studying his computer screen when she stopped in front of the open door. He looked up, not in the least surprised. Or so it seemed. He nodded to her and she walked off, leaving me standing there to be examined like a bug under a microscope. But I didn't care. Jack was the least of my worries. But he's important to Cami and she's the one I care about, so I stood my ground.

He didn't invite me in, but I went in and grabbed a chair, anyway. We sat in silence for a painfully long time before I decided to take the bull—or in this case, the jackass—by the horns.

"I know you don't respect me. I know you would've chosen someone else for your daughter. But I also know that you could scour the earth for the rest of your life and you'd never find someone who loves her as much as I do. She's one of the few things in the world that really matters to me, and I won't rest until I give her the life she deserves. Whether you want to be a part of that is up to you. It would mean an awful lot to Cami if you'd stop being so stubborn. And, no offense, but her feelings are the only ones I care about.

"You don't have to care about me. You don't have to respect me. Hell, you don't even have to like me. You care about Cami and that's enough for me. That's all I ever need to know. How much you're willing to sacrifice for her, though, is entirely up to you."

I was ready to leave after I said my piece. But I felt obligated to wait for him to respond, so I did. I leaned back in the chair and laced my fingers together over my stomach and I eyed him. Just like he was eyeing me.

When he finally spoke, he surprised me. I really didn't expect the old bastard to cave. But he did. I was right all along about that, too. Cami is his Kryptonite.

"All right."

"All right?"

He nodded. "All right. I believe you. And I'll give you one chance to prove it. But just one. If you hurt her, I'll castrate you.

And you've lived in the country long enough to know what something like that looks like. You get my meaning?"

I couldn't help but laugh. "Yes, sir. Lucky for both of us that's not gonna happen. I love her. More than I do myself. I'd rather die than hurt her."

"Just remember that. Because I can see to that, too."

I nodded. He nodded. And then he turned back to his computer screen.

That was the best I could hope for from Jack Hines. But that was all I needed, so the rest didn't matter.

Things went much better with him than they did with my mother. When I told her I was going to try to get Cami back, she made it clear that Cami would never be welcome at the house. My mother left in tears that day. But I know my mother. While she might be bitter and hurt right now, she loves me. She'll come around. Eventually. In the meantime, I'll just visit her on my own. And if she comes to visit me, she'll have to accept that Cami is part of my life. That she's *the* part of my life—the most important one. I wish I could take away the hurt, but I can't. And there's no reason for everyone to be miserable until she can see her way clear of her hatred. I'll just bide my time. She'll come around. I know it.

But I'm not worrying about that now. And I don't want Cami to, either. I'm more anxious to tell her that I finally got her father to come around, got him to see that I'm what's best for her, that no one will ever love her like I do. That alone makes it all worth it. Cami's worth everything. At least now more than one person knows that it's become my mission in life to give this girl everything she ever wanted. And maybe even a few things she didn't know she wanted.

Until she met me.

THE HAPPILY-EVER-AFTER END

A FINAL WORD

A few times in life, I've found myself in a position of such love and gratitude that saying THANK YOU seems trite, like it's just not enough. That is the position that I find myself in now when it comes to you, my readers. You are the sole reason that my dream of being a writer has come true. I knew that it would be gratifying and wonderful to finally have a job that I loved so much, but I had no idea that it would be outweighed and outshined by the unimaginable pleasure that I get from hearing that you love my work, that it's touched you in some way or that your life seems a little bit better for having read it. So it is from the depths of my soul, from the very bottom of my heart that I say I simply cannot THANK YOU enough. I've added this note to all my stories with the link to a blog post that I really hope you'll take a minute to read. It is a true and sincere expression of my humble appreciation. I love each and every one of you and you'll never know what your many encouraging posts, comments, and emails have meant to me.

http://mleightonbooks.blogspot.com/2011/06/when-thanks-is-not -enough.html

Keep reading for an excerpt from

The Wild Child

Available in Spring 2013 from
Berkley Books

PROLOGUE: *Rusty*

Last summer

Jenna's breathing is deep and even. I'm afraid to move, afraid I'll wake her up. It's worth a numb arm to get to hold her like this before she leaves. Besides, I love the feel of her warm, soft skin against mine. Jenna is amazing in all her forms, but I'd be a liar if I said Naked Jenna isn't my favorite.

The summer flew by like a feather on the wind—too fast then gone without a trace. I never expected to want it to drag out. And the only reason I want it to now is because of Jenna. I have a bad feeling about her going back to school, back to where Trevor, her ex, will be.

At the beginning of summer break, they agreed to see other people, which is why she and I started, ahem, "seeing" each other. But I can't help wondering if that will change when they get back to school. Back to being together. Back to being away from . . . me. I would never in my wildest dreams complain about being a summer fling for a hot girl. In fact, I'd wear it like a badge of achievement, being some hottie's piece of ass or booty call. Wouldn't any guy?

But not with Jenna.

For the first time I can ever remember, I don't want it to end.

Have I told Jenna this? Pretty much. I mean, there haven't been any last-minute confessions or pledges or anything like that. And there won't be, either. I think she knows how I feel. I hope she feels the same way. Whatever that "way" is. The rest I'm leaving up to her.

And hoping she makes the right decision.

The "right decision" being me, of course.

Jenna's a free spirit. She's the fun-loving, always-ready-to-party kind. She's not the settling down type. I'm just hoping that her feelings for me will change all that.

I sigh as I look down at her beautiful face—bronzy skin, exotic-shaped eyes, jet-black eyelashes and eyebrows. She's completely relaxed in sleep, dozing against my chest.

As I watch her, I feel the frown wrinkle my forehead. I have a bad feeling.

ONE: *Jenna*

Present day

I don't know why I'm nervous. I'm going home. That's it. No big deal. I'm going home just like I've done every other summer for the last zillion years. First from prep school then from college. This is no different.

Only it is. Or at least it feels that way.

I just graduated college with a degree in business and marketing, but that's not why I'm nervous. I just landed job interviews with two huge companies in Atlanta, only a few hours away from home in neighboring Georgia, but that's not why I'm nervous. My best friend is getting married to the man of her dreams and I'm the maid of honor, but that's not why I'm nervous. It's Tuesday and it's May, but that's not why I'm nervous, either. No, it's none of those things. I know what's making me nervous, I just don't know why.

It's Rusty.

This is the first time I've been home since I left to go back to school. Things seemed fine at the end of last summer. We were both happy and promising to see each other as soon as possible, to call as often as we could. Only that didn't happen. None of the good stuff we'd talked about and planned to do had happened. Things just got hectic and crazy and they changed. Then there was some girl named Layla, as well as Trevor, my ex. It wasn't long until what Rusty and I had just disappeared. Vanished into thin air. Evaporated. Without a trace.

Except for the twinge of pain around the scar on my heart. That has never gone away.

I'm relieved when the buzz of my cell phone interrupts my funky thoughts. The Caller ID shows my best friend's beautiful face.

Cami.

"Where are you?" she asks before I can even eke out a greeting.

"I'm almost there. Don't get your panties in a twist. That's Trick's job," I tease.

I hear her giggle and I smile. That's my cue that my tardiness has been officially overlooked. She's a softy and I know exactly where all her soft spots are.

"Now I can't even remember why I was mad," she admits. I can hear the smile in her voice. "How do you do that?"

"It's an old Jedi mind trick, handed down from my father's father's father's father's father's father's—"

"All right, smart-ass. I get the picture. So, how far out are you?"

"Maybe five, ten minutes. It wouldn't take me so long to get there if Mr. Hot 'n Sexy hadn't gone and won a couple big races and built you a freakin' mansion in the middle of BFE."

"Stop your grouching! You love it out here and you know it."

"Sheeyeah! Not even! You know I'm dying to get out of this town the instant I come back. If only you'd come with me . . ." I pout.

"No can do, *chica*. I'm exactly where I want to be."

I sigh. "I know. And I couldn't be happier for you."

And that's true. Although Cami's life isn't at all what she thought it would be, she's found that the surprises are what she needed most and likes best. Surprises like her sinfully gorgeous fiancé, Trick.

I just wish the surprises in my life had turned out so well . . .

"Jenna, it'll be fine. Stop worrying about seeing Rusty."

She can read me every bit as clearly as I can read her. And through a phone no less!

"I'm not worried per se."

"Okay, whatever you want to call it, just stop it! You're both mature, rational human beings who love Trick and me. I trust you to keep the past in the past and focus on having a good time with your best friends. We're all adults here."

"You do realize who you're talking to, right?"

Cami laughs. "Yes, I realize who I'm talking to. No, you're not the world's most adult adult, but you're the queen of having fun despite pretty much anything. That's the girl who will win the day. I know it. I'm not worried."

But she is. I can hear it in her voice. I'm adding stress to her life, the kind of stress she shouldn't be feeling and shouldn't be subjected to, especially not the week of her wedding. And I have to make sure it stops. Right now.

Shaking off my doubts and misgivings, I assure Cami I'll be there soon before I hang up. There will be plenty of time for fear and regret later. The next few days are all about Cami. Besides, I need to concentrate. I've got some work to do before I get there, emotionally speaking. I need to have some damn good armor in place by the time I see Rusty again! And that's likely going to be within the hour.

What the hell is the matter with you? You're still the same hot, charismatic, confident chick you were the day you twisted Rusty around your little finger. If anybody should be fearing for their heart, it's Rusty. Rusty who's about to get hit with a Jenna bomb of awesome. And he's not the only one. That damned girlfriend of his oughta be afraid, too. She'll have to go through life with Jenna bomb of awesome shrapnel embedded in her treacherous ass.

Jenna strikes again!

I laugh out loud at my ridiculous inner monologue. It's worthy of Stuart Smalley in every cheesy, possible way. All I need is a goofy guy in a cardigan telling me I'm a neat girl and that, gosh darn it, people like me!

You're a crazy person, Jenna Theopolis! But you're a kick-ass crazy person. Just remember that and you'll be fine.